IRISH EYES...

Ally glanced back at the sidewalk, but he was still there, tall, tousled sandy-brown hair, with that infernal grin on that devilish mouth of his. He had his hands stuck in the pockets of his low-slung faded jeans and his shoulders looked entirely too fine in the chambray shirt with rolled up sleeves. It was the same look he'd affected on their evenings in Ireland, oh-so-long ago. A devil in disguise: she'd learned that lesson the hard way. All these years later, she was not fooled by him anymore—there was no school-girl urgency as there'd been all those years back. Those chocolate-brown eyes of his were just a trap of the worst kind and she wasn't going to fall for them again.

"He's the one—a guy I met just after I left home," she said to Lila. "I thought I fell in love—until the jerk dumped me out of the blue and went off with a local girl." And scooped out her heart and stomped all over it.

"I really don't need him messing with me right now." She glanced back at the gate and dammit, dammit, dammit, he was coming through. That was Séamus—always pushing in where he wasn't welcome and expecting to use his considerable Irish charm to get him by.

Lila patted her shoulder. "Then why don't you head inside and I'll deal with Mr....?"

"O'Hearn. Séamus O'Hearn."

"An Irishman, Ally?" Lila cocked a brow at her and half smiled.

"I know. I know. I should have known better, but he's darned charming. Watch out for it."

BOOKS BY THE AUTHOR

Romance
Ashes and Light
Shades of Moonlight
Judas Kiss
Second Spring
A Different Nightmusic
Shadow Play
Unlocking Her Heart
Unlocking Her History
Unlocking Her Grace

Fantasy
***The Cartographer Universe* series:**
The Warden of Power
The Cartographer's Daughter
Afterburn
Aftershock
Aftermath
Afterimage
Terra Incognita
Terra Infirma
Terra Nueva

Mutable Things
Emberstone
Ice Dragon
Crystal Courtesan
Impossible

UNLOCKING HER GRACE

Karen L. Abrahamson

**Dedicated to the Peachland that used to be
and
to the best that it can become.**

UNLOCKING HER GRACE

Prologue

At ten p.m. he deplaned at the Kelowna International Airport to the fawning goodbyes of the flight attendants. The cool night air swirled around the broad shoulders of the body he wore, cleansing him of the tired stink of sweating humans that he had tolerated on the long overseas and transcontinental flights. The body crossed the tarmac, carrying a windbreaker folded over one muscled arm, a single brown leather carry-on bag over a shoulder, while he nestled, for the moment, in the body's brain—its most important passenger.

The airport lay in the heart of a long narrow valley with night-darkened, kindling-dry hillsides of pine to either side. Here and there a lone point of light exposed a lonely dwelling house, the type of place where one could do what they wanted with the inhabitants and no one would hear them scream.

He uncoiled and stretched in the body's brain, sniffed the darkness and welcomed it in, inhaling the faintest scent of silver. What passed for blood in his bloodless existence quickened in his breast.

Silver. Old silver. The body's head turned and he lifted its face to draw in a breath.

Southward. That was where it lay, beyond the backwater city of Kelowna with its too-bright lights that polluted the blessed dark sky. Once Creation had been filled with only darkness, but then day formed. Bright light and heat, and though his kind could exist in such places, they did not like it. They preferred to inhabit the dark cracks of the earth and coil round the minds of others, nursing magic as they gathered power.

But this time the body had to be guided more closely if it was to accomplish the mission he had set for it. It would drain his power dangerously, but it was worth it.

Long, athletic legs strode across the concrete and pushed inside the terminal to recycled cool air. Female eyes turned in admiration toward him and he knew that he had chosen well. This body—this body was ripe for the task, with tanned flesh in a form that women found attractive. The body wore jeans and expensive-looking Italian loafers, and a denim shirt he had chosen to match the eyes. It sauntered across the arrival hall in a loose-hipped, confident way. Outside again, the air was heavy with the scents of sage and pine and cool water. Water of the deep, cold lake that would play a part in his plans.

At the parking lot before him, the body fished in his pocket for the key fob that had been delivered to its Berlin apartment. He pushed the button. Out in the parking lot, a beep-beep-beep came from the only Humvee he could see.

Inside, the vehicle smelled of new leather as the body adjusted the seat, turned the engine on, and cruised out of the lot. In no time at all he was cruising highway 97 southward through the strip of neon lights that was Kelowna and westward across the lake. It was as unimpressive as he remembered. None of the grandeur of mountains like in Switzerland. None of the roar of waves from the ocean, and definitely none of the night life of Berlin.

This was... small. A small city that undoubtedly housed small people, which would make it somewhat more difficult for this splendid body to blend in. But that was what this body had been chosen for—its skill at blending in until it was simply too late for its targets to save themselves.

If Kelowna was small, the lights of his destination farther south spoke of not much more than a village strung like a beggar-woman's rhinestone necklace along the lakeshore. A few more lights scattered up the hillside behind them. None of the glamour of the City of Light and none of the salt sea scent of the Riviera.

Just how had his precious possession ended up here in a village named after a fruit? Peachland. The land of peaches. Never his favorite fruit—too easily bruised and made inedible. He preferred enjoyments that did not show their injuries quite so openly.

When the body reached the lone stoplight on the highway, it turned the Humvee toward the street that followed the lakeshore. A block south it slowed and then pulled over. The dash lights turned the body's hands green as he studied the familiar scene before him. The hedge and small garden separated the large white house from the street. The house's red trim was tarnished black by the night that seemed to claw at the well-lit front porch that ran the breadth of the front of the house. A set of false torches lit the porch with a soft golden light, illuminating a group of people seated there.

What he sought was there. His essence thrummed like a sticky spider thread, vibrating at the quiver of a fly to alert its owner. He had been right to risk himself by once more coming halfway around the world.

The women were there.

There were five, as he remembered. The body pushed a button on the door and the driver's side window rolled down, allowing in the night-tinged scent of lake water and power-imbued silver. For a moment vertigo took him and the body stirred of its own volition. He should not lose control so easily. He reasserted dominance and leaned forward to see whom he faced this time.

One, auburn haired, presided over the group from her seat in a high, peacock-backed, wicker chair, but she, as yet, had been untouched by the curse. Another, also untouched, reminded him of an ancient queen of Egypt he had served, with night black hair cut in ruthless bangs that matched the severe masculinity of her camouflage trousers and sleeveless t-shirt.

The hands tightened on the steering wheel at the sight of the third woman, the tiny blond who had escaped him. Beside her on a loveseat perched another who had frustrated his attempt to recover what was rightfully his. Her hair hung to her waist, and she carried the taint of the curse undone—no longer the haunting scent of the silver she had borne.

The breeze swirled along the lakeshore, stirring the leaves of the trees and the waves on the water. It lifted the long blonde hair of the last tawny-skinned female. The currents of the night brought her scent through the window and he inhaled and closed the eyes. Old silver and magic—that was what he sought. Its thread of scent overlaid an aroma of warm cloves, baby oil, and sweat that sent a titillating arousal through the body.

The spider vibration increased as the woman raised her hand to shift her hair and the torchlight caught on the silver encircling her wrist. He imagined himself staking that fine tendril of scent, hanging above her, his venom sac distended. He released his hold on the body. It started the car and cruised slowly past.

Her.

His target. The vibration in the spider silk ceased.

The spider—he—was here.

Chapter 1

It was one of those blue-saturated days: blue sky, blue lake, blue docks floating on the water, as if she'd amped up the blue on the RGB scale of her camera. She stood by the Private Party sign by the front gate and watched the crowd of people—women, mostly—fluttering around in the heritage house's front yard. The two-story white-with-red-trim house gleamed in contrast to the blue in the Okanagan sun, its broad, covered front porch offering a welcoming shade. Usually the porch was home to a well-used grouping of wicker furniture, but today—the grand reopening of *This and That: Jewelry and Unsung Treasures*—the furniture had been pushed to one end of the porch to allow room for display tables and circulation of the well-dressed people.

The store stood on Beach Avenue in the small, south-central British Columbia town of Peachland, but not in the center of the town. No, *This and That* sat a half-mile along the lakefront on Beach Avenue where the town was slowly being transformed from a place of small, 1950s single-story bungalows owned by Peachland's old families, to sleek, glass-fronted, modern homes and condos owned by new money from the Alberta oil field or offshore riches made in the Orient. Ally had known it was eventually going to happen—from what she'd seen in the world, you couldn't stop progress—but it was still like a gut-punch and hard to see. She'd come home from Zanzibar desperately seeking the safety and sameness of the sleepy small town with its almost empty beaches and despairingly little to do in the mind of a teenage girl. Instead she found a destination spot for day-trippers from Kelowna, and the town she remembered was disappearing under the weight of new housing developments, eating the orchards above the town, and the gentrification of the old town's heart. But not here.

This and That held onto that comfortable past like an oasis in the desert. The house had been Lila Weber's grandparents'. After they had died, Lila had restored it and, with the partnership of two friends, had been determined to make the jewelry shop work to ensure the house could stay in the family and hold onto the town's old grace. They'd succeeded, too, from what Ally could see. The old copper hanging planters bloomed with red and white geraniums and purple heliotrope, and the store's white paint and red shutters shone in the sunshine. A little soft focus, or less contrast in the photographic post-processing, and the place would look like it was filled with magic; and magic was what people wanted when it came to buying the beautiful pieces of jewelry found at *This and That*. It specialized in artisanal jewelry brought from all over the world, as well as specialty custom pieces made by their in-house designer, none other than Regulus, better known as Reggie Lewis to her friends.

After the store's recent unfortunate break-in and damage, Lila and company had decided to turn lemons into lemonade and had seized on the opportunity to update the store and make their grand reopening a publicity event.

Mingling female customers formed shoals like tropical fish, their bright summer dresses setting off their tanned legs and arms as they moved between the porch and the refreshment tables on the front lawn. Two young women, one blonde, one brunette, hovered over a display of earrings on one of the lawn tables. With their heads close together, one pointed something out to the other and there was such open longing on their faces that Ally raised her camera.

Click-brrr. The Nikon D4 hummed in her hand as she shot a few frames, then checked the image. It was good. Thank goodness

Lila had agreed to ask all attendees to sign a photo release before attending so that photos could be used in promotional materials. It really was an excellent event. Lila and the others had outdone themselves and the setting certainly helped.

The breeze off eighty-mile-long Okanagan Lake dispelled the afternoon heat, the blue waves slapping the gravel beach that was just across the street from *This and That*. Blue sky formed a bowl overhead, held up by the gray-green mountains. Uneven benches of land terraced the hillsides and spread lodgepole pine forests, orchards, and wineries down either side of the lake. Out on the water were the ubiquitous power boats, pulling water skiers and their wakes sluggishly behind them. A few sailboats flew before the brisk wind and, closer in to shore, a yellow and a blue kayak cut across the water like dragonflies.

A gust struck her in the face and she turned to shield her camera lens in time to see the wind catch the corners of the tablecloths on two of the refreshment tables. The cloths flapped up and the wind caught hold and began to drag the cloth back over the table. Platters of small quiches and finger food began to slide toward the other side of the table. Ally leapt and grabbed for one cloth, yanked it down. Grabbed another and pulled it back in place as Chloe Main, Lila's partner, rushed to help her. Together they used rubber bands Chloe happened to have in her pockets to loop around the table legs and catch the corners of the tablecloths. When they were done, they stopped and took stock.

"You were fast," Ally said.

"Not as fast as you." Chloe looked resplendent in a body-skimming caftan of white with a seed-pearl-and-jet torque necklace and matching earrings, an outfit that was a far cry from the practical khaki trousers and silk shirt Ally wore. But then, when you're a working photographer, you don't get decked out. Even Chloe's jewelry would be in the way and Ally'd be scared to move around, get down on the ground in such clothing. Even the silver bracelet Ally had on her wrist felt awkward and in the way.

"You getting any good shots?" Chloe asked. The two of them stood by the table and Chloe sampled what looked like smoked salmon and capers on a tiny curled cracker crisp. She nodded in appreciation.

"A few. People admiring the jewelry. A few of the entire scene. It was a good idea having everyone sign a photo release and having them wear a blue dot on their shoulder if they didn't want to be photographed. It's given me a lot of freedom to shoot. The shots of the scene will make lovely advertisements for the place. The people shots are giving me ideas. It might be nice to have a few scattered around the shop or in a portfolio if you think you might want to do other events."

Chloe nodded thoughtfully. "You know, we can't thank you enough for helping out with the photography. I mean, this is really taking advantage of you—sort of a busman's holiday given you're on vacation and all."

Ally shook her head and felt a twinge of unease that she quickly pushed away. "Not a vacation. More like a sorting period." She sighed. "I haven't really wanted to talk about it, but I just needed some space to regain my focus. For some reason, Peachland seemed like the perfect place to do it." And a good place to forget all the stuff that had gone bad with her life, not to mention maybe distract herself with some nice, down-home men. After years of sampling the exotic masculine wares around the world, it would be nice to reset her meters on some good old North American beefcake.

Chloe shaded her eyes to study the party. "God, it's hot. How can you stand it in long pants like that? Everyone else is wearing as little as possible."

Ally looked down at her khaki trousers. "Is it? To tell you the truth, after Zanzibar and the humidity of the Indian Ocean, I hadn't noticed. The lack of humidity changes the light, too, now that I think about it. Over there, it's like there's a haze over everything and everything shimmers a little as if it's a mirage." Zanzibar floated through her memory again, like a giant dhow with a tree-colored, three-cornered sail. Zanzibar and her ultimate failure. She didn't want to think about it because then she might have to deal with it.

Chloe raised her brows. "You okay?"

To steady herself, Ally raised her camera and took a few frames, though she wasn't really aiming at anything. Looking through the lens had always been a safe place, all that convex optical glass between her and real life. It was why she'd been so attracted to photography as a kid—you didn't have to be involved with family problems or worry about friends. "I'm fine. I'm just getting my sea legs under me again is all. It's taken me longer than I expected to get over the jet lag."

"Didn't figure on landing in the midst of a mystery, did you? You regretting putting it on yet?"

For a moment Ally didn't get what Chloe was talking about. She had to let Zanzibar fade away. Then Chloe nodded down at the bracelet on Ally's wrist. The darn thing had somehow snagged on the camera strap. She gentled the strap from around the silver links.

Ally shrugged. "Mystery? That just makes it more interesting." Regret? She had too many other regrets to worry about a silly bracelet. She held up her arm so the sunlight caught in the row of small, ornately-made doors that comprised the bracelet that had consumed the lives of the women at *This and That* since it showed up in a box of estate jewelry about two months ago.

Each of the doors on the bracelet was unique. While all were made of silver, each looked like a door from a different part of the world as if—like a photographer—the maker was conducting a study of the graceful forms doors could take. One looked like it was made of wood planks and had an arched top that was surrounded by tiny grape clusters. Another appeared to be the kind of door you found in North Africa: iron strapped with large iron bolts. Another door had leaf-shaped hinges and a fourth had what appeared to be almost elfish hinges. The fifth looked like a traditional Dutch door with upper and lower halves, and the sixth had what looked like raised, square lintels with a small Fatima hand door knocker. The last, and the one that had caught her eye, had a small gargoyle face for a knocker.

The problem was the bracelet brought trouble. Not only did the darn thing have a nasty habit of refusing to unclasp once it was on, it had come to the store after the apparent murder of the estate sale agent who had sold it to them and the suicide of the man who had run her over with his truck.

Since its appearance at the store, the bracelet's first wearer, Kylee, had nearly been abducted and the second wearer, Chloe, had nearly been killed. All that and the break-in at the store, too. It was enough to make all of them want to lock the bracelet up or destroy it, anything but wear it. But there was something else about the bracelet. Somebody or something was looking for it. In all the years she'd been traveling around the world as a photographer and with her charity, she'd heard a lot of strange stories. Some had proven true, like how certain Indian Shamans could seem to levitate, certain Amazonian plants seemed to foster psychic powers, or how curses actually seemed to work in some African villages. But this was Canada, and the story she kept hearing said that something kept possessing people to try to get at the bracelet wearer. That was, well, just a tad unbelievable. Almost as unbelievable as the Okanagan Lake monster that she had believed in as a kid.

After all, she had been wearing the bracelet for a week now and nothing had happened. At all.

"Still not quite sure what to make of it, are you?" Chloe asked. As the second wearer of the bracelet, she'd had a hard time of it.

Ally nodded and touched her own neck. Chloe's still showed faint bruising from where she'd almost been strangled. "I keep waiting for the other shoe to drop—or to meet the man of my dreams like you and Kylee."

"You haven't had any bad feelings? Visions?"

"Nah. That's your thing, not mine."

Ally ran her hand around the bracelet. The silver was downright cool and never seemed to get warm. Though she could see its charm, she didn't quite understand why she'd volunteered to put the thing on. No, not volunteered—more like leapt at the chance—snagging the bracelet off the table and putting it on before anyone could protest. Everyone else had been afraid, but hey, she was a risk taker. "I figure I'll wear it until it falls off on its own and then I'll get on with my life."

Fat chance of that. She certainly wasn't satisfied with this life anymore. Yes, she helped people through her philanthropic organization, *Get the Picture,* and she liked the smiles she'd been able to put on people's faces through the help her organization provided to dig wells, build schools, and protect the environment, but every time she looked in the mirror, there was nothing smiling back at her. She felt barren and bleached out, like a photograph that had been seriously overexposed and no post processing was going to fix it. The color was gone and so was the passion. She really felt the urge to just, well, run. Heck, she'd done it a few times before in her life. It wouldn't hurt her if it became a habit.

But she managed a grin for Chloe. The other woman had finally unbound her usually braided hair and the luxurious length reached below her hips. Outstanding as it was, it wasn't even her best feature—that was her eyes, which sometimes turned almost lavender but at this moment were luminous blue. Ally raised her camera and shot a few frames, with Chloe becoming increasingly embarrassed.

"I'm outta here," she finally announced, her fingers held up in a crucifix mode to fend off Ally's devilry. She quickly disappeared toward the porch amongst the customers.

"Excuse me! I hate to interrupt, but I promise I won't take a lot of your time." Lila Weber's amplified voice cut through the conversation, and the crowd of women on the lawn went quiet. All eyes turned to Lila, standing on the porch at the top of the stairs with a microphone.

A college friend of Ally's, Lila was a beautiful woman of lustrous curled chestnut hair and hazel eyes. At five feet eleven, she was built like a model and might have once considered such a career, but instead she'd been 'discovered' by a movie studio and had become an overnight sensation in what became a cult classic film. After that brush with stardom, she'd removed herself from the spotlight entirely. No one, especially her fans, understood why.

What she didn't realize was that, just by being Lila, a spotlight would always find her.

Today she was dressed simply in a black shantung silk dress that hugged her curves and yet withstood the heat. A single silver pendant shaped like a heart hung on her breast, but the heart was wound with chains and hung with a lock. Her matching earrings were tiny keys. Regulus designs, both of them. They just had to be.

"I'm interrupting all your lovely conversations to say thank you for coming today and thank you so much for your years of patronage. *This and That* has been in operation for five and a half years now. I can't believe it's been that long. We've grown, and I like to think you've grown along with us as we've experimented with jewelry and other wonders brought in from all parts of the world.

"Today would never have been possible if it wasn't for some very special people who are very important to me, so I'd like to introduce them to you. First off, the one and only Reggie Lewis of our very own Regulus Designs. Reggie, come up here."

The dark-haired woman funneled through the crowd and stepped up onto the lowest porch step. Today, she'd actually eschewed her usual camo pants and black sleeveless t-shirt for a sleeveless, vaguely oriental looking, crimson blouse and white flowing trousers. She waved, her Celtic knot tattoos flexing around her biceps.

"In just a few weeks, she'll be off to Milan to finalize the first showing of her beautiful creations on the runway there. She tells me I'm going to have to give up this lovely piece, too." She feigned a pout and stroked the necklace.

There was applause all around, and Ally stepped outside the gate, snapping photos as she went, to frame the scene. Something made her glance sideways and a masculine figure down the sidewalk looked way too familiar, a ghost remembered from an Irish country road. It couldn't be.

"Next up is Chloe Main, who has been the store manager and the face of *This and That*. Chloe's still going to be here, but she'sstepping back a bit from her store duties to focus on her crystal healing business that will also be operating out of this location." Chloe stepped up to join Reggie with a hug as the applause sounded. Ally kept snapping pictures of applauding bejeweled hands and of the three glorious women standing on the porch.

"Chloe's shift of focus has left a huge void to fill, but we've been fortunate to be joined by my high school best friend, Kylee Jensen. Kylee is a marketing genius and the person we have to thank for this wonderful event today. She will be stepping into Chloe's role and managing the front of the store most days. She's also going to be responsible for growing our venture into private jewelry parties. Thank you, Kylee!" Another round of applause as the petite, sunshine-haired Kylee joined Chloe and Reggie at the bottom of the stairs.

"That's the *This and That* team, but on a special note, we are fortunate to have an old friend of mine join us for at least a short while. She is a philanthropist who has worked with the United Nations in places like Ethiopia, Kenya, and Tanzania. She is a world-recognized photographer who has worked with National Geographic and used the results of her art to raise money for her charity. Today she is photographing our little event. Please welcome Allyson McVay and, if you're so inclined, I've set out a little donation box if anyone would like to help her charity."

Ally cringed, but obeyed the call to join the others on the front porch. She stepped up to receive hugs from the other women she had gotten to know so well over the past week of her visit. She'd met Chloe and Reggie five years ago on a brief visit. Kylee, though, was new.

She smiled at the crowd, then made excuses that she needed to get back to photographing so she could slide through the crowd and ease out the gate. She shot like mad as Lila made a show of cutting the ribbon over the front door and announced that the shop was officially open for business. She invited people to come in.

The swirling currents of femininity edged toward the front porch and Ally shot off another few frames as the brightly clad women flowed up the stairs.

"Well, well, well. It's quite the day. If it isn't my very own little AllyMcVay." The too-familiar rhyme spoken with a too-familiar and too-wished-to-be-forgotten Irish lilt.

She whirled around, praying it *was* a ghost of her imagination.

Not a ghost and not her imagination.

Séamus O'Hearn, Irishman, hunk, and the man who had broken her heart, trapped her in his arms and kissed her in front of everyone.

Disaster.

Chapter 2

The damn woman got her elbows between them, and pointy elbows they were. She wielded them like daggers and forced him to let her go. She fell back from him, breathing heavily, her tanned face gone dark with anger. But her hair was still burnished honey gold and her eyes were still the deep, deep blue of the sea that he'd drowned in long ago. At the moment, though, they'd gone stormy.

"Happy t' see me, Ally-girl?" He grinned. By the expression on her face, she was anything but happy. "I know, I know, it's been a few years, but I got it into my head that maybe it was time to mend some fences." He shrugged like it really didn't matter, when in fact the weight of the world rode on this meeting. Well, perhaps not the world, but his world, certainly. A relationship he never should have ended. A little matter of personal redemption. He'd come here to see whether it was possible to fix what never should have been broken, and he'd always figured humor and affection were the way to get past a woman's anger—at the moment, though, it didn't seem to be working.

"What. The Hell. Are you doing here?" A nice bit of angry white had formed around her lips as she ground out the words. Not exactly his Ally's best look.

"Why, I came to see you, o' course. And the town. You talked a lot about this place before ya took off way back when. Figured I needed to see if fer myself." He took a slow turn around to scan the town. Nice enough. Good big bit o' lake, like a Scottish loch, only kinder-gentler looking. Houses strung along the lakeside. A bit of beach. Sun and warmth and none of the humidity that had made the east coast of Africa damned unpleasant. "Looks good."

He swung back to her, but Ally was gone, her height, blonde hair, and stiff shoulders making her stand out in the crowd of women in the yard as she quick-marched away.

Not exactly the welcome he'd been hopin' for on the long, transatlantic flight. He'd been figuring on something a tad more romantic—maybe a run down the lakeshore into each other's arms, followed by a romantic dinner and a meal of other kinds. It had been a wild bit of fun when they'd fallen into bed together before. He'd thought that with all that time for thinking she'd had over the years maybe she'd have come to forgive him.

Apparently not.

"Damn ya, woman. Yer not makin' this easy." He worked his shoulders and set to follow her. After all, an Irishman was always good fer a party.

§

It was Lila who stopped her. Ally let the press of women carry her up the stairs and onto the shady porch, but before she could escape inside the house, Lila caught her arm and pulled her out of the crowd to the relative quiet past the now-empty display tables to the wicker couch and chairs.

"Are you all right?" Lila asked, concern on her face. Her gaze flickered beyond the overflowing copper flower pots to the sunlit, oh-so-eminently male figure on the sidewalk.

"You saw that, did you?"

"I'd've had to be blind not to. I take it he's someone you're not particularly happy to see."

Ally glanced back at the sidewalk, but he was still there, tall, tousled sandy-brown hair, with that infernal grin on that devilish mouth of his. He had his hands stuck in the pockets of his low-slung faded jeans and his shoulders looked entirely too fine in the chambray shirt with rolled up sleeves. It was the same look he'd affected on their evenings in Ireland, oh-so-long ago. A devil in disguise: she'd learned that lesson the hard way. All these years later, she was not fooled by him anymore—there was no schoolgirl urgency as there'd been all those years back. Those chocolate-brown eyes of his were just a trap of the worst kind and she wasn't going to fall for them again.

"He's the one—a guy I met just after I left home. I thought I fell in love—until the jerk dumped me out of the blue and went off with a local girl." And scooped out her heart and stomped all over it. "I really don't need him messing with me right now." She glanced back at the gate and dammit, dammit, dammit, he was coming through the gate. That was Séamus—always pushing in where he wasn't welcome and expecting to use his considerable Irish charm to get him by.

Lila patted her shoulder. "Then why don't you head inside and I'll deal with Mr....?"

"O'Hearn. Séamus O'Hearn."

"An Irishman, Ally?" Lila cocked a brow at her and half smiled.

"I know. I know. I should have known better, but he's damned charming. Watch out for it."

She took Lila's invitation and, feeling something of a coward, ducked through the door into the crowded store. It was a good room, with pale lavender-gray paint on the upper walls and the darkly-stained wood wainscoting around the lower four feet of the wall that matched the hardwood floor. A cash desk sat in one corner, ably attended by Kylee Jensen. Above the desk was a shelf that held a seated golden Buddha and a small brazier that trailed a myrrh-scented tendril into the air so the whole room had a sultry, exotic feel. The windows along the front were open to allow in the breeze, but even that couldn't wholly alleviate the heat of so many bodies on such a warm day.

The effect was like she'd been pulled down in a deep, slow moving current. The way the displays were set up in the store encouraged the shoppers to slowly circulate around the room like worshippers at Mecca. That would work well in a less crowded store, but now the brightly clad women formed clots around the displays that left others unable to see the wares. They'd have to circulate around again. But there were other things to see. Brightly colored pashmina scarves were braided into a dark-stained wood dowel ladder that ran up one corner by the window so the sunlight made their colors gleam. The earring cabinets filled one wall and were an obviously popular destination given the number of women hovering there. Glass cases above the wooden wainscoting carried crystals, and silver and stone pendants of various colors. Chloe was there to describe them.

Reggie was holding forth at a special display of her designs, and she had a pad and pencil handy so that she could sketch a design on the spot for one of the customers. There was an excited crowd around her asking all sorts of questions about her forthcoming show in Milan.

Ally sank back against the wall by the door and let the women stream past and around her as a set of heavier feet trod the stairs outside.

"Excuse me." Lila's smooth, husky voice. "May I see your invitation? This is a private party today, but the store will be open for regular business tomorrow."

That was Lila, always thinking about tomorrow. She wouldn't just chase the interloper off—which was a darn shame, given Lila could be forbidding if she wanted to be.

"Aah, now. Ya see, I'm not a customer at all. I'm an old friend of Ally's come for a visit."

His footfall said he went to move past Lila and Ally froze.

She would not have a confrontation with that man. Not here and not now. What the heck was he doing here, anyway? How had he found her? Had it taken thirteen years for him to notice he missed her? Or had he just had a bad day and decided he'd come find her to share his misery? Séamus O'Hearn was one of those men who had slipped into and out of her life. Since Ireland, she'd found comfort with someone else. A few someone elses if the truth be known.Well, maybe more than a few. She didn't need Séamus O'Hearn weaseling his way back into her life and her heart like a kid placing rabbit ears above a friend's head in a photo. It was not going to happen. She had other things to worry about, like who was responsible for the collapse of her charity's showcase project and whether the charity could survive what had happened.

So she'd called Lila and come home to do some serious thinking. Who knew an old troublemaker would turn up? He was like an imp from his homeland who brought no good with him.

"Mr. O'Hearn, it seems Ally doesn't want to see you now. As this is neither the time nor the place for a scene, I'm going to suggest you come back after the store is closed or, as I mentioned, tomorrow. I will not have you bothering my friend."

Ally waited, breath held, to see what he would do, because although he was basically a good person, sometimes Séamus could do the stupid thing and truly offend people. She would not let him wreck Lila's grand opening. If she had to, she'd drag him away and deal with him. She chanced a glance out the window to find Séamus busy studying his feet.

"Well then, would ya give Ally a message fer me? Tell her that after all these years I've come to my senses. Maybe it's time she came to hers. She could at least talk to me."

Ally fisted her hands. High time indeed. It wasn't her that did the leaving. Sure, she left Ireland, but that was only after he'd had time to take her heart and clog it into pieces so small they could never be recovered. She heard the clump of his footfall on the stairs and rolled away from the wall herself as Lila stepped inside and made a show of wiping her hands.

"Dealt with."

"Thank you. Now I'd better get busy." She hefted her camera and shot a jillion more frames of the crowd inside the shop. Happy smiles, faces reflected in glass, with the indistinct shapes of the jewelry beyond. Items selected for purchase lying on black velvet trays next to the antique, scroll-sided cash register that was, in-and-of-itself, a piece of art. The mannequins with their ropes of chains and pendants, the pashmina display, and the humanity of delighted faces caught in the light and shadow of the room. Then there was the door closing behind the last customer, the deserted tables out front, and the business of cleaning it all up.

The five of them collapsed on the wicker couch and chairs after they'd been moved back into their historical position on the porch near the shop's door. Lila looked pleased, Chloe and Reggie a tad frazzled, and Kylee positively elated.

"That was the best sales day we've had since I arrived here. We had seven thousand dollars in receipts and we ended up with about fifteen other, more expensive pieces on layaway plans," Kylee said. Her big blue eyes were glowing as she shoved some of her chin-length bright blonde hair behind her ears. "That is a good day of business."

"There was a lot of interest in the crystals, too," said Chloe, combing her hip-long hair with her hands and then starting to braid it. "I gave away a zillion business cards for the healing sessions, and there were a lot of questions about the properties of the different stones. I think Kylee's right. We should make sure that with each stone sold there's some information about the stone's properties and also something about how to keep the stone cleansed and charged. We might even want to consider having a small stock of books about the stones so that people who are really interested could buy one." Chloe looked around the group and got nods in response.

"So who's the guy, Ally? He's got a cute accent," Reggie asked. As usual she looked like a modern-day Cleopatra, with her black hair cut in stark bangs that set off her dark brown eyes and high cheekbones. The soft silk clothing she wore belied the warrior woman she usually was. Unfortunately, she also took great pleasure in asking hard questions when she wasn't making jewelry or taking care of her ten-year-old daughter.

Ally shook her head, her hand finding the bracelet on her wrist. After the heat of the room, it was finally warm, too. "An old—acquaintance, Séamus O'Hearn. And yes, he's Irish and has one of those lovely lilting accents that make North American girls want to throw their panties at him, but not me." Her hand closed a fist around the bracelet and heat seemed to radiate from it. She released it and sagged back in her chair. "Sorry. It just makes me angry that he nearly made a scene at your party. He shouldn't be here. Not at all. It's been what—twelve or thirteen years since I last saw him."

She glanced up in time to see glances pass between the other women.

"Before you get any stupid ideas, Séamus is nobody to me. We had a fling once, years ago when I first started traveling. I thought we were in love. He had other ideas and dumped me for someone else so I left Ireland. Stupid of me to let a man chase me out of a perfectly lovely country. But it's over. Ended. So completely ended."

"So what's he doing here, now?" Kylee asked, her eager blue eyes clearly already scheming. "All these years later, a man doesn't just follow a woman out of the blue."

"Stalkers do it all the time," Chloe said softly, her lavender gaze troubled.

Kylee turned to stare at Ally and all the others looked at her, too.

"Is he stalking you, Ally?" Lila asked.

Ally sighed. "Not that I know of. At least I didn't think so until he showed up at the gate. Scared the hell out of me, he did." And just why was that?

Reggie stifled a grin.

"What? What are you smiling at?"

Reggie shrugged. "Nothing really. Just that for a moment there, you actually sounded like him."

Chapter 3

This was not going as he had planned. It had seemed like such a simple thing. Show up. Apologize again for all that he'd done to injure this woman—not just the ancient stupidity that had ended his relationship with her, but also for his latest transgression. His grandmother had always said that the past was the past and there was no need to worry about the future if you took care of today. At the moment it didn't feel like it.

The fine day had aged, placing shadows on the café table where he'd decided to wait. It was an odd little place, not at all what they would have considered a café back home. More like it was a big city coffee chain plunked down on some backwater lane: Baristas rushed around making specialty coffees inside; a lineup of patrons long enough that it must have emptied half the houses in the town; a cool glass case filled with decadent pastries. All of it inside a shop that had shed its outer front and side walls to let the breeze inside and spill tables out onto the broad concrete sidewalk. And him sitting here amongst them feeling sad.

Wallowing, more like.

Damn thing was, he had set Ally behind him as an unrequited love that he'd lost due to his own youthful stupidity. That was, he had until circumstances had brought her and her work to his attention on his latest job. Then, when he'd realized his recent actions had hurt her again, he'd found out where she'd gone and followed after. He just hadn't had the guts to actually tell her in Africa. So now he was here. The sight of her this afternoon had electrified him and made him realize just how much he had missed when he lost her. All those years wasted. Had she found her relationships with other men as unsatisfying as his relationships with other woman had been? There probably hadn't been any shortage of men for a woman like Ally. A long ago jealousy swam up to his brain and he didn't like how it felt.

Come back tomorrow, the auburn-haired lass had said, but it made no sense to wait 'til then when he had come all this way to say things today. A light wrinkle of waves had cast themselves on the lake that was far too blue and calm—not like the Irish Atlantic at all, and not like his emotions. The hillsides, too, were strange—not the green hills of Ireland, but not the dry brown escarpments of East Africa either. Even the wind felt strange. Not the moist, cool air of his homeland, but not the humid heat of the Indian Ocean either. Here the full afternoon sun could burn a man, but there was none of the wilting humidity.

No, this was a pleasant enough place. He could see spending at least a little time here, even if the café was an oddity and he was missing the easy pints that were available around most corners in tourist places like Nairobi or Mombasa.

He shoved the coffee he'd been nursing away. Never could get rightly passionate about the stuff the way that the Americans and Canucks could. Why a coffee on a hot day when a pint would better quench his thirst? He caught the eye of one of the café's bus boys and the lad sauntered over.

"Can I help you, sir?"

Sir. It had a nice ring to it, but it was more like something they'd call his father. "I'm wondering if there's anywhere around these parts a man could get a beer."

The busboy looked him up and down, maybe taking in his denim and his long legs besides. "Well, if you're up for a walk, there's the Sundowner Pub down in the old town."

"The old town?"

The lad stepped out through the tables and pointed down along the lakeshore. "Down past the marina toward the old eight-sided church. They've got a patio, too, if you order dinner."

"Then dinner and a pint it is." He pushed up from the table and glanced back at his rental car, parked back in the shade of the tall cottonwood trees along the water—it could wait for him there. He set out along the lakeshore, admiring the long legs of the late afternoon joggers in their spandex leggings and the way they bounced in all the right places, but there wasn't a one of them that could hold a candle to a young Ally McVay.

A few hundred feet down the beach from the café, the white and red house waited. When he came even with it, it was clear that the party was over. The tables were cleared from the front lawn and the small sign in the window said closed. He hadn't said he wouldn't come back today. In fact, the lass he'd talked to even suggested that he come back at the end of the day. Dinner and a pint could certainly wait if he could mend fences with Ally. He really needed to apologize. In fact, he might have been better off if he'd led with that when he first spoke to her. Damn.

He went through the gate and across the lawn that hadn't quiet sprung back from all the traffic this afternoon. Once on the porch, he glanced out at the lake, glowing like a hope in the afternoon sun. Well, hope was all he had, wasn't it? That and an apology. If the darn woman would only do the graceful thing and accept it.

The trouble was, Ally was nothing about grace. She could be a fekking banshee when she decided and he was a fekking fool thinking anything else. But he'd found out where she was and he was going to put things to right. Period.

He knocked on the glass-windowed door and waited. Knocked again and peered into the dimly-lit shop. It was a fair-looking spot. Gleaming glass cases. Dark hardwood floors and expensive-looking odds and sods around the walls. Trust Ally to have tony friends.

A dark, feminine head poked through a beaded curtain at the rear of the shop, spotted him, and froze like an earthworm on an icy morning. Then she disappeared back through the curtain, whoever she was. Damn. That was no way to treat an honest man.

He knocked again and thought he heard hurried footsteps and voices. What? Did it take a committee now to decide to take pity on a poor fella at the door?

Then the curtain parted again and Ally stepped through looking grim-faced and dour as if attending her own funeral. Three other women ranged behind her like a fekkin' witches' coven.

She pulled the door open, releasing a tinkle of sound from a bell above the door and the sweet scent of incense and the whiff of cloves that he'd always associated with Ally.

"Well hello, darlin'. I thought given yer little party's over we might have a word." He glanced past her at the other women and blazed his most charming grin and tipped his head. "Ladies. Can I borrow sweet Ally for a moment?"

From the hard line of Ally's mouth, she wasn't going to say yes. There was a rigidity about her jaw and shoulders he'd not seen before.

"Come on Ally, a man needs to apologize, don't he?" He used his best smile, but it didn't really seem to be helping.

"Fine. We can talk, but only so I can tell you to get the hell away from here—me—my friends." She glanced back at the phalanx of women who seriously looked like they could do him harm. "I'm okay, guys. Thanks for your support. We'll just step out on the porch for a moment before Mr. O'Hearn leaves."

She ushered him out the door and pulled it closed behind her before crossing her arms over her chest. "So? Let's hear it."

Shite. She really wasn't going to give him a chance. He'd never get his point across if he just blurted it out.

He nodded at the wicker settee. "Have a seat, would ya? I've got more than two words to say."

Begrudgingly she sat in one of the chairs, her back to the wall of windows, her arms still crossed. Her expression told him it really didn't matter a damn bit what he said.

He settled on the settee across from her. Well, Mrs. O'Hearn never raised a quitter, did she? He leaned forward and considered touching her hand, but settled on catching her eye. It was hard, that cold blue like the fekking Atlantic after a blow.

"Ally. It really is good to see you again."

She said nothing, just continued to study him so he felt like one of those frogs he'd dissected in school.

"It's a long way from Ireland to Peachland. A lot of water under the bridge and all that."

She rolled her eyes. "Would you get to the point, Séamus? There are five of us aiming to go out for a bite and we're going to lose our reservation because I'm talking to you."

Her deep blue gaze had gone hard as stone and her jaw was as set as a granite wall. Well, in for a penny, in for a pound. "I came because I heard you left Zanzibar. I heard you were sick and I wanted to make sure you were all right."

Bloody tool. That wasn't it by half.

She raised one brow and went to stand. "Then I'm fine. I *was* sick in Zanzibar. Malaria, but I got over it. Thank you for asking, but a phone call would have been sufficient. You certainly didn't need to come halfway around the world to ask, and what were you doing checking up on me anyway?"

She looked down at him with those forbidding eyes. But the lips weren't forbidding. He remembered the softness of that mouth too well.

"Ally, please. There's a lot more you and I've to discuss."

She shook her head, her mane of hair shaking around her shoulders. "No, there's not. Thank you for checking on me, Séamus. That was kind of you."

She reached out to shake his hand like a fekking *business* partner. Not a lover. Not the man she'd woken up beside for twelve whole months until the idiot man ran off like a fekking tool.

He stood up to face her and accepted her hand, felt her shake it and himself directed to the stairs and out to the road. When he looked back, she was standing there, her arms wrapped around herself as if she was trying to get warm.

What the hell was he doing? He should head right back up there and tell her how he felt. Tell her what he'd done. Tell her how he'd been the fool his father had always named him. The trouble was, those rock hard eyes of Ally's said she'd never believe him.

Fitting, perhaps, given one of their last times together had been to Blarney.

§

Ally blew out a breath and almost collapsed. Her legs had gone that wobbly before Séamus finally turned and started walking. He looked lonely with his head down, his hands stuck in his pockets, heading down the road toward town. There was none of the bad-boy-and-loving-it jaunt in his stride that had first caught her eye when she was only twenty and newly arrived in Ireland. It had been the way he tossed his head and the wind caught his thick brown hair. And then he'd turned and captured her in the impish glow of those brown eyes of his. She'd been sure she understood where the legends of tricky leprechauns came from—not that Séamus was in any way small. No, he'd been built like one of those brawny Celtic warriors in a romance novel. Still was, if the breadth of his shoulders and the lean line of his hips and torso were any indication.

The sun had lowered over the western mountains, placing a warm, sweet-light glow on the mountaintops across the lake. The lake itself was a cool blue that offset the little fizzle of old flame that Séamus raised. A good thing, because she was *not* getting involved with Séamus O'Hearn again. For all the chemistry they'd had, she was far better off sticking to her no-attachments rule. It was healthier, safer for her emotional equilibrium and, given her frequent travel, far more convenient. She could take her pleasure where she found it, without all the trouble of a relationship.

"Ally, honey? You all right?"

She looked back as Lila slipped an arm around her shoulders. Her auburn-haired friend looked her in the eye, while lavender-eyed Chloe and black-haired Reggie came up on her other side. Pixyish Kylee stepped out on the porch to watch Séamus follow the curve of the lake toward the center of old Peachland.

"I'm fine." Ally found a smile. "I mean, he's gone, right? I guess I'm just a little sad—and mad that he's here. I mean, what's he doing coming here and dangling the idea that he might still want me? But I am so not getting into one of those on-again-off-again romances. To me, that's just another form of torture. No, give me a new man every week."

She grinned at her friends. "Speaking of which, we should get going. Who knows, there might be a man on my horizon after all this—just not Séamus O'Hearn. We need to celebrate!"

She caught Lila's and Chloe's arms and danced them back into the house. "Time to get our purses and head out. Kylee, what time did you make the reservation for?"

"Six thirty," said Kylee, following with Reggie, both still wearing their event finery.

Ally checked her slim, men's-face Rolex that had been a gift from an Emeriti sheik who had been her one-time lover. "That gives us ten minutes to get there. Everybody feel like walking?"

The *Blue Hills Restaurant* was probably the most popular in Peachland and had become a bit of a destination for people from Kelowna, both for its eclectic food and the ambiance. The place was a huge log structure, open to the road and the lake view with an open-air, stepped terrace that led to an indoor pub and a fine dining restaurant on the second floor. The terrace was a favorite of the summer people, where they could come for good food and drink with only a cover-up over their bathing attire.

Ally took it all in as they strolled up to the hostess's station. They were five minutes late after their quick-march down Beach Avenue, but the hostess welcomed them in and seated them at a table on the first level next to what looked like an old stone well. Ally settled in her seat and then craned around. The tables were all full—some with families, some with couples, and the one next to them occupied by a lone-wolf male.

Interesting.

Some of the tables were under cover of a half roof around the edge of the terrace, while others, like theirs, took advantage of the fading sunshine. The log walls gleamed and the wonderful smells of good food were overwhelming. "Wow. Is it just me, or has this place changed? Didn't it used to be a little hole in the wall Italian place?"

Lila nodded and sipped the glass of water their server promptly brought. "Used to be—until Peachland got on the map. Now it's a classy little town," she said with her best classy, gum-snapping dame accent.

"I hope the food's as good as the view," Ally opened her menu but threw a pointed, sidelong glance at the guy who was dining alone.

He was worth the second look: broad shoulders covered in a light blue polo shirt, dark hair that just covered the collar. High cheekbones, she could tell by his profile, strong nose and jaw. Strong physique, too, judging by the muscled biceps, and yet he had elegant hands. Séamus had had elegant hands, too. It was one of the things that had first attracted her to him. He'd been a musician in an Irish band, and the way his fingers had played across the guitar strings had gotten her wondering what else they could do—and got her not a little hot and bothered.

But that was long ago, before she discovered just what kind of man Séamus O'Hearn was.

This man, however, was definitely interesting. Hmm.

She caught Lila looking at her and ended her assessment. "So today. It went off without a hitch, didn't it?"

There was more debriefing over the event and Kylee prattling on about enquiries she'd had about additional—smaller— jewelry parties at the store. Chloe had also had some bookings for her healing business and the store looked like it was going to continue its success. Lila ordered a bottle of white Zinfandel as they considered their menus.

"It all looks so good; what do you recommend?" Ally asked. Chloe was sticking with her favorite spinach salad with goat's cheese and candied pecans. Lila was going for a chicken club, and Kylee was wavering over a small pizza done Napoli style with thin crust and fresh artichoke and tomatoes and cheese on the top. Reggie had a salmon burger, but Ally broke down and ordered the same burger the lone guy was eating, complete with bacon and melted blue cheese dripping out of the side. There was something about the way he held himself. And his hands. Definitely his hands were attractive. She wondered what they'd feel like on her skin.

He must have felt her regard because he glanced in her direction and she almost choked on her wine. *Holy mother of God, those eyes.* Piercing blue, like the blue through the Greenland ice-field she'd once photographed for a piece on the impact of global warming. But when he smiled, he did way more than warm her—it was like her pilot light got turned up to roaring. There was *nothing* cold about this blue-eyed fella.

She smiled in return and he nodded and went back to his meal.

"Earth to Ally? Anyone there?"

Reggie's voice. A basket of breadsticks had appeared on the table along with the wine and just how had she not seen them arrive? She frowned. Shrugged. "Sorry. I guess all my brain cells just went for a fantasy holiday. You were saying?"

"I was asking how you're doing with the bracelet. It's been a few days now. Any issues?"

Ally held up her wrist to inspect the bracelet. "I'd say it's growing on me." It actually felt warm on her wrist for once, and her fingers seemed to slide of their own accord toward the little door with the gargoyle head. It was a gruesome little visage, like something you'd find on Notre Dame Cathedral, not a silver bracelet, but that was part of the charm of the piece, wasn't it. "How's all the research into its history coming?"

That was one of the projects she'd kept her nose out of because, while she might be wearing the bracelet, it really wasn't her problem. The bracelet's provenance, aside from the identity of the retired British Colonel who had owned it, was a mystery and one that Kylee and Chloe and Lila seemed determined to solve. Even Reggie had apparently gotten into the act by taking scrapings of the silver and sending them out for analysis. The results hadn't come back yet.

She had better things to do with her time, like decide just what she was going to do now that her Pemba Island project was more or less in ruins.

Kylee and Lila looked at each other. "We divided up Colonel Bristol's journals, but that's still a whole whack of reading for both of us," Kylee said. She chewed on a breadstick for a moment. "I have to say I probably haven't done as much reading as I should have. I've been a little distracted." A little self-deprecating shrug as she raised her hands. "Relationships—what can I say?"

"You're saying my brother is getting in the way of you doing what needs to be done," said Chloe with a deadpan face. "I could talk to him for you. Maybe tell him to back off and give you some space?"

Color flooded up Kylee's face. "Don't you dare. I happen to like—getting distracted."

"I'll just bet you do, honey," Ally said. "Chloe has a very—distracting brother." She wiggled her brows and enjoyed how the color seemed to go even darker on Kylee's face.

"You guys should talk," Kylee said. "Chloe, you're spending an awful lot of time with a certain cop and you..." she swung around to impale Ally with a not-so-menacing glare. "You have men following you halfway around the world, so I suggest that you both have had a little distracting of your own."

The little minx could hold her own. Kylee Jensen might be small, but she wasn't going to take teasing lying down. "Well, it's the distracting I'd like to have now that would be more fun." She nodded in the Lone Wolf's direction. "Séamus—he's just a blast from the past and not one I want to think about."

"Now that sounds like a story that needs telling," said Reggie, refilling their wine glasses.

"It's a story I don't even want to think about."

"And that's simply not an acceptable answer," Reggie said, topping up Ally's wine and waving for another bottle. "A man follows you this far after all these years and you refuse to see him and expect others to deal with him; well, that certainly sounds like someone who owes us a story. What do you think, Lila?"

Lila laughed and shook her head. "I suppose it would be a fair trade." She met Ally's gaze and made a small what-would-it-hurt gesture with her head. It was true, because it was ancient history, or she wanted to think of it that way.

"Séamus and I go way back. We met not too long after I left on my adventure. You remember, Lila."

"Sure do. She was bound and determined that college was just filling her head with useless stuff when what she wanted and needed was to be out there doing and getting on with her life. No one believed her when she said she was quitting until she up and showed up at campus for a last goodbye because her flight was leaving that evening. Silly, brave adventurer, that's Ally."

"Bold," Chloe intoned. "The word for her is bold."

Reggie nodded and leaned in beside Ally. "She's got a word for each of us. Her intuition and," she waved her hands a little, "all that woo-woo stuff. I, apparently, am 'steel,' for whatever it's worth, and Lila, what was your word?"

Lila just smiled secretively, but then relented. "She called me 'old'."

"Chloe!" Kylee rounded on the lavender-eyed woman with the mane of hip-length hair. "How could you say that about Lila? I mean, look at her!"

Chloe held up her hands helplessly. "The words just come to me. Like you, except you got two—heart and capable."

"Yeah, yeah, yeah, 'but not a capable heart'. I remember."

"So you were telling us about Séamus," Reggie said as their dinner arrived.

For a moment there she'd hoped that her friends had been sidetracked, but no such luck apparently.

She sighed. "So I decided Great Britain was where to start because they at least spoke English. There, I met up with two girls who were headed to Ireland, so I went along. We traveled, sampling the pubs and doing some walks, and eventually we found ourselves at a pub in a little village in Cork County where they had music playing. Séamus was in the band. We hit it off.

What can I say?" She bit into her delicious-looking hamburger and seriously hoped that was the end of the grilling.

It had been pub food like this she'd been eating, though nowhere as good, when the band took a break and a tousle-haired lad had wandered to their table.

The others were looking at each other expectantly and as Ally swallowed, Reggie set her burger down and leaned forward, "Well?"

"Well, what?"

"Don't leave us at you meeting him. What happened?"

Ally scanned the faces, seeking some other focus, but four sets of eyes all looked at her with the same question. "Isn't it enough to know we go way back?"

Four heads shook side to side in unison like a troupe of marionettes. She sighed.

"Fine." She made them wait through another bite of burger. "So we hung out together. He took us on a few hikes in the area, mostly along the coast, but when the girls wanted to move on to another part of the country, I stayed behind. Things got pretty hot and heavy and for a year we were pretty much inseparable, but then one night he was playing at a pub and I wasn't feeling well so I stayed back at the place we'd rented together. He didn't come home. When I saw him next, he'd apparently hooked up with an old girlfriend, because when I finally saw them together it was pretty clear what had happened and that he was waiting for me to get the message and move on. I didn't say anything. Heck, I was embarrassed the way I'd been mooning over him and thinking about having his babies and so on. So I went home, packed my pack, and high-tailed it out of town. I ended up in Africa and the rest is history." She glanced at Reggie and the others. "Now go talk amongst yourselves on some other topic of conversation. I want to eat this delicious burger before it's cold."

She made a show of focusing on her food while surreptitiously keeping an eye on the Lone Wolf at the next table. He'd been here long enough that he clearly was alone, or else he'd been stood up, but she couldn't imagine any woman doing that to a guy who looked like him. He glanced over his shoulder and their eyes met again, his so smoldering hot so she wanted to fan herself. Instead she gave him a little eyeball heat of her own.

When his lips curved, Yowza! Her toes curled in her sandals.

At the table, Lila was talking about her latest plans for a major buying trip. It was going to be a long loop through Asia and northern Africa, with a side trip to Mauritania because of Kylee's description of the silver jewelry there. She was planning to leave in the early fall after the start-of-school travel rush was over.

For a moment the conversation made her throat close. Once, she'd thought of Africa, or at least Zanzibar, as home. She'd loved it there and had chosen to live there because of the proximity to Pemba Island and her project. When she'd left Zanzibar, all she'd been able to focus on was how what she'd thought of as her life work was now in ruins. The environmental project. Her photography, which had once sustained her, now fighting an uphill battle against her own apparent loss of passion and growth of the ubiquitous smart-phone photograph. Why buy an art card or framed photo when you can take a picture yourself and e-mail it home?

"Maybe you can check out where Colonel Bristol found the bracelet," Kylee offered, her bright voice cutting through Ally's morose thoughts.

She chewed another bite of burger and dabbed a crisp fry in ketchup.

Lila's brows rose. "Do I look like someone who is going to go tramping through the desert trying to follow in the footsteps of a group of soldiers who tried their best not to be seen? I don't think so. At least not in this footwear." She grinned and held up her foot, today sleekly encased in ankle-high laced legionnaire sandals with three inch heels.

Kylee shook her head. "You can do anything you put your mind to."

"There is a limit and my limit is anything that includes camping, Kylee. And anything that involves living for days without taking a shower. You and Ally might go adventuring into uncharted territory, but that's not me."

Kylee shook her head but grinned. "That's not good. Not good at all. How are we ever going to find out anything about the bracelet's provenance if we're not prepared to stretch ourselves to get the information?"

Lila stabbed a piece of lettuce from the side salad that came with her chicken club sandwich. "Maybe the same way you're going to stretch yourself to get the journal readings done. We are never going to find out anything if we don't find the section about how he came by the darn thing."

Ally looked back and forth between her friends and then back to the blue-eyed wolf. Reggie and Chloe were discussing the merits of polished stones versus cut crystals. The bracelet felt heavy and warm on her arm and she ran her fingers over it. Reggie had told her that she thought the bracelet was very old, judging by the corrosion in some spots on the surface. Ally thought she might be right, not from the looks of the piece, but from the way it felt under her fingers. Her camera dials started to feel like that after a while, her use gradually smoothing away the sharpness of edges on dials, the colors on letters. The bracelet felt like it had been rubbed, like she was rubbing it, by many hands.

She had an image of feminine hands down through the ages, small and large, some young, some roped with age, some scarred, some covered in ornate henna. It was the kind of image she could create in Photoshop, images layered upon each other. It would be a strong image representing the passage of time through an object. Something to consider doing. It could be the final shot of an exhibition of various women wearing the bracelet.

If the darn thing ever came off.

She was disturbed from her thoughts when a shadow fell over her and the table.

All the conversation stopped. Four female faces looked up expectantly and Ally followed their gazes. The Lone Wolf stood beside their table, beside her to be exact.

"Excuse me. I did not mean to interrupt your party."

Strong voice with a hint of growl that made her insides tremble. He had a hint of an accent that suggested northern European overlaid on almost a Midwestern drawl. Odd.

"What can we do for you?" she asked, pleased that she could find her voice when her mouth felt totally dry. He had a deep, smoky scent coupled with something floral, that didn't quite go with the heat she felt off his body. It took everything she had not to toss her hair. Instead she looked up at him with a question in her eyes.

"Actually, it was you I needed to talk to. I saw you sitting here with your friends and I had to meet you."

"That's very kind of you," Ally said. She held out her hand. "Allison McVay. Ally to my friends."

"Very pleased to meet you, Ally. My name is Abel Khan." His blue eyes caught hers and wouldn't let go. His grip was warm, dry, and strong, and a steady pressure on her hand that could lead her so many places. For a moment she felt dizzy with all the possibilities. He produced a card from somewhere and placed it on the table beside her. It was silver with black embossing. *Abel Khan*, it read. *International Affairs*.

Well, wasn't that most promising.

"I was hoping that perhaps you could get in touch with me if you are interested and we might go for coffee or dinner while I am in town," he said.

He leaned past her to turn the card over. "This is a local number where you can reach me. Please call." He smiled down at her, seemed to almost bow, and then was gone, striding down the restaurant's terraced stairs and into the street where she lost sight of him.

Chapter 4

The murmur of the voices of the restaurant patrons gradually snuck into Ally's awareness. Beyond the restaurant, the deep blue lake lapped the grass-covered slope of lawn that led up to the town's stone cenotaph, and the mountains across the lake had gone golden. The cenotaph flag flapped in the brisk breeze that blew a little cooler now that the heat of the man beside her was gone. The air was redolent with the scents of their meals: well-grilled meat and salmon, the rich tomato sauce and cheese of Kylee's pizza. The day lengthened around them into the lingering warmth of twilight and all Ally could do finally was remember to breathe.

"Oh. My. God," Kylee said. "Is this what your life's like? Handsome men just fall at your feet?"

Ally looked down at her meal, suddenly not hungry because her gut had gone all fluttery and soft with the first signs of lust. "Well, he didn't exactly fall at my feet... but yeah. I meet a lot of men. For some reason they just appear to me." She grinned. "I guess that's my gift—men. I never met one I couldn't have as long as I wanted."

Except one, but she wasn't going to think about that.

She picked up the card and slid it into her purse.

"You're not going to call him, are you?" Chloe asked. "You know nothing about him. He could be a rapist and murderer for all you know."

"Or he could be the man of my dreams. But don't worry, Chloe. *If* I call him, I'll have checked him out first. I'm a big girl. I know how to keep myself safe."

Chloe shook her head. "You be careful. That bracelet can get you to do stupid things. It's like it makes you take chances you normally wouldn't and you already take chances."

"Chloe." Ally caught her friend's hand. "Thank you for your concern. Now can we not talk about my love life anymore and discuss something else? Read any good books lately?"

There was head shaking all around. Everyone was too busy.

So there was more talk of the store and the things to be done. The list was long. "I'll tell you what. I'd like to get out and do some photography, and I need to figure out how to deal with the situation with the Pemba Project, but I won't be doing either all day every day. How about if I help with reading the journals? I have more time on my hands than the rest of you and if it would help you out, well then, I wouldn't feel like such a freeloader. Speaking of which..." She snagged the bill off of the table to a chorus of protests. "Least I can do."

Having finished three bottles of wine along with their meals, they were all a little tipsy when they left—well, all of them but Reggie, who had to drive; but then Reggie didn't need wine to be fun. They banded together, giggling as they crossed the street to the sidewalk that ran along the water. Ally stood there a moment, leaning on the metal railing that stopped drunken customers from falling the three feet down to the water.

"I think I forgot how beautiful it is here, you know?"

Lila came up beside her, her chestnut hair gone dark in the light. Above, the indigo sky was streaked with apricot and red. The clouds caught the color and held it, though the mountains across the lake had gone dark.

"When I heard about the Okanagan fire, I worried that everything would be gone."

Lila shook her head. "Not gone. Changed. Renewed, actually. The fire cleared away the old to make way for the new. The mountains across the lake are going green again—finally. It's good to see. There's even been mountain goats spotted down by the lake again."

Ally looked at Lila, whose lovely profile was so strong in the fading light, and wished she could feel as renewed as Lila was describing. "Thank you for letting me come and overstay my welcome."

Lila chuckled. "Why does everyone say that? You're my friends. I love you around me. Do you know how empty that big house can feel at times? All I can say is thank goodness Chloe and Reggie agreed to be my partners in the store. The way Kylee's working at it, we might have to make it four."

"Maybe you're the one who should call Abel Khan. The two of you would be a spectacular couple," Ally teased. "I can see it now—all your beautiful babies."

But Lila seemed to stiffen. She turned away with a small shake of her head. "I think he was smitten with someone else. He's yours to call or not, as the case may be."

The others were straggling down the sidewalk, Reggie threatening to do a cartwheel and Kylee and Chloe apparently leaning on each other and egging her on. Yes, they all had enjoyed their wine. What a gaggle of friends they were—so different each of them and yet they sort of fit together and made the greater whole that was *This and That*. For a moment Ally felt like an outsider and wished she had something like that.

In Zanzibar, for all that she'd been there off and on for close to ten years, she still wasn't *part* of the place. She lived there, she just wasn't part of it, just like her camera kept her separated from the world's events. It was part of why she'd started the charity— to get out from behind the camera—but now the charity itself was threatened. The success of Pemba's environmental project had brought the donors and that money had allowed her work to continue and spread. With Pemba gone, the donations had already partially dried up and though she loved photography, she just couldn't seem to muster the energy for it anymore.

She struck out after the others, her hands in her pockets, listening to Chloe, Kylee, and Reggie's laughter. Lila floated along with them like a fairy tale princess, her hair caught in the wind. Wind caught Ally's blonde tangle, too, and only succeeded in tangling it worse. She sighed. She might not have what these women had, but she'd used her life to do something else with meaning.

She'd founded her charity and left it in good hands so that she could use her time to do what she did best, which was to take pictures that captured the world's attention, and used that to mobilize help for sometimes horrible situations. It kept her moving, not weighted down by places and things, not to mention attachments.

Other people walked the boardwalk beside the water, enjoying the last rays of sunset reflected on the water and the warmth of the day still seeping up from the pavement. A few hardy folk even splashed in for an evening swim. Others performed their nightly canine duties.

What a strange place this was compared to Zanzibar. At this time of day, she and the other expats would be on the balcony of the venerable Zanzibar Hotel sipping a beer and watching the sun set fire to the horizon. The tri-corner-sail dhows would coast past toward the harbor and she'd sit and drink too much with her friends—okay, that was the same—and then, by mutual agreement, they'd pair off. She'd retire with her current paramour to her little apartment with the carved-wood-and-iron door and trunks, the potted plants, her books, and her bed, to lose herself in a physical encounter that would ring in the end of another day.

"A penny for yer thoughts." The soft Irish accent yanked her around. Séamus, looking windblown and thoughtful. He stood beside her, not touching, his hands in his pockets just like her. She pulled them out. Hands in pockets was a habit she'd picked up from him all those years ago.

"What do you want, Séamus? I thought you made it perfectly clear that we were not supposed to be together. I've moved on."

"Is that what ya think, then? I thought our time way back when showed that we were pretty good together." He rocked on the balls of his feet, but didn't look at her. The wind tugged his hair around his ears and shirt collar, and she caught the old scent he had always seemed to carry—warm hay and green grass and heather after a storm—at least that was how she would always think of it.

"You left me, Séamus. You left me and I felt like a fool because I hadn't seen it coming. You thought you could just pick up with your ex-girlfriend and what I felt didn't matter. You didn't even have the decency to tell me. No, I got over you the hard way. Don't expect me to have any time for you anymore." The pain of that long-ago betrayal was still like a knife in her heart, like the way her heart broke the first time she saw a poached elephant carcass—all the magnificence mangled and lost.

He sighed. "You were a hair's breadth from leaving yerself, luv. You wanted adventure that I just couldn't give. You knew it—you just wouldn't admit it to yerself."

Was that true? Had she been ready to leave? She remembered their fights, but also she remembered the love. She'd loved him so badly her heart had actually hurt.

She shook her head. "Well, I guess that just shows why we weren't meant to be together and why you wasted your time and your money coming here." She stepped back, hoping the old pain wouldn't show, and followed after the others.

"Ally, you coming?" Lila's voice floated back on the cooling night air.

"Right here." She jogged up to the others and Lila cocked her head at her.

"Séamus?"

"The very same."

"What'd he want?"

Ally glanced over her shoulder to where he stood like a shadow on the boardwalk, still looking out at the water as if he could will himself back to Ireland or something. "I'm not sure. Whatever it is, he's not getting it."

"Funny he should show up again after all these years." Lila strolled beside her, a thin shawl pulled around her shoulders. "Have you kept in touch?"

"I sent a postcard to his mom a time or two. She'd occasionally send a letter telling me the news from their home. Séamus occasionally came up. I was surprised that I never heard about a wedding or children—after all, that was what his mom wanted for him. She mentioned he did his degree at the University of Dublin in International Studies or some such thing. It was totally unexpected given all he ever wanted to do when I knew him was play his music." She shrugged. "So no. I haven't kept in touch with him, though I've thought of him a time or two—the road less traveled and so on." She swallowed and a little laugh escaped her. "Silly me. No chance of that ever happening."

"That must have been hard—letting go after you felt so deeply for him. You must have expected more."

More? More? She'd expected the moon. She'd met the man of her dreams and had thrown herself all-in. "Maybe if I'd been older and wiser, I'd have stayed put and talked it out with him, but it probably would have just ended up in a shouting match. We were both younger then and I was a lot more hot-headed. Nope. In this world there are those who take and those who get taken. Unfortunately, where Séamus O'Hearn is concerned, I seem to be the one who got taken."

And she needed to get him right out of her head.

They arrived at *This and That* to find a little green sports car parked at the curb, the vinyl top up.

"That's my ride," Kylee said, skittering across the street as the driver's side door opened and tall and hunky beach-boy-blond Brett Main climbed out. Too bad he was Chloe's younger brother and the love of Kylee's life, because a man like him could come in mighty handy right now.

But Kylee stood on tiptoe to kiss him, then beamed at the rest of them. Brett Main was currently untouchable, and by the besotted look on his face, likely to remain that way. Pity.

"So how'd the opening go?"Brett asked.

"It was fantastic!" Kylee said as he held the car door open for her and she climbed inside. Then he briefly pecked his sister on the cheek, waved goodbye, and was gone.

"Must be nice to have a chariot waiting for you all the time," Reggie said as they watched the car's taillight disappear up the street. "Where's your guy, Chloe?"

"Working. What else. You're a detective—no, make that a corporal in the General Investigation Squad—you're always on call." She finger-quoted "general investigation squad" and made her voice all deep and important. She sighed. "I guess that means it's just me and the other man in my life for the evening. Ta-ta." She waved goodbye and started walking down the street toward home and Clyde, her big old blue-point Siamese cat.

Reggie checked her watch and said she'd better be going, what with her ten-year-old daughter being at home alone under the watchful eye of a neighbor. She took her leave in her old beater pickup and Lila slung her arm around Ally's shoulder. "How does a pot of tea sound?"

She led Ally up the porch to the house and inside, the little ornate bell above the door ding-a-linging at their entry. She reset the alarm and then went through the shop and the beaded curtain at the rear and down the hall to the kitchen.

It was Lila's favorite room of the house, Ally knew, but it wasn't hers. The kitchen was painted white, with sunny yellow cupboards and bright hints of turquoise that reminded Ally far too much of the tropics. It had stainless steel appliances and the stove was set back in a tiled alcove with a copper hood overtop. The walls were decorated with little tropical colored fish in yellow and turquoise. So was the nook that held the table. The back of the house was a line of windows that looked out onto the backyard just above the kitchen counter and the nook. Beyond the color scheme, the whole place was entirely too domestic—not Ally's shtick at all. The place positively screamed home and in-place and attachment to place when she'd sworn never to have that at all. No, better to cut loose because everything changed and nothing stayed the same. She'd seen the changes in Peachland, and in Séamus, and in Pemba. She even felt her own.

She felt old and tired and she wondered where the woman who had once taken on the world had gone.

She leaned against the counter as Lila shifted gracefully around the room, filling a tea bulb with tea leaves, boiling water, and then pouring water into a crooked-shaped Mad Hatter tea pot. She carried the pot and two matching crooked cups to the table.

"Come. Sit."

Ally slid onto the bench seat across from her old friend, her small purse on the table beside her. Lila swirled the pot and played mother, pouring them each a cup. The air filled with the scent of sunny orchards and peaches.

"Hmm. Smells good. What is it?"

Picking up her cup for a sniff, Lila closed her eyes and smiled. "I hope it tastes as good—like peach pie and warm earth." She grinned at Ally. "It's a new blend I bought the other day. There's a local company called OK Tea, that specializes in flavors they say exemplify the Okanagan. They recommended this one, and so far they haven't done me wrong."

She sipped and savored with her eyes closed and nodded. "Another winner."

Ally followed her lead and was pleasantly surprised. Even though tea grew in a lot of the countries she worked in, it really wasn't her favorite drink. Nope, give her a coffee or a beer or a good Irish whiskey if she could get it. She took another sip and set the cup down, feeling Lila's gaze on her.

"You know, you've been here over a week now and you still haven't said why, other than you needed to find your focus again." Her gaze speculated over her cup's brim. "What's happened, Ally?"

Really not what she wanted to talk about, because for some stupid reason, just thinking about everything made her feel like crying. She shook her head. "I don't know if I'm ready yet. I need to understand things myself before I can talk about it all."

"Maybe talking about it will help the sorting."

Lila's steady gaze met hers. Lila *was* a businesswoman. She would understand what a devastation Pemba was. She blew out a long-suffering sigh and nodded. "All right. Here goes. In a nutshell, everything has gone to hell for my charity. Do you remember me talking about the Pemba Project?"

Lila frowned. "Something off the coast of Africa, right? An environmental project?"

"That's right." She remembered the pristine turquoise of the ocean, the white sand beaches, and the colors of the fish among the coral. "Pemba Island is a largish island north of Zanzibar and part of the Zanzibar Archipelago. There are a number of smaller islands around it, mostly inhabited by Islamic villagers. Most of them are fishermen and most of their food comes from the ocean. A few years back I happened to visit one of the islands at the invitation of an Imam on the island. He had started to notice that the reefs around the island were no longer providing the same amount of fish that they used to. He and his people were worried. Where I came in was bringing in scientists to look at the situation. The issue mainly was overfishing because some fisherman were not only selling to the islanders, but were selling to Pemba Island as well. The reefs around the smaller island couldn't sustain that much fishing.

"So together with the Imam we started an education program. The Imam started including environmental stewardship messages in his lessons from the Koran. We started schools on the island and together we worked with the headmen to get them on board. We raised funding to support hiring of local people as environmental stewards and trained them about nets that wouldn't harm the reefs and were still good for fishing. We did campaigns where fishermen could trade in their harmful nets that were also damaging the reef habitat for the new kind." She smiled as she remembered those heady days of weekly trips by dhow up to the small island to visit the Imam.

"The Imam was a very progressive man and the initiative worked. He got the other Imams on the island on board as well as the headmen. And other Imams on other islands around Pemba were also starting to get on board. The people began to police themselves and to question when someone brought in too much fish to the market. The reefs began to see a return to the way they had been and in return, international divers started to come, which meant foreign income for the islanders who guided them."

Her chest had gone tight as she thought about what had happened next. She sighed, but it didn't loosen the tight band of anger.

"Two years ago I got word that a big multinational hotel chain was seeking a location for a resort in the Pemba Island area. It was going to happen eventually. If you saw the miles of white sand beach on these islands, you'd understand it completely. The trouble is, the ecology on these islands is so damned delicate because the islands are really just coral piles pushed up from the ocean bottom. The land is poor for growing and there is very little in the way of natural water sources. Unfortunately, the company settled on my little project island precisely because of the work we had done: the environment was recovering, the population was becoming more educated, and it had the requisite pristine beaches because we'd worked with the headmen to clean them up."

The pain in her chest now felt more like a knife. It cut through her like a disaster photo could cut through the public consciousness. "About a year ago, things changed. Up until then the Imams had been able to hold off the corporation by lobbying the government. The corporation had been blocked and I figured— no, I hoped—they'd move on to another spot. That didn't happen. Suddenly the government approved the resort. I went up to the island. The Imam wouldn't see me. The headmen almost ordered me off the island, and when I spoke to women who had been school teachers and the men who had worked as stewards of the reef, they acted frightened and closed their doors in my face. The man I'd hired to act as the delegate of the charity on the island had disappeared.

"I returned to Zanzibar to regroup and try to figure out what had happened. I finally decided to return to the island, but when I tried to hire a dhow to take me there, none of the captains would take me. One of them, a man I considered a friend, told me that all of the captains had been told that if they helped me to return to the island, bad things would happen to them. As evidence, he pointed to the man who had taken me to the island the last time. His eldest son had died in a very strange fishing accident—his leg tangled in a net that pulled him overboard and held him down. Strange that he didn't use the knife in his belt to cut himself loose. He still had the knife in his belt when he was found.

"So the charity lost our key project, and without it to showcase our work, it's a lot harder soliciting donors. The interest of the other islands in participating in the project faded and without donors we're dependent upon the income from my photography, but that's gone down, too. People figure their own photos are just as good to remember a place as the copy of my photo that they could have bought in a shop."

She met Lila's regard again. "So. My business and my life are in ruins. Any helpful suggestions?"

Lila went thoughtful as she sipped her tea. "That's a lot to take in with my head half fuzzed with wine. Did you try to deal directly with the hotel chain?"

"I tried. I sent them letters and tried to phone. I got the runaround every time—or nothing at all. I don't think I got any response to my letters at all."

Lila shook her head. "Well, maybe you should sleep on it and let me have a chance to think about it. I might come up with something."

Like that was going to work. Now that she'd talked about it, it was like something prowled inside her. She was pissed and she needed a way to work off the anger. She fumbled her purse open and pulled out a certain business card.

"And maybe finding a distraction to keep my mind off it would be even better." She showed the Lone Wolf's card to Lila. "This'd probably distract me, don't you think? No commitments and a whole lotta pleasure—enough to not think for awhile. He looked like he was up to the task." She forced a grin, setting aside her feelings. "Don't you think? He was a pretty yum-yum kinda guy."

Lila's head made a small motion—no—but she looked away and seemed to sigh, then looked back at Ally. "He was good looking, I'll give you that, but is sex really what you want, Ally?"

"Hey, it's gotten me this far in life, hasn't it? And a life without sex—well heck, what would that be like?" She shook her head, the entire concept foreign.

"How about full of other things? I've been celibate for a while and I'm not unhappy," Lila said quietly. "There are friends and a home and a business to be passionate about. Sometimes—if you're lucky—there's love."

Ally snorted. "I'm a realist, Lila. I thought you were, too. Love—well, I'd begun to think it was a myth until I saw Kylee and Chloe with their guys. But then again, it could just be momentary infatuations in both their cases. Who's to say it's going to last for either of them? And right now I don't have either love or my business."

"My, we *are* in a negative mood tonight."

"Not negative, I just know what can happen. I—I've seen it happen too often with—friends." Friends, travelers she'd met—herself. Mostly herself because of the man she'd left standing on the boardwalk tonight.

She tapped the card with her fingertip. "Nope. I think this fellow might be just what the doctor ordered. Think I'll call him."

"I thought you said you were going to check him out first."

She grinned. "I think a little in-person interview will do the trick perfectly." She slid out of the bench seat and stood. The kitchen wall clock read ten p.m. A little late, but not impossibly so for a booty call. "Thanks for the tea, Lila. I'm not sure whether talking about my situation helped or not, but it's been a nice evening. Now I think I'm going to take care of things my way."

Lila caught her hand and looked up at her, far too serious for this conversation. "Ally, think about this a moment. Both Chloe and Kylee said the bracelet seemed to influence their judgment so that they didn't always make good decisions. Maybe you should sleep on this decision before you act. Please."

Ally looked heavenward. Pu-lease. Sure, she didn't usually run off immediately like this, but... "It's a piece of jewelry, Lila. That's all. Don't tell me you believe in that nonsense."

"Well..." Lila shook her head. "At least be careful. You're wearing the bracelet now, and that means you're a target. And—if you ever want to talk more—or if I think of something to help—well, just know that I'm here for you."

She looked so worried, and worrying her friend wasn't what Ally'd intended when she'd come here. Ally squeezed Lila's hand. "Thanks. It's good to know I've got friends like you in the world."

She let go and left the kitchen for her room upstairs, feeling a bit like a bird lifting off from unstable ground, or as if she was trying to capture a panorama with a wide angle lens. She was going to call Abel Khan and have a wild night. Maybe then she could get her head on straight and solve the Pemba thing and then Lila could quit worrying.

Her room—the guest room—was a calming place of pale mauve walls, a brass bed with a gray-and-purple patchwork duvet, and deep purple sheets that were cool and sensual to the touch. A vase of white freesia that Lila made a point of keeping fresh sat on the mirrored dresser. The dresser was old-fashioned but had been chalk painted in white so it had an antique finish. An aubergine-colored chair with gold tassels on the corners sat in the alcove below the sheer covered window that looked out over the lake. The walls held old black-and-white photos of Peachland and the Okanagan Valley, including one Ally had taken herself years ago before she headed out to have her life.

That was the thing, wasn't it? Her life was really divided into BS and AS. BS—Before Séamus—she'd been a kid experimenting with sex and photography to see what she wanted to become. AS—After Séamus—well, that was a hell-bent run trying to show she didn't need him—had never needed him. At least that was the horrible realization that had come upon her in Zanzibar. She really should be heading back there. Old Zanzibar town had become her business center even though it had almost no infrastructure. Her charity might have an office in Nairobi for international dealings, but Zanzibar was the place she hung her hat and decided on the charities she was going to support, like Pemba. The photos she'd taken on that island had been selling like hotcakes ever since they and a video went viral a few years ago. It was also quite possibly the reason that the island had been targeted by the corporation.

That was what was most devastating. She'd brought the disaster onto the island herself.

Shivering, she plunked down on the bed, pulled out her cell, and dialed the number Abel had written on the card in a strong bold hand. She hoped he was like his handwriting and licked her lips as the call tone drilled into her ear.

On the third ring someone picked up. "Hello?"

Nice growly voice that sounded distracted or maybe like he'd been sleeping. At ten o'clock?

"Hello. Did I catch you at a bad time?"

There was a moment's hesitation and then, "Ally. Hello. You called. I'm pleased."

He certainly sounded awake now, and he'd recognized her voice. That was a good sign, right? That he'd found her as memorable as she'd found him.

"Where are you?" he asked.

"At home. In my room in Peachland. Alone. I don't want to be." There. As simple as that, she'd put it out there. "Where are you?"

There was rustling in the background as if he was sitting up in bed. "At home. In my apartment in West Kelowna. Alone, too. Perhaps we should be not alone together?"

"That would be nice, wouldn't it? Where's your apartment?" She could borrow Lila's car. She'd done it before.

Another hesitation and then, "I'm at the Waterford Condominiums. Do you know it?"

She didn't.

"I could come pick you up," he offered.

Not a good idea given she didn't know what she was walking into. She'd at least want the option of being able to leave when she wanted. "I'll come to you. Give me your address."

He did.

"I'll see you in fifteen to twenty minutes." Then she hung up, but she still felt shaky. It was better this way. She retained control when she went to him. She retained control over when she left. She could keep it clean this way. No emotional bonds. No relationship. Just sex.

With sexual release, she could have her life back and figure out what had to be done.

Chapter 5

The highway was still busy as Ally steered Lila's compact SUV up the steep incline of Drought Hill, north out of Peachland, and then toward West Kelowna. On either side of the highway rose slopes covered with Ponderosa Pine. She swept past a sawmill and into an area of orchards-turned-housing-developments and a few more old-fashioned orchards that were still hanging on. Across the Okanagan Valley, a lot of the orchards were being replaced with vineyards or with Brave-New-World corporate orchards that warped trees into stunted narrow rows so that the fruit could be picked by machines.

She swung down into the slumbering old heart of West Kelowna that had been bisected by the highway and then followed the directions Abel had given her by turning toward the water. The road swiftly fell down the bluffs to darkened fields along the waterfront and a bank of lights from a condominium complex. Those lights and the full moon reflected in the lake's uneasy surface as she followed the road into the complex's circular driveway.

It looked—expensive. She pulled past a security post, giving her destination when asked. Lush gardens grew between the parking area and the building. Four tennis courts were lit by moonlight and an interior-lit pool gleamed blue as the tropics, chaise chairs set in regiments around its concrete deck. She climbed out of the SUV and slipped her small bag over her shoulder. She wasn't here for the night, but she'd brought a few things like a slinky teddy to make her visit more memorable.

The gardens smelled sweet and of lake water. Sprinklers sent a light mist into the air that dewed her skin as she strode to the front door. She buzzed his apartment and the building door clicked open. She stepped inside to a white marble lobby scented of lilies from a huge white floral arrangement. A glassed-in area, unobtrusive in the corner, housed a desk, chair, and closed-circuit TV monitors, carefully observed by a security guard. A little impressed, she hit the button for the elevator. When it came, it was mirrored so she had time to fluff her hair and wonder at the flushed face and too dilated eyes of the woman she saw. She felt breathless and hot and as excited as she always did when entering a new sexual venture.

The elevator dinged and opened on the fifth floor. She stepped out and spotted the open door down the hallway. Abel stepped out wearing a pair of faded jeans that hung low on his hips and a white dress shirt that showed off his tan. It hung open to expose his chest, and with his tousled dark hair and piercing gaze, she almost stopped mid-stride. Her mouth went dry, which made the two fluted champagne glasses he carried all the more attractive.

She could feel his smolder from where she was, but she was pretty sure she was giving off her own heat. She stalked straight up to him and accepted the champagne glass, knocked the fizzing liquid back, and met his gaze. "You going to ask me in?"

He stepped aside and she sashayed ahead of him, inhaling his sexy smoke-and-floral scent.

The doorway put her into a short hallway that gave onto a great-room concept apartment. A huge living room had floor to ceiling windows that looked out onto the night-bound lake.

"Wow," she said and turned to him, noticing the telescope and stand pointing out at the lake. "You must have a heck of a view." She went over and bent to look through it. Darkness. The glitter of moonlight on water. "So what are you looking for?" She straightened and glanced back at him.

By the half smile and speculation on his face, he might have been looking at...her.

"Actually, I'm watching for the lake monster." He leaned on the wall, one brow raised as if waiting for her reaction.

For a moment she didn't react. It was the craziest thing she'd ever heard come out of someone so straight-faced and so damned sexy. "Come again?"

He shrugged. "I'm a cryptozoologist. I'm watching for Ogopogo. There's been an unusual number of reported sightings in the area, and after one of my recent successes in the U.S., I decided it was time to try my luck in Canada."

Now that *was* odd. She hadn't believed in Ogopogo since she was a kid—well, maybe deep down she had, sort of like wishful thinking. If Ogopogo could exist, then just about anything was possible in this big old world. Of course, as an adult, that kind of thinking wasn't generally encouraged. Okay, so she had two choices: get the heck out of here because this delectable guy was crazy; or go with the flow and make love to the body but try to forget about the mind. She took the third option and held out her champagne flute. "I could really use another drink, I think."

He sauntered up to her and stood so close she could feel his heat through her clothes as he poured.

"Let me guess: International Affairs just looks better on a business card."

He grinned down at her. "Something like that."

Something like that, indeed. This man was what she wanted and needed right now, but for a moment she actually asked herself whether she really did. Usually she at least did a search of their name on the internet, but not this time. She gulped down half of the new glass he'd poured and turned back to the window to look out at the water.

"So what is it about you that makes me so darned nervous? I never get nervous."

He stepped up beside her. "Perhaps it's because we have this reaction to each other. If it is any help, I was nervous at the restaurant." His hand stroked her back in long steady strokes, then lifted her hair away from her neck and swept it aside in favor of his lips. The moist touch of his mouth made her legs go weak. The progression of his lips down her shoulder, pushing the fabric of her silk blouse aside, was enough to make her breath catch in her throat.

She wanted this man like she'd never wanted a man before. Perhaps it was his infernal good looks or perhaps it was that he was just so—different. Who chased sea monsters, for goodness sake? *And* carried a business card that said International Affairs?

She turned to him and he took her champagne flute from her and set it on the mahogany side table that sat at one end of the large gray leather couch that formed a conversation square in the room. Then he began to unbutton her blouse and shoved it back off her shoulders when he was done. She stood there in a lace bra and her khaki trousers—not exactly her sexiest attire, but he seemed to see through them and unbuttoned her fly.

"Turn around," he growled.

She did and he stepped up close behind her, ran his hands down her sides and right into the front of her trousers, fingers diving under the lace edge of her underwear. "Hmm," he hummed in her ear and one hand pulled loose and with a flick of the fingers her bra was undone and sliding off her shoulders.

His hand found her nipple and squeezed at the same time as his other hand thrummed a spot between her legs that sent pleasure scorching through her. Her head fell back involuntarily onto his shoulder as a shudder cut through her.

"My, you are beautiful. Look." He raised his chin toward the night-blackened window and she saw them framed there, her naked from the waist up, her trousers shoved low on her hips, her body shivering from his touch. It was erotic as hell and almost voyeuristic, titillating because someone on the water could see them.

She swung around as he pulled his hand free of her panties, her breasts against his hard chest. "Your turn, mister."

She quickly smoothed his shirt off and then expertly unbuckled his belt and pulled it free. Then, eyes never leaving his, she knelt before him and unzipped his fly. The gods were looking out for her, because the guy had everything she wanted and more. She eased his jeans and underwear over his hips and helped him step free, then took him in her hands and ministered to him. His balls tightened in her hands and she released him to stand and strip her trousers and panties off. At that, he caught her again and turned her around, so she straddled his heavy cock as he pulsed his hips and fondled her.

It was good that he liked to play like this. Feeling his arousal, his lips on her shoulder, her neck, her mouth as she turned her head to welcome him. And all the time there was this erotic show going on before them, better than a mirror, for the mysterious darkness muted their figures and threatened to swallow them up if they weren't careful.

"Bend over a little," he whispered in her ear and she obliged him. She heard the rip of paper, caught a glimpse of him rolling a condom on, and then he pressed inside her—gently at first, but she was ready. Then hard—abrupt as their first meeting, as abrupt as her first gulp of champagne—and she came with the first explosion of what she hoped would be many.

He had her by the hips as she arched her back for him, and he plunged into her, the room filling with the sound of the slick wetness of their union. Then he grabbed her shoulder and pulled her back to him, pulsing his member inside her so she thought she might faint. His hands slipped over her breasts and down to their moist joining and stayed there to play as he ran his length slowly in and out of her and she ached for more.

"Deeper," she whispered. "Harder."

He released her, pulled out, and walked away, leaving her breathless and half-crazy as he padded naked as a tanned god across the white shag carpet to the fridge for another bottle of champagne; then he padded back to her, magnificent in his aroused maleness. He caught her hand and the two champagne goblets and pulled her away from the window toward another room.

"Now," he said. "Now's when our play begins."

§

It was five a.m. when Ally dragged herself back home, parking the SUV in the carport in the rear of the red and white house and crossing the yard and patio with its wicker furniture and bright turquoise and yellow pillows for the back door. The air smelled clean and still carried the wonderful cool remnants of the night just as her flesh still carried the sensations of her time with Abel. The sky was palest blue stained golden and the sun had just raised its head above the mountains in what photographers called sweet light. She'd come close to breaking all her rules about not spending the night with a man.

It had just been so—refreshing.

And satiating and enervating and—and—and—

She ran her hands down her sides and felt his palms slide over her flesh. Damn. She could just about come again merely at the thought of what they'd done together. He'd been—knowledgeable—more knowledgeable than her and that was something, after distracting herself all these years with fellow travelers she met as she had her adventures.

The hours with him had passed quickly, each of them seeking the ultimate pleasure in each other's company; best of all, without any emotional attachment. Hours later they'd lain beside each other in the coming dawn in his room. His bed was wide and bound with dark sheets of crisp cotton that only accented the softness and hardness of their flesh. The sheets were tangled under and around them, the playthings they had used tossed aside in favor of the oldest positions in the world. The door to his bedroom patio was open and allowed in the sound of the wind and waves as he'd lifted himself above her and run his sensual mouth over her still-burning skin.

She'd shivered at his touch. She'd ached when he stopped, but the light was rising over the mountains on the far side of the lake and she had promised herself she would not stay the night. Staying the night meant something she wasn't about to give to anyone. So she'd swung out of bed and padded for the shower, insisting on taking it alone, and then with the briefest of conversations and a kiss goodbye, she'd left him with her number and departed, hurrying down to the car and home.

Or Lila's home, at least.

She felt a little sheepish letting herself in the back door and disarming the alarm. She stood there, listening. The house ticked around her. The kitchen, gradually filling with the nascent daylight, still held the faintest hint of last night's peach tea. Let Lila have her long girl-talks. Give her a good roll in the hay to clear her head.

She felt—good. Maybe not whole—not yet, but she could put her thoughts together again, and that was a good thing. Maybe she could figure out what to do with her life now. She might have told Lila all was well, but really she was at a crossroads. The reverence for master photographers was waning. With the loss of donors, she'd had to let almost all her staff go and her accountant was recommending that she close her Nairobi office to keep costs down. Her own income had decreased until she was living on the bare minimum so, even if she'd wanted to, she couldn't afford to live in Peachland anymore.

Not unless she wanted to get a job, and what the heck was she trained for other than photography?

The sexual high she was feeling seemed to wane with each stair she climbed to her room. By the time she got inside to where the light streamed in through the cracks around the blinds and sheer curtains, she was feeling sheepish and exhausted. By the time she stripped out of her clothes and collapsed on the duvet-covered bed, she was as depressed as ever.

Yes, depressed. She had to admit it to herself. Abel had been a *very* pleasant distraction, but he hadn't helped her feeling of futility and uselessness. What the heck was she going to do? She was a photographer. She'd created a dream life for herself, or so she'd thought—the ultimate freedom to go where she wanted, do what she wanted, have the men she wanted.

And at the moment it all seemed just a tad, well, old and yellowed, like a photograph that desperately needed restoration. Even last night's booty call seemed a little tawdry.

She rolled over on her side and tugged the duvet up over her. Cocooned like a caterpillar, she fell asleep, wishing she could find her butterfly wings again.

Chapter 6

The early sunlight on the lake made the entire Okanagan Valley seem t'glow like the Irish landscape, even through the smear on the hotel room window. Séamus shoved the cheap plastic blackout drapes farther apart and leaned against the window frame. The supposedly newly renovated room of the Beach Hotel still smelled of the cigarette smoke of previous occupants. Or else the ventilation system from the outdoor patio of the Sundowner Pub downstairs was sucking in the smoke and feeding it into the room.

Leastwise the scent seemed t'go with the place. The room was small and decorated in plastic and polyester. For ease of cleanup, he supposed. He could picture more than a few drunken sods staggering their way up the stairs to the rooms the pub had to let. Most of the upstairs had been turned into apartments. No place he'd want t' live, though.

He'd been a bleeding fool of a fool last night. In fact, this whole bloody thing was starting to feel like something his countrymen would call a banjaxed mess. He should have stayed put in Mombasa and not tried to put things to right. But then, Mombasa was just a port in a storm, wasn't it? The place he'd put down anchor when he wasn't brave enough to face Zanzibar and Ally.

She might be the woman of his dreams, a dream he'd thought was worth fighting for, but she'd made it damn clear last night that she wasn't having any.

He'd burned that bridge behind him, it seemed. He'd let her go fer too long fer any bloody apology to do any good. It felt like all that waited ahead was a life full of right streaky glass like this window. Even his music seemed flawed. It was like nothing he touched would ever be good again.

"Get over it, man. She's just a woman, one among millions."

The unfortunate thing was, she was *the* one amongst all those millions. Just seeing her those two brief times had confirmed it for him, even after all these years. But how was he supposed to make her understand that when the infernal woman wouldn't even talk to him? He slammed his hand against the wall and got an angry, muffled oath from the room next door. Idiot. Tool. Muppet. That was what he was; standing here like some heartsick sow wasn't going t' do him a heck of a lot of good, now was it?

Just what would help, he wasn't rightly sure, but he had nothing to hold him here in Peachland except the idiot notion that Ally might forgive him. The fact he was here said he wasn't quite willing to give up on that fool's hope yet. He needed her forgiveness to clear his conscience for what he'd done in Africa. Then he might be able to get on with his life just as he had these past almost thirteen years. Of course, without her, it might not be much of a life.

He turned back to the room—just large enough for the bed and TV stand and a single straight-backed chair. Bad art on the walls showed an abstract image of something that looked vaguely like the Loch Ness monster in deep water. Ally had once told him that Okanagan Lake held a similar legendary monster—just as rarely seen.

At the moment he probably felt about like those monster hunters who had gone after the wee beast. Coming up empty every time.

"Shite, man. Get yer act together, would ya?"

On impulse he grabbed his guitar and let himself out of the room into the narrow, white-painted hall. It had a new brown carpet that gave off an odd plastic smell, and fluorescent lights that buzzed overhead. Not exactly the kind of place his Dad had planned fer him when he'd pushed him into higher education. Too-right fer an idiot with a guitar, though.

He went down the stairs and came outside at the street beside the pub entrance. Across the road, a common area held green grass, a few park benches, picnic tables shaded under fluttering trees, and a children's playground of swings and a slide. The wind was soft and pleasant, but strong enough to place a light ripple on the water. 'Twould be good fishing weather until the sun got a little higher in the sky and burned the cool away. A light haze on the water showed it was already happening.

He settled on a picnic table in the shade, sitting on the tabletop, his feet resting on the bench, and peered out at the water for answers to his problems. Back home, living in an area like western Ireland, it was hard to get away from a view of the sea. He'd worked out a song or two sitting looking out at the waves, using the pounding surf as the counterpart to the chords he strummed. This lake, though, was too tame. The lake might be deep, but there was none of the mystery and power that the ocean bore.

His fingers found the frets and he strummed a few chords, humming.

Even sitting right on top of the lake, the air was dry. The rocky mountainside across the water had none of the green of home, and none of the grandeur either—not what he'd expected in this part of the world. Still, he could see the attraction of this place. The warmth, the tame water.

Once he might have gotten excited about this new country he was in, but the excitement seemed to have parched right out of him. Nothing a bit of barley couldn't heal, but it was a mite early in the morning. He strummed the guitar again and started singing—softly at first, and then stronger. It was a song he'd written based on a folk story about a girl who watched her lad go away to battle and not come back. His version was about a man watching his woman walk away, and a haunting tune it was, full of recriminations and a chorus about never being able to live again.

Damn fool ideas.

He was just finishing up the last chorus and feeling the tightness in his chest easin' a little when he caught a movement beyond his shoulder. He looked back to see a long-legged female runner come to a stop behind him and lean her hands on her knees. She had auburn hair tied back in a ponytail, so for a moment he didn't recognize her. Then he did. The woman from the shop—the one who had kept him from following Ally inside.

She gave him a quick grin as she caught her breath. "It was you singing. I hadn't intended to run this far today, but your music caught up to me down by the yacht club so I kept going looking for the source."

"Sorry to trouble your ears. I hadn't realized I was singin' as loud as that."

She wiped sweat off her brow and straightened and she was one right *beor*. Beautiful, even, fine as silver-barked birch with those dark eyes and hair. Not as fine as his Ally, but still fine.

She shook her head. "Not loud. There's just strange acoustics over the water. Sometimes I can hear people talking and the only boat is way out on the lake." She held out her hand. "I'm Lila. Lila Weber. I own *This and That* with a couple of friends. I'm Ally's friend."

"I remember. Ya gave me a good reaming out yesterday, if I recall."

She shook her head. "No reaming. I just didn't want there to be a scene during our grand opening. You seem to be able to get under Ally's skin better than anyone I've ever seen."

His turn to shake his head and he looked back at the water, the depths as dark as that part of his heart. "Ya noticed that, didja? It's a talent, but not exactly what I'm goin' for." He shrugged, and far out over the water, a line of something dark disturbed the still water.

"So just why are you here, Mr. O'Hearn? I've got that right, haven't I? That is your name?"

"The name's Séamus. Call me that. Why am I here?" He strummed the guitar again. "At the moment I'm not rightly sure. I guess I came to apologize for something stupid I've done and try t' make things right with Ally. Doesn't look like it's going to happen, though." He strummed an unhappy song about a man lost at sea and the woman left behind pining.

"What's happened between you two? She doesn't seem that happy right now either." Lila slung her hip over a corner of the picnic table and looked at him speculatively.

Ally unhappy? Then perhaps this whole thing *could* blow over. He lifted his shoulders. "What happened? I walked out, is what. An arse is what I am."

"She said you went off with some other girl. Why come after her after all these years?"

He jerked around to look at Lila. "That's what she said, is it? All these years?"

"She said you met in Ireland, but then you split up, so she left."

"All true. Didja know I tracked her down again? Two years ago I realized where she was—the woman's bloody hard to find, you know. She took off from Ireland before I had a chance to come to my senses and realize what I'd missed. So I found her in Zanzibar, but I couldn't quite work up the courage to apologize." He cuffed himself on the side of the head, because there was more to the story than that, but the ugly parts he didn't want to think about. "A genuine wanker, I am."

"She didn't really mention that," Lila said softly. "I wonder why not."

"Probably because she didn't know I found her. I never took the final step and went to see her. Ya see, I knew she'd do this." He shook his head, bitter for a moment at Ally's hardness, but he knew it was just a form of protecting herself.

"You ever think maybe it's because she'sstill hurting?"

He glanced around at her and his fingers ran a little trill out of the strings. "That seems a bit farfetched t' my way of thinking. The lady can make herself pretty clear when she no longer fancies ya."

She gave him a kind smile. "I'll say maybe again, because I do know Ally and I know she draws men like flies and she eats them like honey, but I've never seen her not be able to deal with one before. What happened between you?"

What could he say? "I got scared is what happened. Scared of the changes I knew I needed to make to be happy and more scared that she wouldn't like the thing I was becoming—so I went back to my girlfriend before Ally could turf me out because I wasn't what she wanted." He strummed a sad chord on his guitar and shook his head. And then, of course, after leaving he'd really screwed up, but this woman didn't need to know that.

Out on the lake, the dark line of waves had held its shape for an unnaturally long time. He stopped strumming and stood. "What is that?"

Lila clambered up on the table beside him and frowned. "I'm not sure. Looks like one of those wave formations that some people say are Ogopogo."

"The lake monster." He looked at her in disbelief.

She held up her hands. "Hey, don't ask me! I just live here; and across the lake, Rattlesnake Island is supposed to be Ogopogo's home. Some divers there even found a carcass that they thought might be a new species in a cave down deep. The lake's deep enough. No one's got anything definitive, but there are still people researching it. Where there's hope and all that." She cocked a brow.

"Sounds like a whole lot of bollocks to me, but I take your meaning." He looked back at the hotel with its faded tan siding and less than pristine green awnings. The place had had a facelift, but it still didn't match the refurbished look of the rest of the scrubbed-face town. "I figure to stay a few more days and see what happens, but if the woman won't even talk t' me, it's kind of hard to put things right, isn't it?"

"Ally can be stubborn. I know that, but I'll see if maybe I can soften her up a little for you."

At that he turned to her. "Why'd ya do that—take my side? Yer Ally's friend. I'd think ya'd be trying to knock my block off."

She chewed her lower lips for a moment and then shook her head. "Let's just say that Ally doesn't strike me as someone very happy right now. She says she's come here to find her focus again. Maybe you can help her. Or maybe you'll find out that she just really needs you to leave. If it's the latter, I'll ask you to not make a fuss and go quietly. Okay?"

She met his gaze and there was a clear expectation that he honor his side of the bargain or she wouldn't either. Finally he nodded. "Thank you, Lila. Yours is the best offer I've had all day."

She flashed him a grin and started jogging back the way she'd come. Then looked back at him over her shoulder. "The day's young. Who knows? Maybe you need to bring that guitar of yours down to *This and That*. Or maybe you'll spot Ogopogo."

Chapter 7

The clock on her bedside table said nigh on noon on Sunday when the sound of footsteps in the hallway outside her door brought Ally out of her cocoon. Perhaps not out, but she rolled over and stared at the white ceiling with its crown moldings, or at least what she could see of them with only the light sneaking in around the window blind. The moldings were old-school graceful, just like this house and just like Lila. You didn't see Lila Weber running off to spend the night with the first good-looking man she laid eyes on, but then that had always been a difference between them. Not that men didn't flock to Lila, but there was always a certain reserve about her.

"Unlike you," she said to herself.

"Ally? You awake? I was just going to make some lunch and I thought I'd see if you wanted something."

She threw off the duvet, stood, and almost fell over from the spike impaling her skull right behind her eyeballs. Hung over? How the hell had that happened? She pulled a robe around her shoulders, shoved matted hair out of her eyes, and opened the door to peer, bleary-eyed, out at Lila. "You're asking me about food?"

Lila's hazel eyes widened. "Uh. Yes? Lunch. Or breakfast if you prefer. If you don't mind me saying, you look like hell. What happened?"

What indeed. "Let's just say that my date went a little longer than expected and I didn't get much sleep." She blinked and tried to find some moisture in her bone-dry mouth. She'd photographed drought-stricken areas of the Sahara that weren't so parched. "Give me five and I can get myself moving. Ten and I might actually be human." She tried for a smile, but didn't quite pull it off. She could tell by the tiny little shake of Lila's head.

"Okay. Ten it is." Lila nodded and left.

Ally hunched in the doorway with the robe Lila had loaned her tugged tight over her breasts. Lila, on the other hand, looked cool and willowy in a pale blue, knee-length shift and white ballet flats as she disappeared around a corner and down the stairs with light, clipping footsteps. Sunday, and the store opened at one.

With a groan, Ally turned back to the room. She staggered across to the window and did a very stupid thing—opened the shade all the way. Sunlight flooded in, adding color to the room and revealing Ally's clothing discarded on the floor. The room actually looked like she felt. Except she felt battered enough to have been run over by a truck.

Nope. Inflicted by Abel, more like. With her permission. In the past, after a night of sex, she'd never felt like this. Usually she felt refreshed and ready to take on the world. She must have just let the champagne get away from her. There had been a lot of it flowing in between bouts of play.

The image of sweat-slicked skin and rock hard abs sent a little frisson of heat up through her. Abel had been, well, *very* able. To the point where she'd had to work to keep up. A nice change, actually. And she'd probably never see him again. Too bad, because she had a feeling he still had a few tricks up his sleeve.

And then there'd been his very unusual profession. Cryptozoologist. Now just how many people in the world had a choice of whether to put that on their business card? She fumbled her purse open and pulled out the card. *International Affairs.* Now there was a *double entendre* if there ever was one. And here she thought she was a rare bird with her photo-charity work.

She shoved her hair back behind her ears and headed for the shower because she really needed to wake up. Along with being parched, she was also starving. A good night of sex always worked up an appetite and that was one thing they hadn't done last night, as if the normal things like food and water were too mundane for the fantasy world they were then occupying.

Had he slept her off, like she had tried to sleep him off?

She lathered herself in the shower for a full five minutes, then tugged a comb through her tangled hair and threw on white shorts and a sleeveless singlet against the heat that seemed to pour through the window. In a pair of flip-flops, she padded down the stairs and went into the wonderful-smelling kitchen.

"Are those waffles I smell?" And bacon and maple syrup and freshly squeezed orange juice.

Lila looked up from tending the waffle iron. The machine clicked and she pulled the top up, releasing a cloud of lovely steam and leaving behind a perfect, golden waffle. "You looked like you could use something special or you might not make it." Lila ran an assessing look up and down Ally's frame. "Better. I'd say you might live. Upstairs I thought I'd brought the undead into my home."

She forked the waffle onto a platter in the oven. "How many can you eat?"

"One. Maybe one and a half." As Ally thought about it, her stomach growled long and loud.

"I'll make it two." Lila poured another waffle of batter onto the iron and closed the top. More steam poured out the edges. Her attention seemed wholly on the waffle iron. "So just where were you so late?"

"Abel's. The guy from the restaurant. You know." She told her about his apartment.

Lila said very little, just set the table. "That's a very prestigious address. Some of those penthouses are worth close to a million dollars."

Ally thought about that and frowned. "Something doesn't quite add up. The place is posh and all done up in leather and chrome, but he says he's a cryptozoologist here to study Ogopogo. You wouldn't figure that profession would make that kind of money."

"He might come from money or have wealthy backers." Lila shrugged. "Funny. Out for my run this morning, I might have seen the monster; leastwise we—I—saw the wave pattern that a lot of people think is a sign of Ogopogo just beneath the surface. You only notice it when the lake is fairly calm."

The waffle iron clicked again and another steaming hot waffle appeared. Lila brought a plate with two waffles on it, a platter with bacon, and a piece of buttered toast to the table, then slid in gracefully to the nook. Ally eased in across from her, careful of the spike still trapped in her skull, and considered the food.

She was hungry, she just wasn't sure how much her stomach could manage; but she was game to give her best. She slathered butter on the waffles and poured real maple syrup over top, while Lila placed a piece of bacon on her piece of toast and began to nibble.

"You know you're never going to grow up big and strong if that's all you have for a meal," Ally said around maple goodness. She snagged a piece of bacon and took a bite. The salty crunch was perfect counterpoint to the waffle. "Anyone ever tell you you're an angel?"

Lila smiled. "One or two."

"To what do I owe this luncheon largesse?"

Lila arched a brow. "Luncheon largesse? You can't be that under the weather."

"Nope. And I plan to prove it by spending this afternoon gainfully employed as your chief researcher into the bracelet." She jingled the silver thing on her wrist. "And just so you know, I'm living proof that a good schtooping does not get the bracelet to come off. Just in case you were wondering."

"I believe Chloe put that rumor to rest." She was talking about Chloe's ill-advised lunchtime romp with a certain police officer. To Chloe's good fortune, it had led to something that really looked like it could last.

"I was just saying that I proved it. It could have been a fluke with Chloe. So who knows what'll get this thing off." She flourished the bracelet again, the small gargoyle's head catching the light.

"I made the brunch—luncheon—whatever—because I really think we need to talk and you've been avoiding talking ever since you got here. Why didn't you tell me about Séamus before now? I mean, we've known each other for years... It's like a part of your life you've just amputated."

Ally's heart did a thunk-thunk like a camera on a too-slow shutter speed. She felt shaky enough. "Uh... I didn't really think it was relevant to where I was at the times we got together." She had a sip of orange juice to try to find her composure. She did not want to be talking about Séamus right now. "Like I said last night, all water under the bridge."

"But Séamus was someone very important to you... He hurt you very badly." Lila didn't meet her eyes.

Hold on a minute. There was something going on here, beyond rehashing the tale she'd told her friends over dinner. "So—what? Oh my God, you went looking for him! You've been talking to Séamus."

Lila shook her head and nibbled her bacon, as she considered her answer. "First off, I didn't go looking. I was out for a run this morning and heard the most haunting music. I had to find out where it was coming from, so I followed the sound and found him playing his guitar in the park across from the pub. He's good— really good, in fact. So we got to talking about why he was here. He wants the chance to have an honest talk."

"No way. No how. He walked away from me, Ally. Fool me once, shame on you. Fool me twice and shame on me. I'm not about to make the same mistake twice."

Lila raised her eyes to Ally over the rim of her orange juice glass. "Funny hearing that from you. I thought you were all about the casual sex and no commitments." She set the glass down. "Just sayin'."

If she could have spluttered, she would have. "What the hell's that supposed to mean?"

"I don't know." Lila stacked her juice glass on her plate, her bacon and toast finished. "Why don't you tell me why you set different rules for one Séamus O'Hearn than you do for the guy last night? You can walk away from Abel without any problem and possibly see him again, but Séamus you can't even talk to and you once cared deeply for him." She slid across the nook seat. "Want some coffee? I'm going to make a fresh pot."

She got up and almost stomped over to the coffee maker without waiting for an answer. Ally watched her go, trying to sort out her response and just why Lila seemed put out.

"You know this isn't really fair, bringing all this up when I'm in a weakened condition."

"Gee. I thought you said a wild night out helped to give you more focus. Clear your head or some such."

"Darn it, Lila! What is with you this morning? Why are you attacking me?" It wasn't fair. Her head hurt and so did her chest when she had to think about Séamus O'Hearn. Everything inside her just went—tight—like a spring wound to breaking. It did that when she thought of Pemba, too.

Across the room, illuminated by sunlight like a portrait, Lila stood with her hands pressed palm down on the countertop, her lovely profile suggesting that she struggled with what to say. Finally she turned to face Ally, resolve on her face. "I want to help you Ally. But I just don't understand this thing with men. I know you've been like this as long as I've known you, but all these guys—they don't make you happy. But then you talked the other day about Séamus in Ireland and you should have seen your face. You got this soft smile as if the memories made you happy. When was the last time you were happy, Ally? You seem like you've lost something—the spark you used to have when we were in college. I'm afraid that these guys—these one-night stands—are just a way to hide the way you're really feeling."

"And that, ladies and gentleman is a really good example of armchair psychiatry." Ally looked down at her half-eaten waffles and slid out of the nook. "I'm not hungry anymore and I think I'll pass on the coffee. Thanks for breakfast." Or for ruining it. She pushed past Lila and out to the hall and up the stairs to her room, to collapse in the chair by the window, shaking.

How dare Lila suggest such a thing! As if Séamus meant anything more than any other man. He'd just been around the longest, that was all—a prolonged roll in the hay. She looked at her suitcase against the wall and was tempted to just pack up and leave.

Back to Zanzibar? There was a time in her life when she would have done anything to travel to some place so exotic, but now she'd lived there and the bloom was off the rose, the mystery and clear bright tropical colors of youthful exuberance had gone sepia with age and her own more-jaded outlook.

God, she felt old and—well—weary of everything, and she didn't know how to put things to right.

She could spend time at her Nairobi office and sort things out there in preparation for closing. She really had to put in an appearance before the last of her dedicated staff were let go. It broke her heart to have to do it. She'd been part of hiring each and every one of them. They'd done so much by financing local good ideas, instead of importing international aid organizations that brought in their canned programs that often didn't work at all. Or they made things worse.

Like maybe her Pemba Project had made things worse by setting up the island as the perfect target for unscrupulous developers. Maybe her organization's time was over. Maybe it was time to give up.

Across the room, her cocoon of duvet looked mighty tempting. Roll up in it and let the whole darn world go away. But that had never been her way. When Séamus had dumped her, she'd walked away and put all her grief and anger to good use photographing in Africa and then starting her charity. It had worked, too. The result had made a lot of good things happen for good people.

So rolling up in a cocoon and hoping the world would go away wasn't an option now, either. She either needed to fix things or find a new direction for her life. She seemed to be much better at finding new directions. She stood up and looked at herself in the broad mirror above the dresser. Without her makeup she looked young—almost like the girl who had backpacked through

Ireland—except for the squint lines from too long in the tropics and the fatigue lines from last night. She rubbed at the deep blue bags under her eyes. She definitely hadn't done herself any favors in the sleep department, but she wasn't going to waste anymore of the day. She fluffed her blonde mane and abandoned her room for downstairs.

She found Lila still in the kitchen, just loading the last of the dishes in the stainless dishwasher. She straightened and met Ally's gaze and nodded.

Ally rocked on the balls of her feet, her hands stuck in her pockets. "I'm sorry. I shouldn't have popped off like that. You were just trying to point out some issues you saw. I had no right to get angry when you've been so good to me."

Without a word, Lila crossed to her and gave her a hug. "I'm glad you got that out of your system. I am your friend, Ally. But sometimes it's friends who have to hold the mirror up for you, when you're being foolish."

Ally hugged her back and then held her away. "I might take umbrage with the foolish bit, but you will always be my good friend, Lila. I cannot thank you enough for letting me come into your home. So as I said, it's time I earned my keep. If you've got those journals around, I'm happy to get started looking at them as long as you tell me what I'm looking for."

With a nod, Lila led her to the small bedroom upstairs that had been converted into her office. Neat filing cabinets filled one wall, where a closet had once stood. A corner desk filled the space under the window with printer, fax, and scanner on the desk, and shelves of books on the walls. A box of clipped together reams of photocopies sat on the floor.

"These are the journals of Colonel George Bristol. He and his wife were the owners of the bracelet before it came to us in an estate sale. We know nothing about the bracelet except the little bit that his children knew. It was Colonel Bristol's bracelet, not his wife's. How he came by it, we don't know. All we know is that his son says that the Colonel was protective of it—he didn't like the kids touching it—and that he apparently used to call it his 'luck.'

"He was just another junior officer in the British Army Expeditionary Forces in North Africa during the Second World War. I don't know how much you know about the war there, but it was all about trying to defeat Germany's General Rommel—the Desert Fox. Rommel basically beat the pants off the Allies and they were retreating to Cairo. Apparently Bristol was part of a rear guard that delayed Rommel long enough that the Brits reached Alexandria and were able to mount an offensive that drove Rommel back into the desert and to eventual defeat. From that point on, Bristol had a much more notable career so that he even has a Wikipedia entry. He spent time in East Africa during the war as well, but afterward he immigrated to Canada and lived here until his death. He could have come by the bracelet at any time, but Reggie suggested that some of the wear on the bracelet might be from sand, and Chloe had visions of a sandy environment, and Kylee has got it into her head that he found the bracelet while he was in North Africa. So that gives you a place to start, okay? We want to know where it was found, what he knew about it, etc." She motioned at the office. "You're welcome to work here if you like."

Ally hefted the box up off the floor. "You've got that lovely patio out back and I haven't seen a single person use it. I think I'll work out there."

Lila nodded and went to leave, but then stopped. "About your other problem—the Pemba Project. You know, a lot of those international hotel chains are owned by larger multinational corporations. What about checking into who owns the hotel chain and trying a more personal approach to the owners instead of their manager?"

"You know, that's a really good idea. I will do that. It shouldn't be that hard to find out who owns Lux International."

After Lila left, Ally trundled the journals down the stairs and out through the kitchen to the backyard. It was hot, darn hot. The kind of hot that with the sun blazing down, and protected from the breeze off the lake, the heat would bake right into your bones. A very good way to get rid of the remains of her headache and the used up feeling of her body. Retrieving her sunglasses and electronic tablet from her room and a bottle of water from the kitchen, she arranged one of the wicker lounge chairs with its turquoise and yellow pads and settled with the books and her water beside her. Give her heat any day. After Africa at the equator, who needed an umbrella here in the temperate zone?

It was hot work, made hotter by the subject matter. First of all, she sorted the journals according to their dates. Then she did a Google search on her tablet to find the general dates she should be concerned with. The battle of El Alamein was the turning point in the war for North Africa, so 1942 would be her target date. She dug out those journals—far too many of them—and started reading.

George Bristol wrote with a cramped cursive style that made him difficult to read. Thankfully he seemed to have a gift for story, so his tales weren't boring. He had been with one of the units left to fight a delaying action near Mersa Matruh to give the British time to build up their defenses at El Alamein. Inland from the coastal town, he and his small force had been pinned down and nearly captured when the German Panzers found their way through the mine fields he and his troops had laid. The British had had word to bug out and wait at a specific location for pick up, but the transport never appeared. With the German forces between them and the road to Egypt, that left Bristol and his five men scrambling overland to get back to their forces.

She kept reading, but Reggie showed up in shorts and singlet and stopped to talk for a bit before heading into her jewelry workshop. The fans of Regulus Designs roared to life, blowing even hotter air onto the patio. With her bottle of water finished, Ally marked her place and carried the box of journals into the kitchen and through to the shop. At the moment there were no customers, just Chloe and Kylee pouring over a book.

Ally stepped through the bead curtain into the incense-scented shop. The tendril of smoke rose from a small brazier behind the scroll-sided antique cash register. The space was filled with the rich gleam of glass and artisanal jewelry, along with the flowing drapery of the pashmina scarves. She really should do a still-life study of all the shiny surfaces. The room was a veritable kaleidoscope of interesting textures and reflections.

"So all that hard work yesterday and no customers today?" Ally said as she lugged her box toward the front door.

"We figure they're all just saving their money for a few days," Kylee said.

"So we're taking advantage of it. I'm just showing Kylee what to have printed on small cards about the attributes and care and feeding of healing stones." Chloe said, and stepped out from behind the counter. She wore one of her usual shapeless caftans, this one in deep aubergine that went so well with the lavender-gray walls Ally was tempted to go grab her camera. Chloe's thick hair was back in its hip-long braid as she looked Ally up and down.

"Is that a little wear and tear I'm seeing on my friend?" she asked innocently.

"What? Is Lila telling tales now?"

"Nope. She just mentioned running into your ex and that you had been out on the town last night."

"It wasn't exactly on the town. Or out, for that matter," she said and made her escape out the door.

"You're not looking that 'bold' this morning, Ally. More like 'bowled over'." Chloe's voice followed her out through the screen door.

Grumbling about nosy friends, she thunked down in the shade on the wicker loveseat, took a long pull of her new bottle of water, and continued reading. The front porch was a pleasant change from the rear patio. Here in the lovely shade, she could enjoy the warm breeze off the lake. The summer sounds of laughter and the splash of water were a far cry from the Zanzibar harbor sounds of fishermen and the small cargo dhows that sailed the east coast of Africa just as they had right back to the time of Arabian nights. And there was the smell of the harbor, too. Not just the miasma of drying fish, but the wicked stench of cloves and the island's other spices had permeated everything when the wind was right. At times, when she smelled cloves, she could close her eyes and conjure up the images so permanently imprinted on her brain. Of course here, the scent was of suntan lotion from the beach-goers and coffee and fresh baking from the café down the road.

Bringing herself back, she opened the journal she'd been reading and carried on with Colonel Bristol's adventure in the desert as a few customers straggled into the store. He and his men knew that with the German army advancing and their limited weapons, food, and water, they didn't stand a chance if they tried to follow the coast; so under Bristol's leadership, they struck out farther inland, intending to curve back toward El Alamein when they were clear of the enemy. They had one jeep, with three-quarters of a tank of petrol, that they managed to hair-pin back together.

In Peachland, the afternoon was fading and families were breaking out their propane barbeques to make dinner. In 1942 North Africa, things started to get interesting as Bristol and his four comrades had to take cover from a sandstorm.

"Do you mind if I join you?"

Her stomach did a flip-flop and felt like it jammed somewhere between her heart and her spleen as she looked up from reading to meet Séamus' dark eyes. He carried a battered guitar case over his shoulder. Even though every part of her rebelled, she remembered Lila's lecture. Yeah, it had been a lecture, though she had yet to think about Lila's words beyond immediately rejecting them.

"Let me guess, Lila invited you." She turned back to her reading because she was not going to be the cause of another scene. Shrugged. "It's a free country last time I checked." *Jeeze, Ally, could you be anymore bitchy?* But that was what you got when you put her on guard. If anyone knew that, it was Séamus O'Hearn.

He settled himself in one of the chairs—not Lila's high-backed chair that everyone seemed to think of as her throne, but one of the nice armchairs with the turquoise and mandarin colored cushion. He didn't say a thing, just sat there looking out at the lake. It was a picture, with the white clouds reflecting in the water and placing gentle, moving shadows across the far side of the lake. Photos of the lake she could do a lot with in digital post-production, soften the focus a little, take out the contrast, and the place would *glow* like the magical place she'd always thought it was. She looked over the top of the papers at Séamus and caught him looking at her as his fingers skillfully tested and tuned the guitar's strings. The way he held the instrument, the loving way he touched it—that was another picture. His dark hair shielding his eyes as he tested the strings evoked little shivering sounds from the instrument. He did have lovely long fingers. Once upon a time it was Séamus in just such a pose that she'd fallen in love with. She suddenly felt barely twenty again, her heart so big in her chest it was going to burst right open.

Until he'd left her heartbroken. That wasn't something that was easily forgotten or forgiven or solved.

She swallowed and her hand sought the comfort of the silver bracelet. It was still warm from her time on the patio, and seemed to sooth her as her fingers smoothed over the metal and found the little gargoyle door. Its small deformed face made her smile. Then she realized she was tapping her foot in time to a tune Séamus was playing softly.

"What's the song?" she asked.

"Well, this little piece doesn't really have a name, now does it? I wrote it a long time ago and never thought to give it a name."

"It sounds happy and sad, both at the same time, like when I think of Africa: all those great herds of animals so beautiful to see and so many of them slated for extinction within my lifetime."

"I guess that's sort of the way I was feelin' when I wrote it." He looked down at the strings and brought the music forward a little louder.

"You always were a musician at heart. I was surprised you never pursued it."

He didn't say anything, just kept playing the haunting melodies that were the heart of so many Celtic ballads. She tried to turn back to her reading, but the way his fingers moved over the strings kept bringing her back to watch him. She kept waiting for him to sing because he had a lovely bass voice that always made her think of singing in Saint Fin Barre's gothic cathedral in Cork. The place had the two towers and the high arched ceilings that reverberated the voice as if the golden resurrection angel herself called out to God.

Séamus had that kind of voice.

Chapter 8

It was going better than he'd expected. The front porch of the red and white heritage house had become a small hideaway for the likes of Ally and him. There'd been times in his life when he'd imagined growing old in a place like this. Perhaps the scene he looked out on woulda been more rolling green hills and peat bog than lake and rough desert mountain, but the feel was the same. Companionable—that was the word. It was companionable sitting here beside Ally, strumming his guitar while she thumbed through her papers.

She looked bloody beautiful today, with her long blonde hair falling over her forehead and down over her shoulders. Her profile was classic Greek and she had the longest tanned legs he'd ever seen, right now propped up on the porch railin'. Pretty as a picture and she didn't even know it. Didn't know how his heart beat in his chest just lookin' at her like that and thinkin' of their times together in the past.

Hell, he could still have this, instead of the illusion, if he hadn't been such a dick.

He almost choked on the words of the song—words he'd written at twenty when a certain girl had flown out of his life because of his own idiocy. Too afraid to commit so he had figured he'd cool it for a time—there were lots of other girls to be had before he settled down. The trouble was, he'd let the right one get away. By the time he'd realized it, he couldn't find her and then it had just seemed like too much time had passed. And now—well, now he'd gone and done the unforgivable and all he could hope for was that she might—someday—forgive.

Out on the street a group of people paused to listen to his music. They eventually faded away and a new group took their place.

Ally glanced up from her reading, a thoughtful expression on her face. Then their eyes met and he had to look away for fear she'd see what he was thinking. The song faded away and she smiled.

"You've still got one heck of a voice. I remember when I first heard it. I swore you could melt the panties off every girl in the room. Probably did, too. Didn't you?"

"Come on! It's a passable voice, but I got none of the tenor that makes the girls swoon."

She grinned at him like a sister and he almost winced. So, was that what she wanted from him then? If it was, it might break his heart, but he just might do it. Better to have Ally as a friend in his life than to lose her altogether.

She dog-eared the page she was reading and set it in the box of stacked papers, then looked up at him. "Believe me, there was plenty of swooning."

"And that's a nice thing to say even if it ain't true. Can't make a living with a voice like this, for true."

She blinked and for a moment it looked like she was in pain. "Can't make a living as a lot of things these days." She stood up abruptly and picked up the box. "I think it's time for me to go pull my weight and help with dinner." She started toward the front door, her movement shredding the precious small space his music had created for them, like Atlantic waves taking down a sandcastle. Then she stopped and looked at him, truly met his gaze. "It's been nice, this afternoon. Thank you. The music was beautiful."

He didn't know what to say, so he opted for nothing, just a single nod of the head, preferring to hold onto the gentle music inside. But from out on the road a car horn honked and a rugged black Humvee pulled into the curb. Its arrival stopped Ally.

The driver's side door opened and out stepped a man. Black hair, pale eyes. Even in the heat, the wanker wore a leather jacket and jeans that rode low on his hips. He eased around the car and stopped at the gate and lifted his chin. A lad like that could have any woman he wanted. Money always could, and he was good looking, t' boot.

Please let him be here to pick up Lila Weber or one of Ally's other friends. His stomach went a-crapper and his mouth went dry as the fella pushed through the gate and strode on great long shanks up to the stairs. He glanced in Séamus' direction and nodded as Ally set the box of papers down and went down the front steps to meet him.

"Ally," he said. "I've been thinking about you. I was driving around and wondered if you'd like to get together tonight? So I pulled up the address you gave me."

Séamus' heart sank. He made a point of plucking the guitar strings, but the sound came out crazy as he was feeling at the moment.

Ally seemed frozen a moment.

No, Ally. No.

Then she took a deep breath and nodded. "Sure. I would. What time?"

Séamus about threw his guitar and punched the wanker in his nose.

"How 'bout I pick you up at around nine?"

She shook her head. "How about I meet you at your place."

The dark-haired bugger shrugged. "Suit yourself. I thought we just might have a little fun on the way."

And with that he left, sauntering like some bleeding posh movie star back to his car. He climbed in and, with a bleat of the horn, pulled away. Ally waited until he was gone before she turned back to the house and climbed the stairs two at a time. She grabbed the box and turned to him.

"See you." She didn't say when. She couldn't, or wouldn't, even meet his gaze as she went inside.

The rill of music he'd been feeling was long dead inside but jealousy surged up, alive and well.

§

That had been—awkward.

In fact, she felt a little queasy as she passed through the shop and nodded at Chloe. She shoved the beaded curtain aside and headed down the dimly lit hall for the stairs and her room to dump the papers. In her room the sunlight no longer streamed through her window. Instead, the room was in shadow and it was the low mountain peaks across the lake that still caught the five o'clock sunlight. Almost sweet light. She should be hauling out her camera and seeing what she could do with that most precious light of the day. But she hadn't even pulled out her camera, though she'd lugged her equipment halfway around the world with her. Other than the grand reopening, she just hadn't come up with a subject that piqued her interest enough to actually pull her favorite Nikon out of her bag. What was up with that? From the time she was in high school, she'd rarely been separated from her camera gear. What was different now?

She'd been too busy feeling sorry for herself and letting herself get distracted in the hopes that all her troubles would just go away. Instead, it seemed that she was cultivating new issues.

Seeing Abel and Séamus together just left her more confused. Abel was the kind of man she preferred. Available physically, not emotionally, and that was fine by her. No emotional attachments meant things were cleaner. And he was good in bed. Great, in fact.

So great you spent the morning cocooned in your bed and wishing you were dead?

She shook her head and shoved the documents into the corner, then used the bathroom to wash her hands and face and headed down to the kitchen.

Séamus was a different story. He was every bit as attractive as Abel, though in a different way. Séamus literally oozed Ireland with his music, the lilt in his voice, and the twinkle of imp—make that leprechaun—in his eye. It was hard to stay mad at him. Even this afternoon when she'd been ready to tell him to just leave her the hell alone, his soft way of being 'in the music'—as he'd always called it—had managed to calm her. It had actually been nice sitting there together. Maybe there was the possibility they could be friends.

Friends. She tried that idea on as she pushed into the kitchen and wasn't sure. Good thing Lila was up in her room and wasn't here to ask hard questions. It had been bad enough dealing with Chloe and Kylee's raised eyebrows when she'd passed through the store from the porch with the box of journals.

She rummaged through the fridge and came up with chicken and salad fixings. The thought of frying or baking something and adding that heat to the room didn't appeal to her, so she set the chicken marinating in the fridge in a mixture of oil, lemon, and fresh herbs, and stepped out to the patio. The direct sun might be gone, but heat still radiated up from the patio stones. It made for a pleasant spot with cooler air circulating.

The barbeque was a stainless steel contraption protected by a vinyl tarp that she stripped off. The burners caught first try and she left the grill covered to heat and went back inside. Lila had come down from upstairs, having traded her blue shift for a pair of black Bermuda shorts and a coral-colored t-shirt. She was busy washing lettuce.

"I take it this is what you were thinking?" she asked.

"Close enough." Ally nodded. "Chloe, Reggie, and Kylee going to stay for dinner?"

"I asked them. Kylee's a no-go because she wants to be with Brett. Reggie's got Mom duties. Chloe says she has to run home and feed Clyde and maybe change into something more comfortable, but she'll be back. She just left from locking up the store. It was a slow day today—only seven sales." A few more leaves of romaine went into a sink of ice water. "So how was your afternoon? You feeling better?"

Ally grinned. "A lot better, thanks. It was an okay afternoon, especially after my headache went away. I got a lot of reading done."

"That's good, then. Learn anything interesting?" There was a double meaning there, Ally knew. Lila knew everything that went on in her house. She'd sure as heck known Séamus was here. How could anyone miss that gentle music of his? The man could spin a tune.

She decided to keep the focus on the research. "Actually, yes. He was with some of the rear guard for the British after their disastrous Battle of Gazala, where Rommel outflanked the British forces. Unfortunately, he and his men got left behind in the confusion during the retreat and so, to escape capture, they took off into the desert. Bristol wrote that he was pretty sure that the British would make a stand near El Alamein because the front was narrower there and Rommel couldn't outflank them because of the Qattara Depression." She held up her hand at the question in Lila's eyes. "I know, I know. I was on my tablet half the time until I found a map of the area and the battles. Then I could follow along. Anyway, as near as I can tell, Bristol and his men took a big detour southward into the desert. There's a lot of uneven ground and they figured to hide there as they headed east for El Alamein. They got hit by a sand storm at one point. That's where I am now. I'll keep going tomorrow, but so far there's been no mention of getting any bracelet. I wonder if he just found it in a market back in Cairo or something."

She'd chopped some artichoke, avocado, and green onions while Lila was tearing the lettuce. Digging in the pantry, she found a tin of mandarin oranges and then also pulled out some slivered almonds. The almonds she browned in butter in a small fry pan, the oranges she set to drain and then grabbed the chicken from the fridge and went outside to throw the breasts on the grill. When she went back inside, Lila was whisking some salad dressing together.

The bell from the closed shop dinged out front announcing Chloe's return as Ally pulled plates and silverware together and set them on the counter, then went outside to turn the meat. Lovely grill marks had browned onto the breasts. She brushed more marinade on them and went back into the kitchen as Lila dug out sunflower-patterned napkins. Chloe was tossing the salad. She was dressed in spandex shorts and a loose, sleeveless, yellow shirt that flowed down to her hips. Her long braid she'd rolled up into a bun behind her head.

"I brought wine. There's benefits to having a brother in the business," she said as she gleefully pulled the cork and poured three goblets of a bright yellow wine. "Unoaked Chardonnay."

Ally rescued the chicken from the flame in time and brought a platter of mouthwatering smelling meat back into the kitchen. "So I'm thinking we help ourselves and retire to the patio. It is lovely out there."

They followed her lead and soon the three of them were seated in the comfortable wicker chairs around the coffee table, the plates on their laps.

"So, not much business today," Ally said as she took a bite of chicken. It had a light tang of the lemon and herbs, with the slight char of the grill. Mmm-mmm. She glanced up at Chloe, who shrugged.

"Not a lot of customers, but we got a lot done. Kylee and I put together the text for all the little fact cards on the stones. Then we decided to try some samples, so Kylee ran up to the stationary store in West Kelowna for some cardstock. It worked like a dream. We'll have to try them out on some customers and see what they think." She closed her eyes over a bite of chicken. "This is so good. Lila, you've outdone yourself."

Lila shook her head. "Don't look at me. This was all Ally."

"Well, I hope you got her recipe. This is a great marinade. Light but tasty—sort of like those men of yours, Ally." She shook her head. "Just how do you do it? I swear I didn't see you lift a finger out there and yet you have one good-looking guy serenading you and then some hottie swings by as well. The guy from the restaurant, right? That's more male hotness than this place has seen in a while. Jas excepted, of course."

Jas being her hot police detective main squeeze.

Lila looked a question in Ally's direction and Ally sighed. "Yeah. It was a little awkward having Abel show up while Séamus was here. But Séamus and I are, at best, only friends." She shrugged. "I don't see the problem." She took a bite of the salad.

The spice of the salad dressing meshed with the sweetness of the orange and artichoke and the salt of the nuts. The almond crunch was counterpoint to the softness of the avocado, like the perfect contrast in a photo.

"This is the guy you were with last night?" Lila asked.

Chloe glanced between them. "At the restaurant, right?"

"No. *Not* at the restaurant," Lila said.

Chloe's eyes widened a little and Ally looked heavenward. "So I went out with the guy. He was cute. I needed a little relief so I called him. We got together. It doesn't mean anything."

"And you felt so much better today." There was a little snide in Lila observation.

"Well then, I guess you won't be too happy to hear we're getting together again tonight." Ally chewed her suddenly off-tasting salad and set her fork down on her plate. "I was going to ask if I could borrow your car again, but maybe I'll see if I can rent one for the next while. I wouldn't want to offend you, Lila." She stood up. "I think I'm going to get some more reading done. Thanks for the wine, Chloe. It was great."

She carried her plate back to the kitchen, cleared the food into the green recycling and put the plate in the dishwasher. She made her escape upstairs but not without being conscious of the two other women watching her. She hadn't expected this kind of judgment from them. They were treating her like a slut or something—which she wasn't. She just knew her body's needs and followed them, much the same as men had always done. All this fuss just didn't make sense.

She called a rental company and arranged to have a car delivered this evening, then sat by the window—opened—to read and let the sounds of the evening in. In North Africa, George Bristol and his men were taking cover from a sandstorm out in the desert.

We were fortunate in that we found a cave. Perhaps not a cave as we would see in Britain, but a depression in the stony landscape held what appeared to be a slight alcove. The five of us abandoned the jeep to the storm and huddled there, wind whipping about us, sand blinding. I was sure it was going to blind me, the wind and dust tearing at my eyelids. Then John Hodges made a sound and the five of us tumbled back into a cave. The dust and wind followed us in, but the darkness behind us and the depression and alcove outside lessened its fury considerably. By the flame of my lighter, we saw that we were in a cave and that what had given way to allow us in was an actual door of wood set into the stone. It was such an odd thing to find in the desert that for a moment I considered taking my men and leaving, for who would build such a thing?

Beyond the strangeness of the door, the cave was exactly that—a cave. Dark, with earthen walls made of the rough sand and stone sediment that made up the desert floor, and yet it had a strange scent to it as if something had burned in here just days ago, yet the floor and walls showed no scorch marks. At the rear of the cave we discovered human remains, though by the look of the bones and the shreds of cloth, they had been here a very long time. With nothing else strange to see, we drank a small part of our water and I took first watch to allow the men to get some shut-eye.

Outside, the storm raged and I wondered whether there would be anything left of the jeep or whether my foolhardy plan to evade the Germans and reach El Alamein had just led us to our grave. The way the storm was blowing, sand was flowing into the depression and had begun to sift inside the door. Were we to wake in the morning to find the entry buried and our way free lost?

I did not dare to waste my lighter fluid, so in the darkness I kept myself awake by digging at the stones in the wall with my jackknife. Then I would clean off each stone and set them balancing on each other. At the least, the click of stone on stone was a more hospitable sound than the roar of the storm, but partway through the night, my exhaustion overcame me and I slept.

I woke to a beam of sunlight falling through the upper reaches of the doorway, the lower portions having been securely blocked by sand that kept sifting into our place of safety. By this light I could see the men still sleeping, and at the end of the cave, those bundles of bones and old flesh. By the looks of them, there had been three. One had fallen before the others, either as protector or assailant, it was impossible to tell. Of the other two, one had been a woman. I wondered what desperation would bring them so far into such inhospitable country and what they were hiding from, for surely such a cave as this, carved from the flesh of the desert, would only be a residence of last resort.

Oh, such happy thoughts. But we were alive and, as if in answer, the sunlight caught on something gleaming in the cave wall next to where I had laid my head through the night. It was small, whatever it was, and shone as if it was silver. It seemed to be part of something that, if I caught the edge of the silver, I could move a little, as if there was some opening beyond the stone. I realized I shouldn't have seen it at all, save for my midnight whittling at the wall. I used my knife blade again on the wall and suddenly a chunk of the sand and stone fell into my hand revealing a small opening in the cave wall.

From this I tugged the precious silver, for so I later learned it to be. A bracelet. A woman's bracelet I would say, but of a likeness I have not seen before. It is comprised of seven small doors of an uncanny likeness to doors I have seen across Europe and Northern Africa. Holding it in my hands, I knew it to be something unique and special, so I packed it away against a time when I might have more time to examine it.

Ally dog-eared the page and let the binder-clipped pages fall into her lap. Outside, the evening had lengthened—still blue skies, but fading. She checked her watch: eight thirty.

She'd found what Lila and the others were looking for. She should be leaping up and crashing down the stairs to tell them, but at the moment she just felt pissed off. She held up the bracelet to catch the light of the incandescent bulb.

"So just what were you doing in the middle of a North African desert, my little friend?" She ran her fingers along the doors, feeling them like braille, sensing them like she was trying to read the level of contrast in a scene. Too much adjustment for light, and the shadows would be too dark to show detail—that was key to understanding the picture. Too much light and you blinded the viewer to everything that mattered in the image. The information she had could help expose the mystery of the bracelet, but at the moment she didn't want to commit.

Or share.

She set the journal aside and went to take a shower. Then, wet hair slicked back in a high pony tail, she put on black spandex leggings, lace bra and panties, and a silk blouse. Still with a little time to kill until the car was delivered, she decided to do a little research into Lux International.

She pulled her tablet into her lap and Googled the name. The luxury hotel's reservations page came up. She scrolled through it and took a look at their properties. Definitely super luxury—the kind that would cater to movie stars and the nouveau riche. But they had a subsidiary as well, with slightly less expensive digs. Wondering which one was destined for Pemba, she scrolled down to the bottom and clicked on the website map.

Hmm. A link to the side was called corporate partners. She hit the link, but the doorbell rang. The clock on the bedside table said nine p.m. The rental car delivery, most likely. She pulled on heels she hadn't worn in a couple of years and clacked down the stairs and through the shop. Lila was there talking to the rental car clerk.

She turned back to Ally, her eyes raking her head to toe. "Ally, please." She caught Ally's wrist and held it up so the light caught the silver. "Think about what I said. This thing influences people. You don't need to do this."

Ally waved her away, not wanting another argument, signed the rental papers for the red Hyundai Sonata parked at the curb, and sent the clerk on his way with the company car sent to bring him back. Then she turned back to Lila and gave her a hug. Lila smelled sweet—of roses—and for a moment Ally almost felt like crying.

"Yes. I do."

Chapter 9

After each daily shoot, Ally usually liked time alone to download and analyze her raw images. Similarly, after her sexual encounters, Ally's usual practice was to just get dressed and go home and allow the mellow release to permeate her being. Unfortunately, Abel seemed to have other ideas.

In his moonlit bedroom with its dark wood dresser and wardrobe, he sat naked as a dark god, smoking a menthol-scented e-cigarette as he reclined against his bed's leather headboard. The indigo sheets were a tangle around him, but he was secure enough in his manhood that he didn't bother to cover himself. No, he sat there as he watched her pad around the room trying to reclaim her dignity and her belongings.

This just didn't feel right and that was wrong. She felt awkward pulling her clothes off the dark hardwood floor when usually she imagined herself a lioness on the Serengeti. What was wrong with her? The sex had been good and she'd been just as adventurous as he had been...

"You look like something out of a myth, clad in only your hair and a silver band."

He'd come off the bed, apparently ready for another round of 'play.' She looked up into his pale eyes and wasn't sure what she saw. Lust certainly, but there was something else foreign and unfathomable swirling up at her from the shadows that left her uneasy. Beyond him, through the open windows, came the first breath of morning breeze, the first bird call. Across the lake, the night faded into gray.

"I thought this was all about a nighttime tryst with no strings. Daytime—it means something else," she said as he caught her hands.

His thumbs rubbed the backs of her hands up over her wrist bones. One stroked her bracelet so she almost shivered. That hand felt tender and wounded, the bracelet too heavy on her arm.

"Perhaps I would like to explore what that difference is. You are an amazing woman, Ally McVay."

She shook her head. "You don't know that. You don't know anything about me."

He pulled her back toward the bed. "Don't I? Photographer. Philanthropist. Creator of *Get the Picture*. I did a Google search of your name. You have given your art for the betterment of others." He leaned down and brushed her forehead with his lips. "Perhaps I'd like to include such a woman in my life?"

If she had been a camera, her shutter would have seized. She couldn't take in what he was saying. *He'd checked her out on the internet?* Why hadn't she done the same? Instead, she stood stock-still, then shook her head. "I don't do relationships. I don't."

He chuckled. "Sounds like you're trying to convince yourself." He pulled her into him and ran his hands up and down her sides.

It didn't arouse her. In fact, it terrified her.

He must have known because he released her and reclined on the bed again. She began to tug her leggings on. "How about we start with something simple? You bring your camera to my research. For cryptozoologists, most of the time, lack of photo documentation and less-than-reputable photographers mean our evidence is not taken seriously. We would have to bring the creature up in a net and drag it to shore and even then science would say we conjured it somehow."

"I'm not that reputable." She straightened the waistband and pulled her silk shirt over her head. Her skin felt bruised, her body soiled.

"Ally. What's this all about?" He swung up off the bed again. "We're certainly good in bed together. Why can't we try to be good together in other ways?"

Dammit, he was being so earnest. If she wanted uninvolved sex, this was over. If she wanted to explore something more, then maybe this was the person. Here she was hesitating when she'd always known what she wanted before. She'd always been sure.

But he was giving her an excuse to get back to the camera— something that she'd been avoiding, and that wasn't something she'd ever done before.

"All right. But this isn't going to be about having sex in all the wrong places. If it's helping with photography, there has to be something beyond a debauched bedroom and your abs to photograph." She found a grin for him.

His answering smile was the same panty-melting grin that she'd seen at the restaurant. She hefted her purse over her shoulder. "Now I have to be going."

"Fine. But you will need to return for ten a.m. I plan to spend the day out at Rattlesnake Island. Have you ever dived before?"

She had, but it had been years ago when she was first developing the Pemba Project. She also didn't have any underwater photography equipment, but he apparently did. After agreeing to meet him at ten at his condo marina, she hauled herself out of there and headed for home.

It was still semi-dark when she slipped into the house and up to her room, feeling bad about the argument with Lila and Chloe the night before. She was going to have to do something about that. Apologize. It was Lila's house; she could expect certain standards of behavior. She'd just never figured Lila for a puritan.

Without turning her light on, she stripped out of her clothes and climbed into the bed. The aubergine-colored sheets were cool on her body, but she couldn't seem to fall asleep. Her skin felt hot. Slimy. Finally she abandoned the bed for her shower. Dawn light leaked in around her blind as she threw herself back into the bed again. Better, but things still weren't right. The stupid bracelet seemed to throb on her arm with a deep, bone-aching pulse that matched her heart beat. She was never going to be able to sleep like this.

Just what was it that was disturbing her? She had an uneasy, queasy feeling in her gut. She should be excited. She'd never been on a cryptozoological hunt before, and underwater photography was a newer skill to explore. She'd been excited as all get-out the first time she'd gone on safari in the Serengeti. She'd been over-the-moon the first time she'd photographed gorillas in Uganda. She should be excited now. Just think what would happen if she was the first person to get a clear photo of the Okanagan Lake monster? Now that would be something that would kick-start her business all over again.

She fell asleep thinking of that.

Deep water. Far above, light flickers on waves as she kicks herself down through the cold water. This far from the sun, there are none of the bright flashes of silver fish bodies passing by, none of the silt-green richness of sunlight through sediment and algae suspended in the water. Deeper she goes, following something that she can barely see in the light from her camera. She glimpses a large dark bulk at the edge of the light, the water streaming past her face as if whatever it is causes a current before her.

If she could just catch up to it, she'd understand so much. She kicks her flippers harder, the compressed air in her mouthpiece tasting of metal and rubber. Bubbles flow away upward, soon becoming the only thing that show which way is up.

But the thing, the creature, it runs before her. She is losing it, losing it. She kicks harder, but it is gone. There is nothing at the edge of her light now. She stops kicking and hangs in the water, catching flickers of silver as she swings the light around, barely catching in time the dark bulk that drives down toward her and slams the light out of her hands, the mask from her face, the mouthpiece from her mouth.

She tumbles through the water, air spewing from a severed airline. Grabbing for it, to clamp it closed, but it is behind her back. When she comes to a stop, her lungs ache for air. Which way is up? Which way is light? She fumbles for the airhose, trying to get a sense of where the bubbles are going. Which way?

She starts swimming, kicking those great fins of hers, praying for a glimpse of something, anything to tell her she is right. Maybe she is wrong. Maybe she is falling deeper, or swimming along the length of the lake. Her lungs are bursting. Bursting enough she starts to hear something. Music. Faint strains of music, like water flowing over her ears.

Her lungs are going to explode. Her vision fades toward black even though she hangs in darkness. The weight of the now-empty air tank weighs her down. She undoes the closures and slips it off, then pulls the air hose to her mouth. A mouthful of air and she lets the tank fall away. The music still plays, full of hope and longing as she kicks. Kicks again, but it isn't enough. The darkness presses in, fills her eyes, her ears, her nose. Inhale once more and it is over.

She never planned on dying this way, but then when did anyone?

She inhales the darkness.

And something rips the bracelet off her arm.

She came up off the bed gasping, her heart pounding, the bracelet throbbing on her wrist. What the hell?

She clamped her hand over the bracelet. Still there, thank God. Sunlight rimmed the edge of the window blinds, and the slightly opened window allowed in the sounds of the waves, of children laughing—and music. Guitar. She knew that guitar, knew the music, too. The soft, heartbreaking strains of the old tunes of Ireland, and there was only one person she knew who played like that. Dammit. What was Séamus doing here disturbing her sleep like that?

Disturbing her nightmare, more like.

She'd been dying, the bracelet taken. If anything, it was the music that tried to save her. And just when had Séamus O'Hearn ever tried to save her? Nope, he'd set her into a tailspin.

But not this time. Something else had done it this time. Had finished her.

Her heart still beat harder than it should and her arms and legs ached from exertion as if she really had been swimming for her life. She felt cold, clammy; and the bracelet—she ran her fingers over it—it felt cold except for one small door. She recognized the single little face in the center.

"You keep on like this and I'm going to start believing all Kylee's and Chloe's stories about you." Was her dream a vision like Chloe had experienced with the bracelet? Was she hearing things like Kylee had heard someone in her house? She pulled the bedclothes around her for warmth on her suddenly frozen skin, then caught sight of the clock. Nine a.m. She'd slept for four hours—an hour longer than she'd planned.

She shoved off the covers and stood, feeling the day swing unsteadily around her. Not a good sign. Maybe she was getting too old for these night-long meetings. Fat chance of that. She pulled on shorts and t-shirt, stuffed her hair into a pony tail and under a baseball cap to hide the bed head from sleeping on wet hair, and grabbed a bathing suit and towel and her camera gear before heading out the door.

She was in the kitchen at nine-twenty and grabbed a piece of bread, slathered it with organic almond butter and honey for energy. Juggling the bread, bathing suit, and gear, she hurried down the hallway to the shop, then paused at the beaded curtain. Lila, Chloe, and Kylee were in the shop. Kylee was helping a customer, while Lila and Chloe were speaking quietly by the cash register. Well, Ally had to face Lila sometime.

She pushed through the curtain, the beads clacking around her. Everyone glanced in her direction, but Kylee and the customer quickly got back to business. Chloe and Lila, however, still watched her.

"Morning," Chloe said. "You're up and going kinda early for you, aren't you?"

She shrugged. "I've had some sleep. Not enough, but some. I've been offered a chance to photograph an expedition to document the Okanagan Lake monster. We're heading onto the lake at ten." She checked her watch. "I don't have much time, but guys, I wanted to apologize for yesterday. I don't know what got into me. I'm sorry, okay?"

Chloe nodded, but it took a moment before Lila followed suit. Her eyes seemed to search Ally's, then she put her arm around Ally's shoulders. "I just worry about you. Especially with that thing on your wrist." She nodded down at the bracelet that looked innocuous and dull in the light of the store. "You be careful today, okay?"

"I always am," Ally said and headed for the door, a little frustrated that Lila felt the need to say that. But on the other hand, she could have taken some time this afternoon and checked Abel out on the internet, but she hadn't. What was with that? She shook her head. She'd been with him for two nights now. He could have tried something, but he hadn't. The little bell dinged above her as she stepped out to the porch, and chords of music washed over her. For a moment the bracelet flared and a warm flush filled her skin. It must have filled her face when she turned to the guitar player.

Séamus, of course. Just what she didn't need. She should have gone out the back way.

He smiled up at her with that lovely wicked smile of his. "Well, aren't ya a sight for sore eyes this morning."

"What are you doing here?" she asked.

"Here?" he looked around himself as if seeing his surroundings for the first time. "Why, I don't rightly know. I was walking along and said to myself, 'self, where would you go if you wanted t' meet beautiful women?' My feet took me right here and there you are. My feet were right, it seems."

"And you always were a charmer. Lila know you're here?" A stupid question, given she must hear him.

He hefted a glass of lemonade. "She said it gave a little aura to the place. Now, what that aura might be, that's another thing, but I'm happy fer the chance to play."

He patted the seat beside him. "Come, sit awhile and I'll sooth away yer worries with a song."

His eyes twinkled a little, just like she remembered, and those musical hands of his seemed to move across the strings of their own volition, creating lovely chords. Ally checked her watch. Not quite nine thirty. It wouldn't take long to get to West Kelowna.

"I can only stay a moment." But she sat down, wondering why she did. She'd been with Séamus before—had seen their relationship fade to black. But there was still something about him—a little bit of the blarney, most likely. "So, seriously. What brings you here?"

His hands coaxed sweet music from the guitar strings, but he wouldn't look her in the eyes. "If I told ya it was you, you'd get up and leave, if I know Ally McVay—and I do. So let's just say I had a hankering to sit on this lovely porch again and get fed lemonade by yer lovely friends."

Okay. She wasn't going to do this again. She stood.

"Where ya going, Ally-girl? Off fer more of yer play?" he said, as soft as a chord on his guitar, but his voice was filled with pain.

Rigid with anger?—embarrassment?—frustration?—she didn't know—she crossed her arms over her chest and peered down at him. "You have no right to even ask and certainly no right to disapprove. But if you must know, yes. Yes, I'm going to play. I'm going to play at being a photographer and try to be the first damn photographer to get a clear shot of Ogopogo." Her voice had risen. "Is that okay with you? Do I have your permission? Why should you even care? You're just going to head off to greener pastures again, because that's what you do, isn't it? Isn't it?"

Séamus sat and took her barrage like a subject in a portrait studio. His eyes stayed fixed on some infinity point until she'd finished and then he looked up at her, patted the guitar strings once, and pulled out his case to stash the instrument away. He stood up. "A man can tell when he's overstayed his welcome. I'll be going, now."

He stopped at the screen door. "I'm off," he called and Chloe came to the door.

"You'll be back tomorrow won't you?" She glanced in Ally's direction and Ally threw up her hands.

Her watch said she was down to twenty minutes to meet Abel's boat and that was a bare minimum of time. She left not hearing the rest of the conversation, clattering down the front porch stairs and out to her Hyundai. Séamus still hadn't left when she pulled away.

Damn him.

§

On the shifting waters of the blue lake, the boat slip at the Waterford Condominiums was comprised of a series of piers that together were shaped like double *H*'s moored sideways to the condo boardwalk along the lake. Ally screeched into the parking lot with one minute to spare, grabbed her swimsuit, camera bag, and towel, and ran. Slip 52c sat inside the arms on the left side of the outermost H. That pier system was separated from the inner system by a fueling station.

She punched in the code Abel had given her to get through the security gate and was running by the time she reached the filling station. Her hair streamed behind her until the wind caught it and tossed it in her face. The sky was blue with high, puffy clouds that sailed like small ships across the heavens. That was one thing about this country: with its folded landscape and mountains, the sky was cut up in small pieces and had none of the haunting grandeur of the Serengeti, where the expansive sky rested on the tops of the acacias.

Different places. Different spaces.

Different people, too.

Unlike Séamus, Abel didn't strike her as the kind who'd wait for her. Come or not—that was her choice. If she wasn't there on time, it was over. She didn't want it to be over, did she?

But just why had she wasted time sitting on the porch with Séamus? She knew she needed to be here. Stupidity. That was why. A need to revisit old pain?

Ahead a large cruiser rumbled in its slip, belching forth a blue miasma of diesel. She dashed past the front of the boat and caught sight of the man untying the dock line. Screeched to a halt and went back to him. Abel. Dark hair a sexy tousle, blue eyes picking up every shade of blue from the waves. He wore a sky blue polo shirt as if he knew exactly what that did to his eyes. A pair of navy shorts and white dockside shoes completed the ensemble.

"Ahoy, Captain," she said, cocking her hip as she faced him. "Permission to come aboard?"

His pale regard slipped from her sandaled feet up the bare length of her leg to her chest to her face. Lingered there a moment and reversed direction, pausing in all the right places as if he was remembering his hands on each one. She sure as heck was. She swallowed.

Casually he checked his watch.

"You almost missed the boat," he said. But then he smiled

She just wasn't sure whether it reached his eyes and for a moment she almost changed her mind about going.

Chapter 10

"I appreciate everything you've done for me, Lila, but I really think this is just wastin' my time. Ally's made up her mind. She's moved on. I think it's about time I moved on, too. It was an idiot idea, me coming here."

He stood on the white-painted porch of the jewelry store, the wind off the lake in his hair and the long walk along the lakeshore waiting for him. His guitar was locked up in its case and ready in his hands. Lila, the auburn-haired beauty whose milky-white skin he was sure was the product of some distant Irish ancestor, stood before him. She was a grand woman, tall, but as willowy as the birch up in the back pasture of his father's farm. Her eyes were gray-green flecked and strong as the old stone walls that held in the farm's yard. Steady eyes, those. They weren't showin' any sign of flinchin' now, either.

She shook her head. "I think you're wrong, Séamus. I know it's hard, but I think Ally's really struggling. She says she came here to refocus, but she really seems to be floundering. This guy she ran off with—she just picked him up in a restaurant two nights ago. He's—he's another of her men. You know." She looked almost apologetic as she said it.

"Yeah. I know. I heard about it in Zanzibar when I got up my nerve to look for her. More of her 'play' is it? It's like she uses it to numb herself." Now. It hadn't always been that way.

Lila sank down in the high-backed chair and looked up at him. "You know, I never thought of it that way, but yes, that describes it exactly. She always liked men—but now… I don't know what got her that way, but it's a tactic she's used for a lot of years. The thing is, I'm worried about her."

"Lila, people have been using sex t' feel better for as long as there've been human beings." And he should be going. It was bad enough he'd made a damn fool of himself coming down here and serenading Ally like some lovesick minstrel. *Fer God's sake, man. Take yer pride back.*

Lila nodded, but two small frown lines had formed between her brows and, in her lap, her hands worked her many silver rings in anxiety. She stared out at the lake but finally nodded and looked up at him. "There's something you need to know, Séamus. You see, I think Ally's in danger, and for some reason she seems to be putting herself out there to make herself a target."

Her grave expression made him pause. "What are ya talking about?"

She met is eyes and motioned at the loveseat beside her. "This'll take a bit."

Leaning his guitar case against the porch rail, he sat.

"Have you noticed the bracelet Ally's wearing?" she asked, brushing her hair back behind her ears and waiting.

"A silver thing. She seems t' play with it a lot. Always running her fingers there like it's something automatic."

"So you've noticed it, too. Kylee was like that. So was Chloe." She shook her head.

He'd met the two other women, but what did that have to do with Ally? "And now you're talking in riddles, love."

She sighed. "Sorry. There's just been so much going on. If feels like years that we've been dealing with this, but it's really only been two months. And everything comes back to that bracelet."

She told him a wild story about the bracelet being found and how Kylee Jensen came to have it on and then was abducted because of it, and then saved. Chloe was next with the bracelet and was attacked in her home, before the perpetrator was stopped. "In both cases, something or someone was after the bracelet. Both

Kylee and Chloe got sensations off of it and Chloe had visions that just about caused her to have a mental breakdown."

"So if the bracelet is such a problem, why don't they just take the blasted thing off? It seems the logical thing t' do."

"Logic would suggest that, wouldn't it?" she said with a smile. "The trouble is, the darn clasp won't work. All of us have tried it. It's like the bracelet won't come off until it's good and ready. In Kylee's and Chloe's case, it wasn't until they'd worked out their difficulties with the man in their lives. The man who abducted Kylee said it was all about the bracelet, and that he couldn't take it off her arm until she was dead. The second man—the one who attacked Chloe—tried to strangle her."

She was lookin' at him so intently that at first he didn't understand. When he did, he felt his jaw drop a little. "Ya think I'm the man Ally needs to work things out with." Shook his head. "Yer tellin' me that some damned magic bracelet has picked me for Ally and that I should hang around until she realizes it?" He hefted himself to his feet and chided himself for a full-on fool. "That seems a might farfetched, don't ya think? Who's t' say that the bloke she's with today isn't the fella she'd meant to be with? Maybe she'll come home today and the bracelet will have come off."

"About time I faced the facts, I'm thinking." He picked up his guitar case and headed down the stairs.

"Séamus?" Lila's voice came from behind him.

He turned back to her.

"If you love her, please stay. At least a few more days. These things—they each seem to have come to a head in a few weeks at the most."

Her hazel gaze searched his. "I can't protect her. Not when she keeps going off every night. That's the thing—at least Kylee and Chloe were mostly around people who could help them, but what if the guy's plan is to get her alone..."

She was asking for help to save her friend. Did he still love Ally enough to do so? If he didn't love her, could he just leave, then? The clenched feeling in his chest and that fact that he was makin' a fool of himself here in Peachland suggested the latter was a moot point. Dammit, he hadn't come here to fall in love again. But the fact that she might be in danger from something or someone made him want to go after her right now.

"So tell me. How come the guy that abducted your Kylee was able to get to Chloe, too? And Ally's with someone—that fella. She's not alone."

Lila sighed audibly and shook her head. "I know it sounds mad, but they were different men and each of them seemed to be possessed by something—something alien. At least that's how they describe it. A homeless man, a contractor, a police officer, an accountant, and a thief have all been involved in this case. One of them killed himself, but left behind a note talking about something in his head. The others all have similar stories. All of them talk about wanting the bracelet." She came to him, where he stood on the stairs. "So I'm scared when Ally goes off with someone she doesn't know."

She caught his free hand as he tried to make sense of her story, and her fingers were cold as ice. "That's all I'm going to say, because I know I'm messing this up. I'll leave it to you to decide."

With a nod, she freed his hand to return to the shop. The little bell dinged above the door as it closed behind her. Well, that was a crap load of confusion to consider. Of course it might just be a load of shite, but the lady was clearly spooked and lookin' for his help.

He went down the stairs slowly and left the yard. The long walk home along the curve of the bay would give him time for thought.

§

Abel's boat turned out to be a brand-new cabin cruiser, complete with head, galley/lounge area, and narrow bunks in a bow bedroom so that the researcher wasn't required to go to shore all the time to provide for basic bodily functions. The pilot's deck sat above the lounge cabin. The deck at the stern contained racks of wetsuits and diving tanks. The interior lounge held banks of electronic equipment.

Ally inspected the boat while Abel, on the pilot's deck, captained them out of the marina and onto the lake. It was a glorious day, with a brisk wind that placed light chop waves on the lake. The sky was scrubbed of clouds now, and the air was so clear it felt like she could see forever. She dug out her camera and took some shots of the rough hewn mountains across the lake, of the sun's gleam on the unsettlingly black wetsuits. The dream came flooding back to her and she stumbled back a step, the day suddenly cold.

Stupid reaction. They were just wetsuits. She pulled the camera up again and shot the tangle of electrical equipment in the kitchen and the lake view through the galley portal, going for more a photojournalist's recording of their venture. Then went back outside, kept a wide berth around the wetsuits, and went up to the pilot's deck. Abel casually steered the boat while fiddling with another piece of equipment.

"What's that?" she asked, coming up beside him and rubbing her arms for warmth. Just let her get some air and sunshine. It had just been a dream. There was no reason for her to feel like the day was closing in around her.

"Sonar." He finished what he was doing and slipped an arm around her waist to reel her into him, but his warmth just didn't seem to sink into her. "So we can see what's under the surface. There have been researchers who've brought sonar before. Some haven't found anything, but one team located a large ping. Unfortunately, they lost it before they could track it."

"So what makes your sonar different?" she asked, studying the innocuous little box and the computer monitor. Feigning interest was so much better than feeling panicked. "What makes you think you'll get anything more?"

He turned his magnetic gaze on her and for a moment she went weak in the knees. "If I turn my mind to it, I can accomplish anything. That and the fact that this sonar is next generation. It can take random pings it hears and discern enough that it can extrapolate an image. It was developed to find aircraft crashed on the ocean's floor. When we find something, not only will we be able to see that something's there, we'll be able to see what the something is. It should deal with the issue of schools of fish fooling the sonar. This monitor shows the electronic signal so we can follow. It connects by WiFi to extrapolation software in the galley."

Ally took it all in, the wind whipping his smoky scent into her nose. "How long have you been doing this—this research?" And why haven't I seen you on Discovery Channel? With his looks, he'd be a star as soon as he was discovered. Not that she'd spent the last ten years anywhere close to a television, but a guy like him she'd hear about.

He shrugged. "Five years. Before that I was trying to make a living as a fisheries biologist and then I joined the military."

And the fitness took. He looked ruggedly, dangerously handsome with the wind in his hair, squinting into the sunshine like a hero.Exactly her type.

"So where did the International Affairs on your card come from?"

He raised his brows at her and looked out at the water. "Would you have been as intrigued if I'd had cryptozoologist on the card?"

She thought about it a moment. "Probably. But I can see your point. So just where does one study cryptozoology?"

He smiled a little. "The answer is, you don't—at least not at any top university. I studied zoology and marine biology and I've been doing this on the side since I got my degree."

"On the side, huh? So what do you do when you're not chasing Bigfoot or Ogopogo?"

His hands tightened on the wheel as he looked down at her. "Do you really want to know the mundane me? I thought this was all about the adventure?"

What could she say? She hadn't told him much of anything about herself and he hadn't asked. No, he'd done the logical thing and googled her name. Now that she thought about it, it seemed strange how little she knew of him. He'd said he wanted them to get to know each other when he invited her out here, and yet there'd been no conversation about each other's likes and dislikes. Strange.

"I figured we'd cross the lake and set up at Rattlesnake Island. We can dive there and try to find the spot where previous researchers found the odd skeleton. See if there's anything else there to see." He smiled down at her. "You might want to get your bathing suit on."

A shiver ran through her and her chest tightened in a way that had to be a reaction to her dream last night. Her heart beat an insane number of frames a second. She was out on the water in the middle of the lake and she was going to dive after having her nightmare.

She wasn't sure she could do it.

They *were* making too good a progress toward the island that sat like a toe testing the water at the base of mountains. The mountains rose in gray granite waves up from the blue water, with sapling poplar trees and young ponderosa pine making a comeback after the Kelowna fire. Along the water's edge lay narrow beaches of white sand littered with fire-blackened wood. A narrow channel separated the island from the mainland. Maybe she could talk him into some play on the beach instead of diving.

Abel cruised around the island and back before dropping anchor in the leeward side so the sun beat down with no wind for relief. "We'll stop here a while, do a dive, and then have lunch. We'll run a search grid in the area of the island before we head back to the marina."

"Sounds good," she said, trying to keep her voice business-like.

She beat him down the stairs and stripped off her clothes, pulling on her bronze bikini. Not exactly diving material, but it might delay the inevitable entering the water. When Abel came down the stairs he stopped dead. "Interesting suit. You think it will hold up diving?"

Not quite the reaction she expected. Not usually the reaction she got from men, either. Usually they were practically drooling at the sight of the tiny bronze bikini, barely differentiated from her sun-bronzed skin. What was it about this guy that both drew her and, frankly, scared her? It was like a photo of a brightly colored tricycle abandoned in the rain could evoke feelings of loneliness. She hefted her camera and took a photo of him, then checked the little screen at the back of the camera. Yup. The focus of the camera lens had always helped to distill the essence of her subjects. Maybe... maybe it was something about Abel's eyes. Dangerous enough that they both aroused her and made her want to run.

He came over to her and ran his hands down her arms to her hips. He took the camera from her and set it down before he pulled her into him. His hands slid under her bikini bottoms. "You are a hot one, aren't you? You want to play now, or wait 'til the dive is done?"

She ran her hands up his chest and unbuttoned his shirt to expose his tanned skin. "Maybe we shouldn't dive at all. Don't we have better things to do?"

A low chuckle rumbled through his chest. "If you are going to be a complete distraction, I might have to rethink having you with me."

He swatted her bum, leaving behind a sweet sting, and stripped off his shirt. His washboard abs and taut muscles rippled in the sun and her mouth went dry. His shorts he stepped out of to reveal swim trunks that didn't really leave a lot to the imagination. She couldn't help but ogle a little.

"Let's go swimming, shall we?" he said and hauled a wetsuit off the rack to toss in her direction.

She caught it and the neoprene hung in her hand like something skinned. Put it on and ignore the alarms going off in her gut, or beg off?

Just what is the problem, McVay? You like the guy. You came with him.

So you had a bad dream about diving—since when do you believe in stuff like dreams?

Maybe since Chloe had those visions and Lila and everyone regaled her with the tales of alien possession. That'd set off anyone's bad dreams.

So get on with it, then, and quit acting like a silly school girl.

She unzipped the suit and found Abel watching her. "There a problem?"

"Nah. I was just thinking about shooting underwater. I haven't done it in years. You've got underwater equipment, right? You said so."

He blinked once. "You said you had equipment."

"Camera equipment," she nodded to her bag. "Digital cameras aren't going to be much good underwater."

His clear blue eyes momentarily clouded over, but then he shook his head. "I'll arrange some for tomorrow."

While she pulled on the wetsuit and fought to get the bracelet inside it, he fished a smart phone out of his pocket, checked something, and dialed. He went down into the galley while talking and came back up with two bottles of water.

"All arranged. One of the camera stores in town rents that kind of equipment. We'll be all set for a deeper dive tomorrow."

She swallowed, but nodded. Deeper didn't necessarily sound better.

Abel helped her settle her headlamp and her tanks, and she remembered enough to check that the airflow was correct. Abel arranged his own tanks himself. Then they climbed down the rear of the boat to the small diving platform at the stern.

In the shadows under the hull, the lake looked dark and murky. Where the sunlight hit it, it reflected back at her with the unfriendly anonymity of mirror sunglasses. Just where the heck was this feeling of doom coming from? She knew how to dive— leastwise she'd dived a few times on tropical coral reefs. The only difference this time was that this was a lake.

And she'd just had a powerful dream of drowning.

Abel caught her hand, so there was no choice. Together they stepped off the diving platform and the chill water closed over them.

They bobbed up side by side and Abel took the mouthpiece out of his mouth. "You remember how everything works?"

She nodded, got her mouthpiece and mask in place, and dove under the water. A touch on her leg said Abel was right beside her.

As opposed to the darkness she'd seen from above, light filled the water. Microscopic algae and sediment shifted like sand around her and turned the light golden. A steelhead trout flashed silver and was gone.

Abel came up beside her, his hair floating like a corona of darkness around his head, his headlamp like a star. He pointed down and nodded a question. She nodded back and they started down, the flippers giving her kicks a languorous feel as the water sleeked past her face. Beneath them the sloping rock of the island gradually came into view, long cords of lake weed growing thickly up from the sides. Fish flashed among the plants, and the sunbeams placed long shafts into the water. Above, the hull of the boat fell away and she felt chilled and very alone regardless of Abel effortlessly swimming ahead and to one side of her.

She kicked after him as he led her down into darkness. The light became fainter until she was surrounded by shades of gray lit only by the lamp on her forehead and the one Abel wore. It was harder to see other than the occasional flash of fish scales that swiftly skimmed away. She kept checking over her shoulder for the surface. It still hung there, but barely—a lighter form of the unending gray-green around her.

Abel swam to their left and found the slopes of the island joining the sides of the mountains that edged the lake. Down farther, and she didn't like this because above the light was quickly fading away, but Abel seemed to be searching for something. They were crisscrossing the island's flanks.

Then Abel pointed at something below them through the murk. The bottom perhaps?

But Okanagan lake was over seven hundred feet deep in some spots. There was no way they'd swum that far down and no way she could do that in this equipment, even if she wanted to. She swam to catch up and caught Abel's foot. He looked back at her. Stopped, his lamplight glaring in her eyes.

Ally pointed up, the universal signal that she wanted to surface. Abel shook his head and pointed down.

The water pressed in around her and suddenly it felt like the tank wasn't giving her enough oxygen. She shook her head vehemently and pointed up. Pointed at her tank and her air hose, and touched her throat. *Get the message, Mister. I can't go on.*

Abel shook his head again and angled downward, following the dim light of his headlamp. What the hell? She'd told him what she wanted and he wasn't listening to her. She had two choices— stay or go—and neither was a good one. As a diver, you were supposed to stay with your diving partner. But as a diver, you were also supposed to do something when your partner indicated distress.

Her air *was* flowing. But Abel's sleek form was quickly disappearing into the gathering gloom. She was going to give him a piece of her mind when they got topside, but she was not leaving him—diving rules were there for a reason.

She struck off after him and finally caught up. Abel glimpsed her and gave her a thumbs-up and pointed below them. Farther down in the murk, a greater darkness was like a great wound on the flank of the island. Abel pointed at her and made a thumbs-up sign, asking if she was okay.

She nodded and he started down again, damn it. In this blizzard of dirt, algae, and darkness, how could he see anything? But she followed, afraid to lose sight of him.

It wasn't a true cave, at least not from what she could see. It was more like a depression in the stone, but then it was hard to see anything through the darkness. She hung on the water, feeling the lake's current shift past her as Abel circled down and around the cave entrance. When he came back to her, he grinned around the mouthpiece and pointed toward the surface.

Finally, damn him.

She started up through the water, finding power in anticipation of reaching sunlight and air. After a few kicks, she looked over her shoulder for Abel.

He wasn't there.

Chapter 11

The silt and algae sifted around Ally through the chill Okanagan Lake water. Her headlamp provided a single beam of light through the water, but otherwise everything was green-gold murk that melted away to darkness. Below her, the darkness was only greater. Had she swum so fast that she'd outstripped him? Was he just following more slowly, or had something happened?

Her heart trip-hammered in her chest and her breath was too rapid. Just how much air did she have left in her tank? She should have her own diving watch to track such things, but she'd depended on Abel for that. Abel who wasn't here at the moment.

Go down and look for him? She knew which way was up. She could find her way back to the boat again.

Fighting her fears, she headed back down, her arms at her sides so her fins sent her swiftly deeper into the darkness.

The slope of the island was just to her right. If all else failed, she could follow it up. She scanned the water around her, but there was no sign of Abel, just the flashes of fish disappearing into the darkness.

It was so frigging dark that her headlamp barely showed anything. Her chest felt so tight she was almost gasping, and she knew that wasn't good. She'd use up more oxygen that way and she needed to conserve it, given she didn't know how much time she had.

Still no sign of Abel, and ahead and below her, the greater gloom of the cave gradually materialized. Had the idiot gone in there and gotten himself into trouble? Because there was no way in hell she was going in there.

But a diving buddy was supposed to be there to help.

Something grabbed her leg and she spun in the water, half screamed, and swallowed water. Swallowed it down as she realized another diver had materialized behind her. Abel. Laughter in his eyes.

What the hell? Her heart felt like it was going to tear loose of her chest. She wanted to punch him, make him pay for her terror. She punched him in the arm, but the water stole any force from her blow. So she turned tail and swam.

Up. Through the blinding murk.

Up. Toward the sun and the boat and air.

Up. Away from the bastard who could drown for all she cared.

Something dark moved through the water to one side of her, too far away to really see more than a shadow. Or perhaps that was all it was, just the shadow of a cloud or a boat passing over the water.

But there were no clouds in the sky and no boats nearby when she reached the surface. The boat was a hundred feet away so she swam over and hefted herself up onto the platform before stripping the mouthpiece out of her mouth and the flippers off her feet. Then she stomped up onto deck, dumped her tanks and wetsuit where they came off of her, grabbed a towel, and went below deck for a drink.

She found beer in the fridge but that wasn't good enough. She rummaged in cupboards and found a bottle of Glenfiddich scotch. She poured two fingers in a glass and knocked it back. Poured another and felt the boat shift as Abel came up onto the diver's platform. She sipped the drink and let its heat feed her anger as she toweled off her hair.

She heard his movements—shifting the tanks, slipping out of the wetsuit—and then he was behind her, pressing his cool, hard chest against her back, sleeking his bastard's too skilled hands down her flanks. His breath was warm on her neck as he nuzzled her. The bracelet flared almost burning hot on her wrist.

She elbowed him in the gut and yanked around when he folded. "You bastard! Do you know how worried I was? You disappeared and I was afraid something happened to you. I had to go back down there alone to look for you!"

He caught his breath and grinned up at her. "Yes, but you should have seen your face. It was worth an elbow to the stomach."

He straightened, still chuckling, and something inside her froze. Asshole. Imbecile. Bastard of the first degree. She was Ally McVay. No one should be scaring the shit out of her like that, but this idiot had. Or she'd let herself be scared, and Ally McVay never let herself be scared. What was happening to her? She swallowed back all the invectives that swelled on her tongue.

She was out here alone with this guy by choice. *Oh my God, she was out here alone and just how was she going to get out of this?*

The same way she'd bluffed her way through her first meeting with rhino and elephant poachers on the Serengeti and managed to win her way into their lives to get her photos; she could do this, too.

Blowing out a long breath she met Abel's gaze. "Sorry about the elbow. It's just—it wasn't any fun down there in the darkness. And I didn't have a watch to even know if we were getting close to the tank minimums. My bad for not having the proper equipment. I won't go down again without it." Her jaw ached from talking through gritted teeth.

He nodded. "Okay. I'll get that sorted out for tomorrow. You'll have everything you need, including your camera housing." He gave her a hug that was too tight. "So how about you make us some lunch and I'll shift the boat closer to that beach you spotted. Afterward we can swim ashore and let nature take its course."

He grazed her ear lobe with his teeth, something that usually turned her on, but she wasn't feeling it. Not even when his hand came up to cup her breast. There was something wrong—whether with her or with him, she couldn't say. It was like their whole—not relationship, because that wasn't what this was—had suddenly gone so far out of focus it was just a swirl of colors.

She stepped back from him, blinking. "So what did you have in mind for food?"

"Stuff's in the fridge." He threw a shirt on over his bathing suit and took himself back up to the pilot's deck. Soon the boat's engine rumbled, she heard the anchor chain clanking, and then the craft swayed and nosed slowly toward shore. Finally she got herself moving and opened the fridge. Beer. Copious cold cuts of various types. Cheese and crusty buns. Mayo and mustard. Not even a tomato or lettuce. For a man with expensive taste, he ate like a common man, or a German, apparently. All he needed was some sauerbraten and schnitzel.

She frowned. Just where had that come from? Abel didn't have a German accent. In fact, he had almost no regional accent at all. But there *was* something about him. His carriage. Her first impressions that he expected to be obeyed. He might have dark hair, but he still had those blue eyes and his features—some people would describe them as Teutonic, with the strong jaw and brow.

The questions bounced around her brain like studying a photo with no key point of interest. She decided against making sandwiches and instead laid out a platter of meats, cheese, buns, and condiments. With a beer for Abel and a bottle of water for herself, she carried the tray and dishes topside and set them on a shaded bench seat.

The rattle of the anchor dropping sounded from the front of the boat and then the craft swayed as Abel joined her on the rear deck.

"What's this?" he asked, scanning the platter with less than approval.

"I thought you might like to build it yourself. Or was this a test to see what I'd make you?"

His brows rose as he stepped closer to her. "Would it matter if it was?" His mouth trailed down her shoulder and his hand came up and plucked loose the bikini string around her neck.

Her top crumpled into his hands and he shoved it down, baring her breasts to his mouth. Her body responded, but her mind was saying no. She grabbed his head and pushed him up and away. "I—I thought you wanted lunch. I know I do."

For a moment those pale eyes froze her to her very core, but then he smiled and he was Abel again. He grinned. "I suppose the woman has a point. There's something to be said for keeping up one's strength." He looked her up and down and pulled a pair of mirrored shades out of the pocket of the dress shirt he wore. They effectively made it impossible to read what he was thinking anymore and that left her feeling a little blind. As a photographer, reading people and what they were all about was part of her skill. She used the ability to bring them to life in a photograph. Landscapes were like that, too, with personalities she had to read in order to capture their feel.

"You know, I'm really coming to appreciate that bikini of yours," he said, lounging back in a padded chair next to the lunch platter to study her. She hurriedly pulled her top in place and sat across from him.

"I'm glad you like it."

He shrugged. "I liked it better when it was half off. Live a little. Try it topless."

Ally shrugged right back. "I have. In San Tropez. I got a horrible sunburn, and being on the water just doubles the risk." *And I don't like the way you're looking at me like a piece of cold cut meat.*

It was true. His face barely changed as he glanced from her to the meat he put on his bun.

"It's too bad you pulled me away to go look for you. I saw something in the water when I was closer to the surface." She bit into her half sandwich—she'd discarded half the bun—and chewed.

Abel looked up at her. "Really?"

"Really. And no, this isn't a way to get you back. As I was nearing the surface, I saw a shadow off to the side. It was big, but I couldn't make out any details. Maybe it was just a submerged log, but it disappeared on its own—or a current got it."

He chewed thoughtfully and nodded, his demeanor suddenly more scientist than letch. "I guess that just means we *really* need to come back here tomorrow. You know what? I think we should head back to the marina. I've got errands to run in town if we're going to have what we need."

She didn't know why she felt relieved, but she nodded. After the meal, she cleaned up while Abel got them started back to the marina and his condo. She was wrist deep in soapy water when something got in her eye. She rubbed away the tears. Just what the heck was that all about? Here she was with a perfectly good guy—great looking, great in bed, and with a very unusual career—even if he could be a jerk from time to time, and she wasn't happy. It was like she wasn't happy with anyone. What was the matter with her? Why did she always treat men as simply a vehicle to physical release? Other women didn't do that—at least not any other women she knew. They were all about relationships and staying power.

Heck, to *her,* staying power only had to do with the bedroom.

Perfect. Her work was in turmoil and now so was she. Maybe she should totally swear off all men for a while.

"So much for you being lucky," she said to the bracelet as she wiped the soap suds off of it. Both Kylee and Chloe had described it as such, and so, according to his son, had Colonel George Bristol. So far the darn piece of jewelry hadn't done a damn thing for her, and wasn't that at least part of the unspoken reason she'd put it on? That and the fact she'd be darned if a silly bracelet was going to frighten her.

But she really could use a little luck in her life.

She had things cleared up and her composure in place by the time they docked. She gathered her things, offered to help lock down the boat, but Abel said he preferred to do it himself. As if he was as tired of her presence as she was of his.

She made it back to her rental car and headed back to Lila's wondering whether the chance to photograph Ogopogo was worth putting up with more of Abel's misbehavior.

Unfortunately, it probably was.

At three thirty in the afternoon, the shop seemed to be busy. Ally came up the porch stairs—no Irish musicians on the porch, thankfully—and pushed into the shop to the ding-a-ling of the little brass bell hung above the door. Chloe was there and so was Kylee, both helping customers, while two others browsed over the earring display. Incense filled the air with exotic sweetness, the pashmina scarves stirred in the currents of air from the open windows, and the newly-stained dark brown wainscoting gleamed. It was a beautiful-looking shop of beautiful things, and the women who worked here and who patronized the shop only added to the grace of the place. On impulse she hefted her camera and shot a few frames, then pushed through the beaded curtain and into the hallway to the rest of the house.

Upstairs, Lila's office door was open, so Ally poked her head inside. "Hey. I'm back."

Lila was at her desk, the computer on. She wore her auburn hair of wild curls pinned up in back, the rest a wild tumble around her face. The computer screen was filled with what looked like Excel spreadsheets.

She frowned and checked her watch. "That was quick. I didn't expect you so soon—or even today, for that matter." She kept her expression noncommittal.

Ally shrugged. "You know me. I can't stick with one man for too long. He might start to mean something." Damn, it wasn't supposed to hurt to say it. It was supposed to be funny.

Lila frowned. "Are you all right? How did the Ogopogo search go?"

She found herself playing with the bracelet links on her wrist. Then she sighed and shook her head. "Not great." It answered both questions. She looked around the room. There wasn't another place to sit other than the floor. "Do you mind if I come in? I'm not interrupting something important?"

"Ally, honey, come in and make yourself at home. I'm just justifying accounts and, frankly, I could use a little break."

Ally went in and sat cross-legged on the floor, feeling tawdry and cheap in her short-shorts compared to Lila's demure look of a plain, light gray shift. She wore a single silver chain with a silver and moonstone Regulus pendant shaped like an angelfish. The fish had swept-back fins that formed an almost perfect circular outline around the moonstone.

"So what's up?" Lila asked, her hands clasped in her lap.

"I saw something out on the lake." Why she led with that, she had no idea.

Lila's brows arched. "Really?"

"A shadow. We were diving, and through the water I saw something. It was big. Maybe..."She thought about it. "It was maybe thirty feet long. It could have been a log, but it was there one minute and then it was gone. I wouldn't expect logs to swim away, would you?"

Lila shook her head cautiously. "Isn't that great that you saw something?"

"Yeah. I suppose. It just got me thinking is all. About all the things hidden under the surface of the lake." Of a life, more like.

"What else happened out there, Ally?" Lila asked. Her voice was soft as if trying to sneak up on a subject. They probably both were.

"I got mad at Abel." She told about the dive and Abel's trick. "When we got back onto the boat, something was just off. I didn't want to be there or with him." She looked up at Lila and then away to her own hands fidgeting in her lap. Okay, this was the hard part and she wasn't sure she could do it. "What's wrong with me, Lila? Why do I do what I do—meet men, sleep with them, and then run away?"

"Oh, honey, that's the million-dollar question, isn't it?" Lila leaned down to put her arms around her and tug her into a hug. "That's part of why you're here, isn't it? It's not just the business stuff?"

Dammit, the darn thing had gotten into her eyes again. She pulled out of Lila's arms and palmed tears off her cheeks. "Sorry. I don't want to mark your dress."

"This old thing? It washes like a dream." Lila shoved her chair back and went to her knees to give Ally another hug. She ran her palm over Ally's head to smooth her hair and found a tissue for her to blow her nose. Then she sat down knee-to-knee cross-legged like Ally and caught her hands. "So why do you think you do those things? I've always wondered." Her hazel gaze was encouraging.

Ally pressed her lips in a line. "I guess I hadn't really thought about it until today. It was all about finding the next guy, having fun, and leaving before he could leave me."

"That sounds like a dangerous proposition. I mean, sure, you get some great sex, but it doesn't mean anything. There's no emotional connection."

That made Ally smile. "I was trying to avoid that." Had succeeded, too. Except once.

"You know, that is really strange. Most people go through life looking for emotional connection and despairing when they never find it. Bonding and attachment are the most important things in a child's development. It shapes their ability to relate to the rest of the world. It gives them empathy." Lila looked her hard in the eye. "You've got plenty of empathy, or you wouldn't spend your life raising money to help others. Why aren't you like that in your personal life?"

A really good question. She shook her head. "I don't know what's the matter with me."

Lila squeezed her hands. "It's not a matter of what's the matter with you. It's what happened to you, Ally. Two different things. One says you're sick. The other says you've found a way of coping with something that happened to you. Maybe that coping strategy isn't best for you, but you can change that. Learn other ways. Figure it out and maybe you can change—if you want to."

"I just feel so darned confused. How am I going to save the charity if I'm consumed with dealing with my inner demons? I need to focus on the business."

"Did you ever think that maybe sorting yourself out will make sorting out the business easier, too? It's like you're fighting a battle on two fronts right now. History will show you that doing so isn't often successful."

Ally nodded. It was something to think about. She stood and gave Lila a hand to her feet.

"I take it the bloom is off Abel?" Lila asked, as she slipped back into her chair and glanced up at Ally.

She shrugged. "Some. There was something about him today. An edge. There certainly wasn't any emotional connection." She held up her hands at Lila's little guffaw. "I know, I know. I'm the person who's been avoiding emotional connection. On the other hand, I might have seen Ogopogo, and that's kind of neat." She ran her hands back through her tangled hair. "God, I am such a mess."

Lila looked up at her. "Yes. But you're still lovely and we love you anyway." She grinned. "Listen, how about we go out for dinner this evening. Just the two of us. We can wander down to the Blue Hills Restaurant and have a nice meal, a glass of wine, and girl talk. Sound okay?"

"Sounds fantastic. Later, then. I think I'll while away the rest of the afternoon doing a little research on Lux International and reading the good Colonel's diaries. Did I mention I found the spot where he's found the bracelet?"

"What?" Lila was on her feet again.

"Yup. It was like Kylee thought. He found it in the desert during the campaign against Rommel. I'll keep reading and I'll tell you more at dinner."

She gave a toodles wave and escaped to her room, but not from her thoughts. Just what was it that kept her from emotional connection?

Chapter 12

The phone call that disturbed Séamus' plans came at three fifty. He was locked in his bleeding cigarette-stinking room, the window open, but even that couldn't seem to get the smell of smoke out of everything. It was like the walls oozed the stuff out for him to breathe. What he was doing, sitting in his room fingering chords on his guitar when outside it was a fine, blue day, he wasn't sure. Maybe it was nerves, because tonight would be the first time he played to an audience in North America. Or maybe it was just that he was still trying to decide whether to stay or to leave Peachland. He looked over at the suitcase stand. That held his backpack. Everything was there. All he had to do was call the airport. The black phone sat on the room's desk, taunting him to make the call.

He hadn't been able to bring himself to do it, regardless of his words with Lila. "Yer a bloody wanker and weak as a cup of a Yankee's tea. Play the gig tonight and get outta here."

He reached for the phone just as it rang. Saved from making the call again?

"Séamus?" The familiar voice spoke through the line before he had the chance to say hello.

"Lila, love. I was just thinking of ya." He set the guitar down and stood up to look out at the day. The breeze filled his face with the scent of water, but it was missing the comfortable scent of brine he knew from home.

"That's a relief. I was worried you'd gone." A pause on the phone. "You haven't made arrangements yet, have you?"

He glanced back at his suitcase and then at the phone. "I suppose you could say I was still considerin' my options. It's a long way to go to change my mind again."

Another pause. "Séamus, you remember that stuff we talked about this afternoon—the crazy-sounding stuff?"

He thought of Ally, running down the porch stairs with her blonde hair flying in the breeze and her long tanned legs. "Yeah. I remember. Silver bracelet that won't come off. Someone after the women who wear it. Fekking crazy story. What of it?"

"I—I want you to talk to a couple of my friends. They've got information that might convince you. I hope you don't mind, but they're on their way over to see you."

Shite. The woman was almost as crazy as Ally could be at times, but in for a penny... And talking with a couple of good-looking ladies couldn't hurt either. "Send them around. I'll be here." He hung up shaking his head, just as a heavy fist knocked on his door.

Groaning, he set down his guitar and went to the door. Opened it. Bloody hell! What were the fekking coppers doing here?

"Can I help ya?" he asked of the big man with an unruly thatch of dark hair. A carrot-top fella stood behind him. Both had broad shoulders and the unmistakable calculation of the constable in their eyes even though both wore jeans and t-shirts.

The dark-haired fella held out his hand. "Jasper Stone.My friends call me Jas. This is Danny Forester. Lila asked us to come."

"Séamus O'Hearn, but then ya knew that, didn't ya?" he said, trying to cover up his confusion. Lila sent police to talk to him? He stepped back to allow them entry to the room. "I'd offer ya a chair, but ya might have to fight each other for it. Not exactly posh, this place."

The dark-haired Jasper settled into the chair. The redhead slung a hip uneasily on the windowsill. Séamus sagged on the bed.

The two men's eyes did a quick, assessing flicker across the room and returned to settle on him.

"Let me guess," said Séamus. "Lila sent you to make sure I wasn't leaving."

The one named Jasper shook his head. "We're not here to stop you if you make up your mind to go." He nodded at Séamus' backpack. "We're here to fill you in—give you information that might help you in your decision."

"That would be what Lila said." He shrugged. "So what is it that's so important I know?"

The two men looked at each other. "Danny, I think you're really the one to start the story." Jas looked back at Séamus. "You see, Danny here was involved right from the beginning, but you've got to understand that this is not the official account at all. If the brass caught wind of what we're going to tell you—well, we'd both be in a psych ward. Know what I'm sayin'?"

Séamus looked from man to man. "You're Royal Canadian Mounted Police?"

Both men nodded.

"And you're tellin' me you believe in Lila's wild-ass story about a silver bracelet and fairies?"

"There's no fairies in this story, friend," the redhead, Danny, said. "Leastwise, none of the Walt Disney kind. Whatever we're up against here is one badass mother." He shook his head. "But that's jumping ahead. You see, I was there at the beginning. I was called out to help with a hit-and-run accident, or at least that's what we thought it was. Some estate agent got run down just outside the latest estate sale she'd held. I was helping out, taking witness statements. One of them was a homeless guy—crazy as a shit-house rat. He was spouting off about aliens in his head and how a pickup truck ran the woman down and then he looked me in the eyes and that's the last thing I remember aside from collecting the victim's appointment book.

"I came to a day or so later here in Peachland, watching a certain jewelry store you might be familiar with. I knew I'd been watching the place. I knew I'd been looking for something. Worst of all, I knew that something evil had been riding me like jockey. It felt like my brain had been scraped from my skull, chewed up, spit out, and stomped on." He shook his head and shivered even though the breeze was warm. "I knew I'd been following Kylee Jensen, the first woman who wore the bracelet."

"We nearly lost Kylee the night of the Canada Day celebration. A neighbor of hers—a nice, unassuming accountant—suddenly got it in his mind to kidnap her. We barely got to her in time." Jasper picked up the story. "When we did, there was something in the guy's eyes that was so old and evil it could make your hair go gray. Then as suddenly as it was there, it was gone, and we've got a raving lunatic on our hands."

Jasper shook his head and Séamus stood. "I'll thank ya for your time and the story, but I don't see what this has tado with me."

Jasper waved him back to the bed, but Séamus went to the minibar and pulled out three beers instead. He handed them around. "Telling tales is thirsty work. I'm guessing you're not working now. The clothes, ya know."

The three of them clinked bottles and Jasper sighed. "With Kylee, the bracelet finally came off when she consummated her relationship with Brett Main. He would have been here, too, but he had some business out of town. With Chloe, it was different. You see, I knew from almost the first time I saw her that there was something between us. She—did not. She had a history that made her certain that there was no one in the world for her.

"She's—different. Sensitive, some would call it. She practices crystal healing and so on and whether you believe it or not, all I know is that the harder she fought the attraction, the worse her situation got. She started having visions that were almost like seizures. It was only after circumstances forced her that she finally committed to try the relationship. Then the bracelet came off, all by itself. Strangest thing I ever saw." He shook his head and took a swig of beer. "You understand what I'm saying?"

Séamus just nursed his beer, considering. "So you're tellin' me that Ally needs to commit to someone or else she'll be in danger. So why tell me? Why not tell her? Not that the woman will listen."

That was the thing. "If ya think I have any sway over Ms. Ally McVay, ya got another think coming. She hasn't listened t' me since Ireland, and even then it was an iffy thing. Now—well, she barely tolerates me."

"That's not what Lila says, and from what I've seen, she's a pretty good judge," Danny said. He peered out the window where the afternoon had waned and the scent of burgers and fries wafted up from the pub below. "Apparently Ally's really struggling now. She doesn't know what she wants, but she's not happy."

"And what? I'm supposed to make her want me? Shite, man. The woman like as turfed me off the property. Then she went trotting off to be with another bloke." A long cool pull of beer down his throat couldn't release the hopelessness of the situation. "I'm about the last person Ally needs. I broke her heart. That's something someone like Ally won't forgive." And she shouldn't. He'd been a right scoundrel, he had. And now—well, when she learned the truth, she'd hate him, wouldn't she?

He upended the bottle and drank it down, hoping for a wee bit of relief from the pain in his chest. He shook his head. "I'm not yer guy. I screwed things up enough between us. I don't want to do it again. Better I get outta here before I cause Ally more pain."

She didn't have to know exactly how badly he'd screwed things up—that the collapse of the Pemba environmental program was his doing. *Ya are such a wanker. Yer Ma would be so proud.*

Something passed between the two men. Both drained their beer, set the bottles down, and stood. "All right," Jasper said. "Since we stole the better part of your last afternoon here, how about we take you to dinner to compensate you for your time?"

"Not necessary," Séamus said. "Besides, I've got plans t' play downstairs during open mike night. Sing my way outta the country, so to speak."

Danny checked his watch. "What time does that start?"

"They told me set-up is at seven."

"Well, then, we better get moving."

Jasper grabbed one arm and Danny the other so there really wasn't much chance of turning them down as they strong-armed him outta his room and down the stairs to the street. They hustled him down the sidewalk as if they were afraid he'd bolt.

"What the hell's going on here, ya blaggards?" He'd planned to grab a burger up in his room, not be dragged along the street to God knew where. But the two fellas didn't seem like mean-spirited folk, more like they had good intentions. He finally relented and went with them.

They turned at a log building with an open, terraced courtyard filled with tables and enough good smells that he could positively inhale his dinner. "This might be a bit rich fer my blood."

"Don't worry about it. Consider it our treat," Jasper growled and led him up through the tables, Danny blocking any chance of escape behind. They'd probably done this sort of thing a lot in their kind of work. The question was just why they were doing it t' him.

The answer came from a circular table in the corner. Two women sat there. Lila he recognized as she smiled up at him, her auburn hair full around her face above a simple gray dress. The blonde with her back to him, he could have guessed if the luxuriant hair didn't give her away.

He stopped dead until Danny gave him a little push to the kidneys from behind.

"Hey Lila," Jasper said stepping up to the table. "You don't happen to have room for us to join you, do you? The place is packed and me and my friends had a hankering for one of those blue cheese burgers."

"Well, Jasper Stone and Danny Forester. What are Peachland's finest police officers doing here?"

"Taking our pal, here, out for his last meal in town." Jasper's strong hand snagged Séamus' wrist and dragged him forward. "You might remember Séamus O'Hearn. I understand he's been at the store a time or two."

Lord save him from 'friends' and acquaintances who were intent on improving his love life. He glanced down at Ally, and if she could shoot daggers out of her ocean-blue eyes, she would. Thankfully, it was Lila, not him, getting the full benefit of the glare.

Lila finished the charade with a gracious wave to the empty three chairs around the table and he found himself, not surprisingly, seated beside Ally. Jasper ordered a pitcher of beer and five glasses.

"This wasn't my fault," Séamus said to Ally.

"I know perfectly well whose fault this is," she ground out through gritted teeth. She glanced at him then and shook her head. "I'm sorry you got roped into this."

He shrugged and had to smile. "There are worse things."

She looked so damned lovely. The fall of her hair around her dramatic features. High cheekbones, lush lips, those bluest of blue eyes, and a patrician nose. Just as lovely as the first time he saw her laughing with her travel companion at the back of a smoky Irish pub while he was playing with the band. He'd been drawn to her then, and he still was. His hand itched to touch hers just as it itched to hold his guitar and make music. So much for his father's dream of an upwardly mobile child in management. It was like he, Ally, and his music were all part of a greater creation, a greater design like the ones the priests went on about in church.

The beer was brought and Jasper poured. Lila and Danny got into a conversation about the investigation into who had orchestrated Kylee Jensen's abduction. It apparently still had yielded no information other than the fact that anyone who had had any direct dealings with the force that was supposedly possessing people could not recall the man's name. Even his description didn't come easily.

"So how'd your day go? You were off on a boat or some such, weren't ya?" Séamus asked Ally.

She nodded, but sighed. "I guess the best answer is interesting." She air-quoted the "interesting." "We dove around Rattlesnake Island. I might have seen something."

"Seen something? Like what?"

"Like maybe the lake monster."

She shook her head and frowned and it suddenly came to him that she was tired—more tired than he'd ever seen her before. "Yer kidding, right?"

But she shook her head. "Nope. Not kidding. There was something in the water with me, but it kept far enough away that I couldn't see it as anything but an indistinct shadow."

"That should get ya a mite excited."

She sighed again. "I s'pose."

They ordered, letting Jasper, Danny, and Lila do the talking, about the weather, mutual friends, and the renovations Jasper had just finished on his house. Jasper had his blue cheese burger, while Danny ordered one with bacon and cheese and Lila ordered a salad. Séamus scanned the menu but frankly, sitting here next to Ally, he just wasn't hungry. She didn't seem to find anything appealing either. And now that he really looked at her, she seemed tense and tired, with deep blue circles under her eyes. Something or someone was keeping her up at night.

A surge of jealousy ran through him, but he shoved it away. There were too many miles and too many other partners between then and now.

"We could share a pizza," Séamus offered. "If yer interested. It looks like they've got something akin to the spicy sausage we used to eat at that little hole-in-the-wall place in Cork."

Her gaze sought and found his. "I haven't thought about that place in years."

He gave her a crooked grin. "But it was good, right?" He was thinking of so many things.

The tension around her eyes seemed to soften. "It was. All right. We share a pizza."

"Done and done." He placed the order and picked up his beer. "Here's to old friends and new ones and taking a chance!" Stupid toast for a stupider situation. He should just be sitting here keeping his bloody mouth shut, because the truth felt like a stone stuck in his craw. He knew things could never work with Ally until she had the truth before her. And afterward? Well, she wouldn't want anything to do with him at all, would she?

Dammit, he'd made his peace with the fact Ally was never going to be his. Not even when he could feel her just sitting beside him, like a force of heat and life.

"It was good back then, wasn't it?"

The question tore him from introspection to total awareness and he turned to look at her. She was looking at him intently, waiting. What could he say? That it was the happiest time of his life? That he loved her so much it scared the shite out of him and he ran like the fekking coward he was?

"Yeah. It surely was. I think I'll always remember the first time I saw you. You and that blonde hair of yours glowing like the sun at the back of the dark pub. Ya were quite the sight, Ally-girl." Enough to steal a man's heart straight away.

"You weren't so bad yourself, you know." She grinned. "Those broad shoulders and the way you didn't play a guitar—you coaxed the music out of the instrument until the thing wanted to sing. Silly, I know. But that's the way it sounded."

The food was brought and two plates for Ally and him. Everyone tucked in. The pizza was good—far better than what he remembered from the little shop they'd frequented in Cork. The tomato sauce was rich, the cheese copious, and the sausage spicy enough to make him pour another beer. He had two through the meal and when there was one piece of pizza left, Ally offered to arm wrestle for it. Her smile made her face light up. It was the best they'd been together since he'd arrived in Peachland.

And now, with the last piece of pizza gone, it was over.

"Séamus, it's almost seven," Jasper said. "Didn't you have some place you have to be?"

"Shite, yes." He checked his watch. "The owners of the pub are having an open mike night. I had a hankering to play." He shoved away from the table and stood, then stopped. "You could come if you like. I could use some moral support." He scanned the people at the table, his survey ending with Ally. "Fer ol' time's sake?" And to delay the inevitable parting?

He was sure she was going to shake her head "no," but instead she looked at Lila and the others. "What do you say? He's quite the musician. It'll be worth your while."

You coulda knocked him over with a feather. Ally wanted to come? It was the most marvelous thing he'd ever had happen. Before he ruined her life and his.

Chapter 13

What the hell she was doing, she wasn't sure. *Why* she was doing it was an even bigger mystery. She'd sworn off the man. She had. But walking beside him, with Lila and Jasper and Danny—just when had Lila come up with this plan of hers?—it brought so many old feelings back to her.

The evening air was still warm, but the breeze off the lightly ruffled lake was cooling. The tops of the mountains across the lake still glowed with sunlight, but the mountainsides themselves had gone gray, as had Rattlesnake Island, resting like a low hump at the bend in the long, narrow lake. Conversation floated around her, from Danny—another most attractive man, just where did Lila find them?—and from Jasper, Lila, and the restaurant tables lining the sidewalk. Across the street, a few boats were tied up for the evening, and the flag stirred around the flagpole over the cenotaph.

They could hear the pub before they neared it. Hard, rocking music blared out of the bar's open doors and windows. The tables at street level were full and there seemed to be a crowd inside as well.

"Looks like you've got an audience," she said when Séamus paused on the sidewalk studying the crowd.

"That can be a bad or a good thing, depending on what kind of music they're liking."

"They'll like you. I did. You're real—not all put-on airs and pretend." She put her hands on her hips. "Are you telling me that

Séamus O'Hearn of Cork is nervous of playing in Peachland?" She held her hand out and he must have seen the silliness of his hesitation. Peachland was a one-horse town. Cork at least had a couple of horses.

"I'll go get my guitar."

He left her there, trying to figure out what was going on, the bracelet a touchstone for her fingers. She'd come home from the boat content to stay in and try to figure out what was going on with her that she had such an aversion to relationships, and yet now here she was with Séamus again. It just didn't make sense. But, then, neither did the thing with Abel. He might not have been trying, but he'd scared her today. Scared her enough that at moments she'd been terrified and had thought she'd seen something in the water. A thirty-foot something. The Ogopogo monster? It couldn't exist and yet maybe it could. She *had* seen something. And, Abel notwithstanding, she had a chance to go back down there tomorrow. If she could get a definitive photograph of the lake monster, the money from that would make all her worries about her charity's finances go away. Heck, she'd likely be set for life. Could she do that? Could she face down the fears she'd had and go back on the boat?

It would give her the chance to decide whether there was anything more between her and Abel than sex. It would give her the chance to see whether there really was a lake monster.

You were terrified, woman.

Yes, but it had been a joke—according to Abel. And he was the one who had used the word relationship, hadn't he? Maybe that had something to do with her being so afraid.

She closed her eyes. If she was interested in Abel, then why was she here? Sure, Lila and Jasper and Danny had as good as locked them in a room together, but it was her who had followed Séamus' lead and suggested they come here.

"How're you doing, girlfriend?" Lila slipped an arm around her waist.

Ally scowled at her. "Trying to figure out why I'm not mad at you."

"You ever think it's because I'm right? I can tell chemistry when I see it." She lifted her chin at the door Séamus had disappeared into. "And then there's this." She clasped Ally's hand and lifted her wrist up to see the bracelet. "After watching Kylee and Chloe, I'd say I almost believe that this bracelet knows what it's doing. Somehow it brought Séamus O'Hearn all the way from Ireland. You have to at least give it a chance. That bracelet has been lucky for a lot of people."

"So you guys tell me. Like Colonel Bristol got through and brought warning. That was the making of the man."

"See? You've just confirmed everything I've been telling you. Now you need to listen to me about the other thing as well. You are in danger as long as you have the bracelet on. You need to take care."

Ally held her away, thinking of deep water just as Séamus returned, grinning, with his guitar case in hand. He led them into the bar and left them in search of whoever organized the open mike night.

"Ally, please listen to me. I'm serious." Lila confronted her again as they found a table and ordered another pitcher of beer.

"Believe me. I know you are."

And now if Lila would only take the hint and leave things alone. Ally scowled at her friend from across the table until suddenly they were inundated with other arrivals. Small, blonde Kylee, with Chloe's brother, Brett, in tow. Chloe herself pulled a chair beside Jas, and Mr. Hottie Policeman leaned in to give her a kiss. Another one effectively off the market. That left the redhead. Out of old habit she eyed him speculatively. Not bad. But then didn't she have enough problems right now trying to sort out her feelings about two men, without adding a third to her dance schedule? It was bad enough juggling two cameras around her neck. Three?

Shudder the thought. And frankly, she just couldn't find the energy to get interested.

Across the pub, the canned music stopped and a microphone squealed before a spotlight on the low stage revealed a gaggle of band equipment and a rotund man with a tangerine-colored Sundowner Pub t-shirt on.

"Good evening folks. Welcome to our monthly open mike night. We've got a few acts for you tonight. Two of the bands are local boys well known to the Sundowner, but we've got some out of town talent as well. One group hails from Vancouver and we've got an act all the way from Ireland, so let's put our hands together for the first group on the bill tonight—Blue Water!"

The crowd applauded as the announcer stepped down and a group of youngsters who couldn't be long out of high school climbed onto the stage to take their place among the band instruments.

A one-two-three tap of cymbals and the band launched into a cover version of *American Woman* that got everyone's feet tapping. They followed it up with a couple of similar songs that got some couples up dancing and Ally's feet hopping under the table. She leaned over to Danny. "You want to dance?"

He shook his head "no." Stymied, she sat back and immersed herself in the music, wondering where Séamus had gone. Her hand went to the bracelet and traced its outline. Just where was all the luck that the others kept spouting off about? Colonel Bristol might have thought the thing was lucky, but it was more likely that he was a brave man who happened to be at the right place at the right time. She could get downright depressed about her lack of luck in *any* facet of her life, but the beer had left her feeling mellow. A hand fell on her shoulder and she recognized the neat nails and small, rough hairs on the back.

"Hey," she said, looking up at Séamus. "Sounds like you've got special billing."

"Everyone just wants t' see the leprechaun." Shaking his head, he slumped in a chair beside her. Then, seemingly on impulse, he caught her hand. "You feel like kicking up your heels, luv?"

The bracelet was heavy and warm on her wrist. What the hell. Dancing with Séamus couldn't be any worse than sitting here feeling sorry for herself. She was this far into madness, a dance wasn't going to hurt anything.

She allowed herself to be led to the miniscule dance floor, but instead of dancing opposite each other, he kept her hand and swung her around, then pulled her into his arms and did a fast foxtrot to the music. She followed and a flush seemed to run through her body.

"You know that you've just scandalized the younger generation who thought you weren't supposed to touch when you dance together—except maybe twerking," she said looking up at him. He really was a dashing character. A humorous quirk to his mouth that always made her think he was laughing at her—and that had helped her laugh at her too-serious nature; those dark brown eyes that always had a twinkle; the broad, muscled shoulders and sensitive mouth. He had a thatch of brown hair that reminded her of the high meadows of Irish mountains. She'd loved Ireland, with its green copses and hedgerows, its crags and rugged coastline. She'd loved the light that seemed to come from the landscape and fill her camera lens and fill up the deep well inside her. Séamus had that kind of light around him. No wonder women loved him.

She swallowed as his eyes met hers. This close she could smell his natural outdoors scent, clean and crisp—unlike Abel's heavier perfume that at this moment almost seemed like a mask to something darker.

He grinned down at her and his hands slipped down to the small of her back. "Ya look thoughtful, luv. That isn't exactly what I was going for."

She inhaled his scent and found a smile, though she was feeling shaky. "Let me tell you a little secret—I'm having fun. It feels like it's been a very long time."

A full-blown grin took his face—white teeth and that twinkle that had once stolen her heart. The way it sped up for a moment, it was almost like he stole it again. Her chest tightened and she pulled back from his arms. "I—I think I need to sit down."

"No. Ya don't. You've been sitting on the sidelines of yer life fer too long. Leastwise you've been missing all the fun. Now dance, damn ya, girl." He twirled her around. And again. And again, as the rousing song came to an end. Then he yanked her into his side again and their eyes locked on each other or at least she couldn't seem to look away as the rotund announcer came back onto the stage to announce a change in performers. Then Séamus blinked, releasing her from the spell, and he led her back to the table.

"That was the most fun I've had since I got to Canada," he said, plopping into his chair and pulling Ally down beside him. He didn't release her hand and Ally felt Lila's scrutiny. The scheming woman was smiling. She untangled her fingers and sat there fuming, but there was no way she was going to cause a scene by storming out.

Besides, what did she have to be angry about? She'd danced with an attractive man—that was all. It didn't mean anything— nothing more than her trysts with Abel. No, she was here because she knew how important music was to Séamus. He'd been crazy about it when they first met, even though he was studying for something else. Music had seemed to be part of him—more important than blood the way it ran through him.

She reached for her beer as talk swirled around her. The new band wasn't quite as good and played rock that was a little bit heavier. The crowd thinned a little and the announcer in the Sundowner Pub t-shirt climbed the stage after only two songs. A third band climbed the stage. They looked like a group of skinny kids complete with long, greasy hair, and for a moment she wondered what business they had here. Heck, were they even old enough to drink? But they set up their keyboard, drums, and two guitars quickly enough.

When they started to play, it was like the entire pub stopped. They were a throwback to the 1970s, channeling the Moody Blues, the keyboard filling in for the London Symphony Orchestra that the original band had had on many of their recordings. She'd discovered the band through Séamus, who had always been a fan of the seventies. She glanced at him and he was turned to the stage, his eyes shining as he listened.

That was Séamus, caught in the magic of music, and she wished she had her camera to capture his expression as a true representation of this man, and yet this was too personal a moment. Her hand snuck onto his and squeezed and he seemed to escape whatever spell he was under. His hand turned under hers and twined their fingers. A tingle rushed through her as their palms connected.

"Their music still moves you," she said.

He shrugged. "Just the emotional wanker in me, I guess. Their music makes me think of longing and how, if we just tried a little harder, we might make these lives of ours a little less futile."

Was he talking generalities or them in particular, because she really understood the nature of futility. His brown gaze was so deep she felt like she was falling, until she released his hand and held onto the arms of the chair.

Séamus stood up, but his eyes were still on her. "I guess that's my cue."

The announcer was back and she hadn't even realized. Séamus walked away and Lila slipped into his chair.

"How you doing?" she asked.

Ally considered. Shaken? Surprised? Disturbed? Happy? "Would you believe that I'm having a good time? I think I owe you an apology because I wasn't thinking good thoughts of you when they arrived at the restaurant."

Lila leaned into her and slung an arm around her. "Apology accepted. He really seems like a nice guy. I thought maybe you just needed to be reminded of it."

"We had a lot of fun way back when," she said with a sigh and watched as the stage lighting was changed to focus on a single stool and microphone as the announcer announced their performer all the way from Ireland. Séamus took the stage and settled on the stool.

"Listening to the Moody Blues always makes me a tad melancholy, so don't expect me t' be playing any jigs and ditties tonight. I've a couple o' songs for ya, though. One's a Gaelic song called *Biodhan Deoch,* or The Drink Would Be In My Lover's Hand—" he hefted a pint of beer and drank "—and the other's something I wrote myself." With that he set down his drink, tapped his guitar a couple of times in rhythm, and launched into a lovely quiet song, his rich bass resonating though the pub and somehow setting her skin tingling all over her body. She couldn't take her eyes away from him and the span of his fingers across the frets, the way his fingers found the strings and his eyes shone as he looked out across the pub—to her.

It was like he spoke to her just as he had the first time she'd seen him, and though she didn't understand the language, she understood the longing in the song. She'd felt it. Felt it still, like a deep hole carved in her chest, an image with its core burned out by overexposure. A loss that she had never been able to fill.

Séamus' hands flew across the strings and his hair fell forward over his eyes as she watched him play. He wore only jeans and a khaki-green t-shirt with some kind of design on the front. When the song ended, the crowd erupted in appreciative applause and he launched into his second song. This, he had said, was his own writing and he'd written it in English, not Gaelic. As with so many Irish songs, it was sad—a tale of longing for a woman lost across the sea after the man betrayed her. The pub was silent as he finished, his deep voice rumbling out his emotion. Then the applause started again and he stood, bowed, and left the stage. As simple as that.

Or maybe not, for her gaze caught on the design on his t-shirt—something that hadn't registered over dinner. A door.

A door blazoned with the image of a gargoyle.

Chapter 14

Séamus felt emotionally drained and yet elated as he pushed through the crowded pub that had turned into a gathering of admirers. Men slapped his back and offered t' buy him a beer. Women stepped into him trying t' engage him in conversation—or something more. He'd seen it before in his days with the band. The experience was both exhilarating and destructive. He'd let it get to him once before and ruined the best relationship he'd ever had.

The announcer had announced a longer break this time—he said to allow them to reconfigure the stage again, but most likely t' refill the drinks. The waitresses were scurrying like mice in a sack of grain. All he wanted was t' get back to Ally. Had she heard his song? Had she realized it was for her that he wrote it—an apology set to music? He'd hoped playing it might absolve him of some of the guilt.

It didn't seem to have helped. But she'd watched him. Yes she had, and her blue eyes were shining almost like they used to. Would she congratulate him? Maybe even kiss him? A smile at least. He could keep warm a long time from one of Ally McVay's smiles.

Then he reached the table. His seat was taken by Lila. She had hold of Ally's hands so hard her knuckles were white as she fought to hold Ally in her chair.

"How could I have known, Ally. Tell me that? I had no idea which door you liked. If I had, yeah, maybe I would have done what you're accusing me of, but I didn't. So I didn't. This thing with the bracelet—it has me spooked too, okay?" Lila looked up at him. "Séamus. Settle something for us. Where'd you get that t-shirt?"

He stopped, looked down at the shirt. How the hell was a man supposed to remember where he got his rags from? But this one he knew. "My ma sent it t' me. Seems the old farm has become a bit of a tourist stop for being a typical Irish farm. The people that come, they fancy the front door. She got the idea from talking to my sister and had some shirts made with the door on the front. She sent me one." He shrugged. "You remember, Ally. The ugly little door knocker ya always said was probably what I looked like when I was a newborn. Ya used to tease me."

Ally looked—stricken. All the tension seemed to flow out of her as she sagged back in her chair, then pulled a hand loose and grabbed her beer glass off the table. She drank it back in one long pull, her throat working smoothly.

"Hold on there, luv. You planning on planting yerself under the table?" He gently confiscated the beer glass—unfortunately almost empty. Lila went back to her chair as he sat down.

Ally was shaking her head, examining the bracelet and scanning his chest. Then back and again. And again.

"It just can't be. It just can't. This has got to be some kind of trick, just like all the photo enhancements out there. Somehow— between you and Lila—you've done some kind of sleight of hand to make this happen."

He caught her hands, gone frigid cold. "What's wrong, Ally? What's got you so spooked?"

She met his gaze then. "Didn't they tell you? According to the bunch of them—" she waved her hand at the table occupants. "According to them, along with the danger of having the bracelet on your wrist, it's also supposed to fix you up with your soul mate or something. At least that's what happened for Kylee and Chloe. The way they could tell that it was the man of their dreams was the man had a door that matched the one they fancied on the bracelet." She looked away as if looking anywhere at all would be better than looking at him. "I happen to have a preference for a little door with a gargoyle. See?"

She held her wrist out to him, and bloody hell, the little silver link was the spitting image of what he wore on his shirt front. He frowned. "That's damn strange, that is."

"Ya think?" Ally stood and swayed. "I think I really need to go home and think about this."

The way her words were slightly slurred, his Ally was definitely feelin' her beer, but the tightness around her mouth said she was definitely gutted as well. Arguing would get him nowhere. He stood up. "I'll walk ya."

"I'll walk with her, Séamus." Lila climbed to her feet.

"Or I can," Chloe chimed in.

Ally turned to them. "Would you all just leave me alone? I need to think. Alone."

With that she shouldered her purse and pushed her way free of the pub. Séamus looked down at the table of people he barely knew and sighed. "This is mine t' deal with, I think."

He went after Ally.

Outside of the pub, the air was much cooler. The air was dry, even though the breeze off the lake didn't let you realize it. From the highway at the base of the hills on this side of the lake came the normal rumble of traffic, but the town just held the sounds of the pub that leaked onto the sidewalk, the voices of people leaving nearby restaurants, and Ally's unsteady footfall along the boardwalk.

He crossed the street to follow her.

"Ally, wait up, luv."

She shook her head, her blonde hair darkened by the night. "I'm not your love. I'm nobody's love—just their fuck-buddy." She glanced sideways at him. "But, then, you knew that." She kept walking, away from him, shaking her head as if she regretted something.

"Ally, you can have any man ya want. You always could." He hurried to catch up to her.

"You know you ruined me, don't you?" She glanced sideways at him as she strode along, head down, shoulders hunched. "I was fucked up enough after my dad left my mom and me. He always told me Mom never loved him—leastwise she withheld sex—something you shouldn't be telling your preadolescent daughter. And then I met you and all the old stuff I'd been doing just fell away. You were the only man I ever wanted to be with.

"But then you up and frigging left me." Her voice broke and she shoved him away, rushed down the street along the shore.

Leave her be or follow? She didn't want anything to do with him, but there was the danger that Lila and the others said she was in. Half-drunk, she was a perfect target and he'd be damned if he was going to let anything happen to her. Doggedly, he went after her and caught her arm. Swung her around just like he had on the dance floor, and suddenly she filled his arms.

"I was a kid. A fool. An idiot. And I figured it out, but it was already too late. You'd left—run away. And then like the true fool I am, I didn't go after you." He looked down into her drink-hazed blue eyes. Take a chance? Bare his soul and take the licking he deserved. "Ally, I always loved ya. God help me, I still do."

She went still before him, her gaze suddenly clear and blue and assessing. "What am I supposed to do with that, Séamus? You hurt me. Badly."

He released her and stuck his hands in his pockets. "I never meant to. Not really. I was scared silly at the way I felt back then—at the way I feel now. Do what you will. I'll probably deserve it."

He didn't even see the fist coming. She drove it into his gut and he almost doubled over. Then she danced back on the balls of her feet, both fists raised to fight him.

"Are ya crazy, woman? What the hell are ya doin'?" he grunted. For a woman, she packed a pretty fair punch.

"Getting my own back," she said, bobbing and weaving in front of him, even if she was half-drunk.

If this was what she needed to heal from what he'd done to her, then he could take whatever she dished out. "Then would ya hit me and get it over with, luv. I'll take m' medicine."

She darted in and her fist found his chest. Another his chin, and she grimaced and leapt back cradling her striking hand. "That hurt."

"And I'm sorry for it."

That seemed to take the fight out of her. Her hands fell to her sides and she cocked her head, her deep blue eyes almost black in the night. "Just how is it that you know how to take the fun out of everything, Séamus O'Hearn? I thought the Irish were supposed to be fun." Hands on her hips, she shook her head. Then she turned and strode off on those great long legs of hers.

He went after her like before. He wasn't about to let a hair on her lovely body be harmed. He caught up to her and walked silently by her side. She was quietly muttering to herself.

When they reached the gate to the store, she paused. "Thank you for walking me home," she said almost shyly. "I don't really need your help from here."

But she didn't open the gate and leave him. She just fingered the bleedin' silver bracelet on her wrist and looked up at him. There was so much sorrow in her gaze and so much confusion. He would have given anything to have seen the clear-eyed dreamer he'd fallen in love with in Cork so long ago.

Lightly as he could, he caught her shoulders. "Ally. I truly am sorry for all that's happened. All your unhappiness..."

Her gaze slipped away to the ground between them and then, before he could finish, she had his face in her palms and was on her toes kissing him.

All the years fell away.

§

The world filled with the warm, clean, green scent of Séamus as the night of soft waves and wind disappeared. The incredible soft-hard of his lips, the heat of his hands as they found her shoulders, then slid down her sides to come around her. She had tried to capture the flooding feeling his touch evoked in her in a thousand photos—to no avail. Then her arms slipped around his neck and he was kissing her back with a passion that made the present go away. She was young—so much younger—and it was not the dry, night-bound hills of the Okanagan around her, but the misted green landscape of Ireland in spring and she was standing outside the Blarney Castle as Séamus kissed her after kissing the Stone of Eloquence.

What in hell are you doing? She was throwing herself at this poor man. Besides, she was angry at him—still hurting after all these years.

After all these years, *why* this man? *Why* was she still hurting? Did that mean something?

She pulled loose and staggered back a step, her fingers to her lips. He stood there, not like the great, hungry darkness that was Abel, but instead like a steady pulse—waiting. Waiting for her to decide. His nut-brown eyes were watchful, waiting, too. His hands hung loose by his sides and that damned t-shirt with the little gargoyle picked up the warm yellow light from the heritage-style streetlight.

"Does your family really have a door like that?" She swallowed, trying to get the emotions that threatened to overwhelm her under control. This was Séamus. Séamus who, after so many years, had come looking for her. She wasn't sure why she asked; as soon as he'd told his story about the t-shirt, she'd remembered the door in question. Had remembered so much more as well, that she'd thought she'd locked away forever, like a storage vault of images suddenly exposed to sunlight.

Séamus and her in his bed, his long pale body spooning hers. Séamus cooking her breakfast, the foggy dawn through their apartment window riming him with light. The two of them going for hikes in the countryside so that he could show her his favorite places. Séamus in the night and the wild, tender way he had loved her.

He stepped up to her as if he were approaching a skittish horse on his father's farm, his hands outstretched. Then they clasped her arms again.

"Did I tell ya I missed ya?" His voice was soft and carried the music of his accent as he stepped up close to her. "Everyday since I was a fool and left ya."

A part of her trembled. A part of her wanted to call him the King of Blarney. But he lowered his head to kiss her again and

God help her, she met him. Wanted his kiss. Parted her lips and suddenly his hands were tangled in her hair and he had her so tightly against his chest she could feel the rush of his heart.

Or maybe that was her own.

Even after all these years there was something here. Something that filled her up as if she'd been empty all these years. When he pulled back a little she stroked his face. His features—older now— but still him, still Séamus.

"This is silly, kissing at the gate like schoolkids. Do you— do you want to come in?" Damn it, why the heck did she feel so nervous? So much like crying? She hadn't felt nervous with Abel, and she *knew* Séamus.

His embrace loosened and he leaned down to open the gate.

She stepped through, smiled back at him and caught his hand, then led him down the path around the side of the house and to the back door. She fumbled her key out of her pocket, managed to unlock it and get them inside the door to the kitchen before he caught her lips again. The scent of Lila's herb garden by the sink and of fresh peaches in a bowl on the kitchen table mingled with Séamus' scent as she kissed him so hard her ears rang.

Not ears. Alarm. She pushed away from him. "Hold that thought." She hurriedly disarmed the alarm and then turned to him. Her mouth felt dry and her palms were sweaty. *Just what was she doing?* "I could offer you a coffee or a glass of wine... " she said looking around the room.

"Ya could. We could sit here and discuss everything that's happened to us all these years, but is that really what ya want t' spend the time doin'?" He stepped in close and looked down at her and she'd never realized just how tall Séamus was—able to look down at her five-foot-nine height with ease. In the moonlight through the window, his gaze was black, but it carried none of the danger of Abel. Instead it promised warmth and something she hadn't thought about in a very long time. A place, a home. Comfort.

But that wasn't her. She was the one who liked danger, wild places, and wilder men. But there was something alluring in

Séamus, too. He might be far from Ireland, but somehow that place shone through him. He brought the safety, the comfort with him.

"I think—not." And with that she kissed his cheek, linked her fingers in his, and led him down the hall to the stairs to her room. At her bedroom door she paused. "I know this might seem silly to ask, but there've been a lot of miles and a lot of men since we last were together. Are you sure you want to do this? I mean, is this just a roll in the hay for old time's sake? 'Cause I mean, I'd understand. We were pretty good in the sack together." Darn it, she couldn't even look at him as she asked. What made this seem to mean something?

"Ally-girl, it was never just a slap and tickle with you, if that's what you're asking." He caught her chin in his palms and raised her face to him. Kissed her softly, tenderly, so she almost forgot to breathe.

When he stopped, she stood there blind for a moment until she remembered to open her eyes. She opened the door, too. And they stepped inside.

The moonlight reflected off the lake water, so the unshielded window seemed filled with silver light. She left the bedroom light off, so the dresser and bathroom door were just shadows, but the moonlight filled the checkerboard-duvet-covered bed with light. She led him there and kissed him, tugging his t-shirt out of his jeans, pulling it up over his head and then tossing it aside. The gargoyle didn't matter. Séamus did. She ran her palms down over his torso and closed her eyes at the rush of familiarity. Her hands remembered. Did the rest of her body? Did his?

She pulled her shirt and shorts off and faced him in lace bra and panties. Dammit, she was shaking. Shook more when he reached out a single finger to trail down her forehead, touch the tip of her nose, her lips, her chin, then lightly graze down over her breastbone and belly to the top of her panties, leaving a trail of fire in his finger's wake.

"Ya look just as I remembered, luv. Just as beautiful."

She knew it wasn't quite true. She had more scars—old ones from a bout of topical ulcers from a sunburn gone septic her first year in Africa—her skin was more weathered, too. And she had lines around her eyes that hadn't been there before. But Séamus hadn't changed at all.

Still a young man's body of rock-hard abs and farm-boy muscle. Had he ended up going back to help out his dad on the farm after she left? She realized that she hadn't asked him a thing about himself since she'd seen him again. "You are the same." She placed her hands on his chest. "The same sweet man I fell in love with all those years ago."

"An' there's a lie if there ever was one. I've got my scars and my demons picked up along the way." He smiled down at her. "We've wasted a lot of years, Ally-girl."

It was so true. She stepped up to him, kissed him as he steadied her shoulders and she undid his jeans and slipped them down off his hips to leave him wearing only blue boxers. Then she stepped into his lean length and let him pull her into him.

Yes, it was the same. He was the same and suddenly she wanted the feel of him inside her more than anything in the world. Let his *feel* of home and safety fill her—heal her. For once more in her life, let her feel it, even if this night was all an illusion.

"Come to bed," she whispered when he released her, and she lay back on the bed.

Séamus stretched out beside her, stroking her side, her belly, pushed the straps of her bra down off her shoulders. At the same time she explored the strange familiar country that was him. The crags of his face were still the same, perhaps a little more wear around the eyes, but the hollows of his cheeks were the same as was the thick mess of his hair. His lips still carried that devilish grin and she had no doubts of the damage they could do to her resolve when they ran over her skin. That, she remembered.

His shoulders were still broad and strong as she stroked them, stroked his pecs and lower, following the narrow midline of his belly down to the concealing waistband of his underwear.

"These have got to go, I think," she said and sat up beside him to tug them down over his hips and then strip down off his legs.

Another flotsam of clothing on her bedroom floor.

He caught her arms before she could touch him, ran his hands down her shoulders, tugging the bra straps with him. The bra hung loose over her breasts and his hands smoothed the cups lower, skirting the edge of her nipples with his thumbs so she caught her breath as her whole body thrummed in answer.

"I think we need to be rid of these bits o' cloth, too, luv." His big hand reached behind her and the bra fell open. "Aah! I still got m'touch." He grinned up at her and tossed her bra away, then tickled her back down onto the bed until he could strip her panties from her.

Hard flesh against her smooth. His guitar-string-callused hands teasing her breasts, her sides, the insides of her thighs as he slid down her body to tongue her.

At the first touch of his tongue, she arched her back. As he found the spot, he stole her breath. As sensation overwhelmed her, she whimpered. The night seemed to flood all around her. It filled her up and smothered her, and Séamus was the only one who could save her. Her body became a single tight drum and he was playing her, playing her tap-tap-tap so she was going to explode.

He must have felt the way her body tensed, for he suddenly lifted himself up and was there above her, the throbbing length of him pressed against her belly.

"Please," she whispered and brought her legs up around his waist. *Heal me. Save me. Make me feel alive again.*

He leaned down to kiss her, a soft kiss that played with her lips and made her even more ravenous for him. Then he pulled back and hefted her hips in his hands to bring her up to him.

His entry was one long, sure stroke and she cried out at the ripple of pleasure.

When he didn't move, she opened her eyes and found him smiling down at her.

"Now there's my girl," he said softly when she went still under him. He trailed his hands down her face to her breasts, then followed with his mouth to suckle on her nipples and slowly began to move inside her.

It was a slow, languorous movement. No rush. No need to seek immediate release. No need to use titillation or mirrors or tools to bring her arousal. This was only Séamus, slowly moving. Slowly pleasuring her with his body, his hands sleeking her skin and coaxing the sensations higher as he moved harder and deeper inside her.

He swept her out from under him and above him, his gaze never leaving hers except to roam her body. The sweat on his brow, the smile on his lips spoke of his pleasure as she took over providing the friction of their bodies.

It was like a dream, one that she had not known that she wanted. And yet, looking at this man—with his devilish smile and his hair briar-tangled, this man who held her hips and thrust his pelvis up to meet her—with all her heart, she did.

§

She was a goddess, a queen, the way the moonlight gilded her body. She rode above him, her arms above her head as she thrust her hips, and yet her deep blue eyes were open and looking at him. The bedroom, for all it was a guest room, still seemed imparted with a sense of her. Or perhaps it was only her scent of cloves that seemed heady and powerful as they moved together.

Her blue gaze seemed to blaze questions at him and he wanted to find the right answers. To draw for her in pictures, or find her a landscape where all the trails led back to her, for that was what he had found over the years. The moments of peace, the moments of bliss were all moments when they had been together.

He ran his hands from her hips up over her breasts to her shoulders and pulled her down to him so her blonde hair fell around both their faces. For a moment they sheltered there, together, his body still firmly lodged in hers. Their breath mingled and he knew she could be wild and adventurous in her lovemaking, but this was not the time for that. This was about emotion. This was about finding.

When he read her eyes, there was so much there it hurt to see. How he had hurt her so deeply she had never recovered, how she had searched and searched for another, how she wasn't sure she could trust her heart now.

He rolled her over under him and smoothed her hair back from her face. "I'm sorry I've hurt ya, luv. It was never supposed t' have been this way."

How could he tell this beautiful creature that he was to blame for even more of her pain than she suspected? He closed his eyes and began to move inside her again. When he looked back at her, he prayed she wouldn't see his guilt and the way he continued to deceive her even now.

Would she have brought him to her bed, if she knew?

But her eyes were closed and her head thrown back, her hands fisted on the pillow under her head. Her breath came in small gasps. Her head shifted side to side. Her utter abandon aroused him absolutely. He lifted himself on his hands and increased his tempo, thrusting deeper, deeper inside her. Her insides quivered as her head tossed, then stopped. Her hands opened, then shifted down to grip his ass. Her eyes opened and it was like everything she had been exposed to her in her life fell away.

Her hips lifted higher and her legs wrapped his waist as she met his thrusts. Sharp cries escaped her as they came together, as the world narrowed around them. There was only Ally. There was only their flesh merged for this moment. Sensation ripped through him. His muscles tightened.

Ally. This was Ally. He had found her again.

He opened his eyes and thrust deep within her. Home. This was home. Home so sweet he never wanted to leave.

Her eyes flashed open, shock and awe in her gaze, a rough explosion pulsing through her that tore him over the edge. Bright light filled his head as he collapsed forward over her, his body pulsing. Smooth hands held him inside her as she quivered and then she cradled his head and rocked him to her.

"Séamus.Séamus," like a song, she whispered into the cleft of his shoulder.

They lay together between sleep and waking as the moon crept over the sky. He watched its progress in the shifting shadows that slid across the walls. After all these years and all the dreams, Ally-girl lay luminously asleep in his arms. He kissed the smooth angle of her shoulder and her hand came up, ran longer fingers through his hair.

"You're awake," he said and nuzzled the back of her neck, her slight movements arousing him.

"I am. I—I wasn't expecting this, Séamus." There were words there she wasn't saying. Was it a disappointment?

"It has been a long time. Strange how our bodies remembered."

She shifted then, to lie beside him, her head nestled in the crook of his shoulder just like she had done years before. Her blue eyes were stained black by the moonlight as she studied him. "We did, didn't we? Somehow our bodies recalled."

She frowned and two small furrows formed above her brows. "I didn't think that was possible. I didn't think this was possible." She looked up at him with a combination of wonder and disbelief.

"It's true, luv. It did and it was all I remembered. It's good t' just lie here."

From somewhere in the house a floorboard squeaked and she stiffened in his arms.

"What is it, luv?"

She pushed away and sat up on the side of the bed. "Lila's home. What if she heard?"

Snaking an arm around her, he pulled her back down and snugged her into him again. "What of it, if she did? It's what lovers do. She's a grown woman. She knows."

She was so still she might have been one of the stones fallen from a castle wall, except she breathed. "You're taking this as if it was fated, Séamus."

"Maybe that's so, but I prefer t' think of it as setting old wrongs t' right, ya know?" he caught a curl of her hair around his finger. So soft, just as she was silken soft beneath her exterior.

She rolled over and stroked his face. "It was good, wasn't it?" She smiled and it was like the very first time he'd seen her at the back of the pub. She leaned in to kiss him. "Totally unexpected. Why now, Séamus? You were the one who left me for someone else."

The way she said it broke his heart. He ran his knuckles gently down her cheek. "But you ran, too, luv. Before a man had a chance to come to his senses. Sometimes 'not-running' is more than doing nothing. Sometimes 'not-running' is fighting for what you want, you know?"

She went absolutely still as if he'd struck a deep blow. Emotions flickered across her face and then she looked at him, her eyes bright. "How did you find me, Séamus? How did you know to come now, just when I needed you the most?"

Her hair was a wonderful tangle about her face, her face flushed, lips bruised from lovemaking, and God he loved her. But this was the time. He had to come clean. The air in the room seemed to vibrate with the words he needed to say.

His heart thudded doom in his chest, but he had to do this. "I tried t' find you in Zanzibar, but you'd already left. Yer landlord said ya'd come here, so I followed."

Coward. Worst of curs. He felt her raise herself up on her elbows but wouldn't meet her eyes.

"Zanzibar? But why now after all these years? How did you know that I needed you?"

He licked his lips, seeking the words—or escape. *Not escape, ya wanker. Ya came here t' do the right thing.*

"Ya see, luv, I heard about yer problems—the Pemba Project going tits-up when some hotel conglomerate bought the island headmen off."

She stiffened beside him and her face turned haunted. Her hair hung in her eyes as she nodded. "It was out of the blue. Somehow they bought off the headmen and got approval for their development. The company brought in outside workers and that destroyed the equilibrium of the island economy. It totally undermined everything and the coral reefs were being raped again. The families stopped sending their kids to school because they needed them to help earn money. In fact it got worse, because with the foreign workers came sexual exploitation of the women and girls."

She'd pulled herself to sitting, her knees to her chest and the tangled sheets around her. "It was horrible. A total undoing and I tried to talk to the company, tried to talk to the island elders, too, but someone had got to them. Someone had bought them off so they wouldn't even talk to me. Even the Imams had been seduced into shifting the focus of their messages." She dug her fingers into her hair as tears filled her eyes. "I don't know what to do, Séamus. I tried everything, but nothing worked. I've never had that happen before. I feel—lost."

He should put his arm around her shoulders. *Just keep his mouth shut and he could pull her into his side and comfort her— have Ally in his life again.*

But it would be based on a lie of silence.

His sighed and the moonlight seemed to tremble around him. "Ally-girl, there's something y' should know. After you left Cork, I did what my Pater wanted of me—I went to university in Dublin to study international business. Hotel Lux International—I worked for them as their Pemba advisor."

Time stopped in the room. Then horror bloomed in Ally's eyes.

Chapter 15

The cold light of the moon disappeared as Ally leapt off the bed and flipped the bedroom light on. The harsh light revealed the stark remains of her tawdry encounter with one SéamusO'Hearn. Séamus, the man who had ruined not only their love, but—*everything.*

The room stank of their sex. The bed sheets were in tangles, the naked man on the side of the bed looked up at her with guilt and dismay in his betraying brown gaze. The incandescent light placed hard shadows on the lines around his eyes that she hadn't noticed before. Séamus had aged. He looked tired and old and defeated—just like she'd felt ever since Pemba happened.

And he was the cause.

"You bastard! What? You came here to gloat? To have a last little fuck just so you could do to me physically what you did to my life?"

He came up off the bed. "No! That's not why I came. I came t' apologize. To beg yer forgiveness. I didn't know it was you, Ally. Your project. Not until it was too late and the damage was done." He caught her shoulders, but she ripped away.

"So it's okay to ruin the environment, just not my little pet projects, is that it?"

"No—that's wrong. I didn't know what they were going to do to the island. It was supposed to be an environmentally friendly project."

She suddenly realized she was naked and grabbed for her shorts and a t-shirt. Yanked them on.

"Get out." She pointed at the door, then realized she'd probably have to disarm the alarm to get him out of the house. When he hesitated she grabbed his clothes off the floor and shoved them at him. "Get your fucking clothes on and I'll let you out. I suggest that tomorrow you climb on a plane and get the hell out of town, because if you don't, I just might come hunting you."

He pulled his clothes on, covering his strong legs, slim hips. The breadth of his shoulders. The body she had just loved. The man she'd fought not to love all these years—until tonight. Damn it, she felt like he'd ripped out her heart again, only this time it might be worse. Being with him tonight, his tenderness, she'd allowed herself to be vulnerable again. To actually step out from behind her camera and feel her heart soften.

And now this.

She was an idiot. Probably always would be where Séamus O'Hearn was concerned. Her Achilles heel—but now those pixels had gone dark in her emotional sensors. Now she could see him for what he truly was—a cheat and a liar.

"Ally-girl, please. Believe me. I didn't know how it was all going to unravel. They looked for my advice because the island headmen had turned them down. I told them to go to the Imams and influence through them as well as the headmen. All I thought they wanted was a bit of beach on the island to build an exclusive resort. It was supposed to be an eco-lodge. At least that was what they told me. Ally, I came because I still love you. Because I hate that we split up all those years ago and I don't know if I can live with myself for what I've done to you and that island."

She marched to the bedroom door and yanked it open. "You can plead ignorance all you want. The damage is done. You lied about why you were here and now you expect me to believe your sorry story about how you love me? Come on, Séamus. All I feel for you right now is shame that I was so flipping stupid that I fell for you again. I'm not angry at you; I'm angry at myself for letting myself believe in you again. Now shut up so we don't disturb Lila anymore than we already have."

She shoved him out of the well-lit room into the darkened hallway and down the stairs, the floorboard creaking protests under them.

Too bad, so sad. She was better shed of him. At the kitchen, the moonlight came through the bank of windows that gave onto the backyard patio filled with blue shadows and silver. Her hand came to the bracelet at her wrist. She keyed in the alarm code and opened the back door. Lake-scented air rushed in, carrying with it the scent of geraniums, baby's breath, and roses.

Séamus stepped up to her again, his brown eyes seeming to drill a hole right down to her heart. She looked away, to the night.

"I didn't have t' tell ya, luv. I could'a kept it a secret, but I wanted our relationship to be based on truth. So I took a chance and told it. I'm still glad I did."

"I'm sure you remember your way around the house. And just so you know, I did some research on Lux International. They're owned by a multinational corporation called Schwarzenacht. I checked the corporate books. I'm going to go see the owner and see if I can get him to fix Pemba and blackball your sorry ass in the process."

He stepped past her, then stopped. He turned back. "Ally, I wish ya'd rethink this—not ruining me, I deserve it. But from what I hear, there's too much danger collecting around that bracelet of yours. Let me stay here to protect you."

In the moonlight the gargoyle door on his t-shirt seemed to glare out at her as if she was the one in the wrong. Her hand placed a firm band over the bracelet. Kylee and Chloe were totally on the wrong track when they said that their men were somehow connected with a real-life door that matched the bracelet. But then, a t-shirt wasn't a real-life door, was it?

She met his gaze and ignored the bruising of her heart. She'd been bruised before and had learned how to harden it. "I don't need your protection, Séamus. I'm a big girl. This—this was the sign of just how poor my judgment is. Now, if you have any human decency, you will stay away. No guitar strumming on the porch. No running into me at dinner or on the street. It's done. Over. Ended, and I want you out of my life."

He nodded. "Goodbye, then, Ally-girl. Keep well."

He turned and trudged across the patio to disappear into the darkness around the corner of the house.

The night ticked around her as she listened for the soft click of the side gate. Gone. He was really gone this time. She inhaled the cool scents of water and green growth, but a tremor ran through her. Her body still felt him. The light strokes of his hands, playing her like a flesh and bone guitar. His kisses that ignited her.The way he stoked her fire with the slightest movement inside her. He was a man of subtle movements and wavering Celtic chords.

And she'd sent him away—had lost him again.

The backyard scene seemed to smear and flow. Wiping her eyes, she pulled the door closed behind her, reset the alarm, and looked around. There was no way she could spend the night in her room. Absolutely everything there would remind her of him, of what she'd lost both on Pemba and in her love life.

Instead she flipped on the kitchen lights and rummaged through Lila's cupboards for herbal tea—chamomile, even though she didn't particularly care for the taste—and put the kettle on to boil. When she had a cup, she slipped into the brightly cushioned nook and wrapped frozen fingers around a mug covered with frolicking cat images. The chamomile steam rose into her face and she inhaled. Took a sip and burned her tongue, and wasn't that just the way of the world—even the things that should soothe you bit you in the butt when you were down.

She sniffled against the pain in her mouth. Sniffled at the pain in her heart and scrubbed at her eyes, hoping it would help.

It didn't. She slumped against the back of the nook, wiped her eyes, and realized she was full-on crying.

Lila found her there, coming into the kitchen so quietly that at first Ally didn't even realize she was there, until a warm arm slipped around her and wrapped a yellow pashmina around her shoulders.

"Lila. Hi." Ally scrubbed her face. "What are you doing up?" Then she shook her head. "I'm sorry. We woke you, didn't we?"

"Actually, I got up because I couldn't sleep. I guess it was all the adrenaline from the dancing—yes, I danced. I got up to make a cup of tea and then realized your bedroom door was open and the light was on. Then I heard the beep of the alarm. You sent Séamus away, didn't you?" She slid in beside Ally and gave her a hug. "What's happened? When neither of you came back to the pub, we all assumed things were going well."

"Well, we all know what they say about assuming." She tried for a smile, but all she came up with something that felt sickly and close to death. Dammit, it shouldn't feel like someone just tore out her heart. *She* was the one who sent him away. *She* was the one who always had her camera between herself and involvement. Even her international development she'd done at a distance, hiring others to do the work on the ground except when she was taking photos. But Pemba had meant something to her. It had shown that people and environment could coexist, *just as she could coexist with Séamus in the world*. More than coexist. There'd been signs that they could be together, finally, after all these years finding each other. And now both were over and done. Kaput.

"It's simple, really. He lied. His coming here was all a lie to confess his sins and gain my forgiveness. Absolve himself of culpability in the destruction of one of the last bits of paradise on the planet."

Lila frowned. She wore purple satin pajamas that whispered around her as she stood, went to the stove to check the kettle, and then poured her own cup of chamomile before returning to the table. "I'm not sure I understand. He came to apologize for leaving you, right?"

Ally laughed and it tasted bitter in her mouth. "I wish. That's what I thought, too, at first. And that I could forgive. We were so young back then." And terrifyingly in love. No wonder he ran. "No, this was betrayal of another kind." She told Lila what Séamus had done. About his work for the company that had destroyed her Pemba Project.

"He came here thinking he could apologize and all would be forgiven." Shook her head.

"And you can't do that?"

Ally shook her head. "How? The guy comes and acts like he wants to get involved again. He even talks himself into my bed—and then he springs this on me? As if a good fuck would make it all go away."

She scrubbed her face. "It'll never go away. He betrayed me."

Lila nodded, her great hazel eyes thoughtful. She nodded. "That's certainly one way to interpret what happened. It is. But there is another possible perspective."

Ally set her mug down, the chamomile suddenly tasteless swill. What was it about Séamus that had people—women mostly—always making allowances for him? "You're taking his side now?"

"No. No. No." Lila made a show of open hands. "I really am just talking about possible interpretations. Séamus could have thought that after making love he had to be honest, because if he kept his secret any longer you'd just think he was manipulating you. After all, you haven't given him much chance to tell you since he arrived in town." She kept her gaze averted, almost as if she didn't want Ally to read her expression.

"You don't agree with what I did." Ally's stomach clenched, whether out of resentment at Lila or anger at herself, she wasn't sure.

"Honey, what I agree with or don't doesn't really matter here, does it? You made a conscious decision and took action on it. That decision has you feeling sad. I don't like to see that."

She was so matter-of-fact and accepting. Normally that would be great, but Lila's little speech reminded her that it hadn't really *been* a conscious decision. It had been a lot like when she stomped out of Ireland—and out of Zanzibar, for that matter—a reaction of the gut. Love, hurt, and anger all tangled up. Where had she learned to just up and walk away when things got hard? Her dad? "He did betray me and the people of Pemba."

"Yes, it sounds like he did and he knows that was wrong."

"Dammit, Lila! You make it sound like I'm the one who wronged him tonight. It was wrong what he did. I can't have someone like that in my life."

"Okay. So he leaves and goes back to something he must be pretty good at—strategizing how to get business done in foreign countries." She sipped her tea. "It's too bad, actually. I think he'd be a lot happier pursuing his music, but I don't think he will without his muse around him."

"What? You're suggesting I'm his muse, now?" Forget the fact that she was going to do her best to ruin his career in business. "Get real, Lila. I have. And now I'm going to get some sleep because tomorrow I am going to go and get a photo of Ogopogo."

Leaving Lila before she could say anything else infuriating, Ally slipped out around the nook and returned upstairs.

The scene of the crime. She walked around the bed and then stood by the dresser, considering. Finally she tugged the sheets smooth and, screwing up her courage, turned off the lights and lay down on top of them. She pulled the duvet over her and lay there staring at the ceiling. When sleep wouldn't come she rolled over on her side and tried to stop the shudders that ran through her. The worst part was when she pulled the pillow into her chest and buried her face in it.

It smelled of Séamus and she couldn't let it go.

§

He'd made a damned desperate mess of the whole thing.

At four a.m.,Séamus sat by the window of his not quite dingy hotel room and stared out at the slumbering town as the sun rose. It really was a right lovely town. The air smelled clean and the breeze was refreshing. The traffic from the two-lane highway was a comfortable low rumble. He could understand how this place could be a home you could come back to again and again. Blue water, pleasant climes, and a bevy of beautiful women, including the little group that had gathered around Ally at the store. Lila Weber and the others he had met must think him a very bad man after what he'd done to upset their friend.

And Ally?

Ally was probably scheming up other ways to make him pay—she especially would be when she realized that he had no intention of doing what she'd asked and walking away. Just walking away would be a coward's way out, but given what those two cops had told him yesterday, he wasn't dropping Ally to fend for herself anytime soon. Nope, regardless of their row, he was sticking around. She'd just have t' get used to it. She might be a hard case, but in this she didn't have a say.

When the sun had lifted its head over the mountains, he roused himself, had a shower, and pulled on his clothes. Then, having rescued his guitar from the front desk of the hotel, he headed down the street that followed the beach to the café just up from the red and white house where Ally was staying. He grabbed a coffee and a bacon and egg sandwich of some kind and settled himself on a park bench just across the street from the jewelry shop.

The coffee cut through the ugly taste of too much failure and too little sleep that filled his mouth. It filled his veins with a jittery sense of impending doom—something that was surely helped along with a lovely bit of cold egg and biscuit congealing in his gut. Not his finest hour, this, what with the only shut-eye coming in that brief interlude between when Ally and he made love and when the world had gone a-crapper when he'd told her what he'd done. His eyes felt like pee holes in snow, and the sunlight off the lake was brutally bright. He hauled sunglasses on and pulled out his guitar. Might as well get the practice in.

A slow Celtic tune limbered his fingers. A couple of joggers stopped to listen.

"You're the fellow from the bar last night, aren't you?" asked a man in spandex, his girlfriend or wife beside him.

"That I guess I am."

"Have you got an album out? We both really liked your music and your voice."

Séamus shook his head. "Not at the moment, no, but it's on my to-do list." If he had one. "Right now I'm just trying to pay penance for some bad shite I've done." He met the man's eyes and smiled. "Woman problems, yaunderstand?"

The man followed Séamus' gaze as the front door of the shop called *This and That* banged open and a right mad blonde came stomping down the stairs and across the street toward him.

"I think I got her attention," he grinned, but the man and his girlfriend took their leave to continue jogging. Probably a wise move, judging by Ally's expression.

"Good morning to ya, Ally-girl. How're ya keeping?" He strummed the guitar, experimenting with a little run of chords while she stood there, veritably steaming.

"What. The hell. Are you doing here?" she gritted out through clenched teeth.

"Takin' my morning coffee." He hefted his cup in a toast. "They really do a fine brew at the shop down the way." He lifted his chin in the direction of the bakery café.

"I told you to leave. Go home to Ireland or wherever you hang your hat these days."

He glanced up at her then. "Last time I checked, this was a free country. I don't see as it was me that went searching you out this morning. I was just sitting here messing with my strings. You're the one as came out." He started a song and began to hum.

Ally rounded the bench to confront him. "Listen here, buster. I don't know what your game is, but it's not going to work. If you think you can get back into my bed just by sitting here being all musical and pathetic—well, you've got another think coming."

He shifted his fingers across the frets, remembering the silken feel of her skin and the way she'd responded to his touch. Then he raised his eyes to her and grinned. "You have it your way, luv. I'll just sit here nursing my coffee and my music."

"Fine. Do that. I won't be here anyway. Abel's picking me up and we're headed out to look for Ogopogo."

"The lake monster I read about?"

"That's right. We're taking Abel's boat out to search for him."

He nodded. "Must have a lot of equipment."

"He does. He has patrons who're paying for it."

"Well, that's good fer you, then. Have fun." He started a more complicated song that required more attention or he'd get his fingering all wrong. A rousing bit of Irish music ran along the lakeshore and he caught of glimpse of people shifting in his direction. That should right piss off his Ally-girl.

"You." She positively growled as she trounced back across the street. He made a point of turning to admire her retreating figure and waved when she looked back at him. The fact she looked back gave him hope, when there was a very good possibility that he had no right for hope at all.

But let her get the damned silver bracelet off her arm first and then he'd have a thought about leaving. Just get her safe was all.

Chapter 16

"That man! I swear he's just doing it to bug me." Ally banged into the kitchen and Lila and Chloe looked up from where they were enjoying a morning cup of coffee while reviewing the books for the store.

Sunlight filled the room and erased the aura of sadness that all the room's bright colors hadn't been able to erase last night. But then the sadness was hers, not the room's. Why she felt so sad was just plain stupid. She hadn't seen Séamus in a dog's age. He showed up on her doorstep as if she was supposed to swoon at the sight of him and when she did—well, then he swung the hammer down, didn't he. Just like some ancient Irish warrior with his war hammer. All right already. She'd been hit, knocked down, but she was darned if she was going to stay that way. She didn't need Séamus O'Hearn. Not for love or companionship, and not for sex either. Certainly not for adventurous sex, which was what she'd grown accustomed to.

Nope, Séamus was all about lovemaking.

And she was not going there. Séamus was history, even if he was playing his guitar across the street. Even if he'd been right in his little dig that it was actually her who had done the running.

"She does not look happy, Lila. I thought last night was all about making Ally happy," Chloe said. She motioned to the seat beside her. "Come sit. Tell Aunt Chloe what's got you all upset."

Ally rolled her eyes, but she sat.

"He's out there."

"Séamus?" Chloe asked, all innocence.

"Of course, Séamus. After I specifically told him to leave me alone and go home to Ireland. Now he'd sitting out there strumming that guitar of his and drawing flies—a crowd—I don't know. Attracting attention, anyway."

"And you don't want to have to listen to him play? I thought he played rather well, didn't you, Lila?"

Lila sipped her cup of coffee and nodded. "He did. But I don't think the quality of the music is the issue. Ally has questions about the quality of the man."

"Oh." The teasing quality left Chloe's face. "What happened?"

"You mean Lila hasn't told you?" Wonder of wonders. "Last night—after we made love—he spilled the beans about why he'd really come here." She told Chloe about Pemba and Séamus' admission of his role. "How am I supposed to trust someone like that?"

Chloe caught her hand. Squeezed. "I think I understand—about trust, anyway. It takes all the time in the world to build trust and only a moment to break it. He was pretty brave, taking a chance and telling you, don't you think? Even if he is a bastard for having done what he did. Funny, though. When I met him, the word I got for him was *loyal*."

"Loyal to Lux International, you mean." It was all Ally could do not to pull her hand away. She closed her eyes and sighed, because she was not going to give Séamus credit for telling the truth about what he'd done to her project. "Listen. I've decided I'm going back on the water to dive for Ogopogo. If I can get a decent photo of whatever it was that I saw out there yesterday, it will fix my financial problems and I can at least get my charity back in the black again. For that I can put up with Abel. Don't worry—after last time, I'm not looking at this as anything other than a chance for a photo. He's coming to pick me up, and before you say anything, I will Google his name just to make sure everything's on the up-and-up. Okay?"

She slipped her hand away and slid out of the nook.

Brow furrowed, Lila looked up at her. "Are you sure that's the best idea? When you came back last time, you were upset. Even if you don't want a relationship, what do you know about him? With the bracelet on your wrist, you might as well have a target on your back."

Ally rolled her eyes. "I've been out with him three times and nothing has happened! So, what? Fourth time's the charm for him? I know the bracelet has you all concerned, but like I said when I put the stupid thing on, I'm a risk taker. I can handle this." She shook her wrist so the bracelet links tinkled together and suddenly felt tired. "This is just a chance to get a photo that might fix my business problems. That's all. If it doesn't—well—no harm, no foul. Now give it a rest. Please?"

She turned to go, then stopped, because she didn't want them to think she was walking away mad, even if she might be a little. "By the way, I read a little more, and after the battle of El Alamein, Bristol talked about being in Cairo and trying to determine the provenance of the bracelet. He made the acquaintance of a man who worked in antiquities. The man said the bracelet was unusual in its style—enough so that he was sure it didn't originate in North Africa. He suggested that it might harken back to the time of Roman domination of the Mediterranean. There was a lot of commerce that brought in specialty items like jewelry and spice from all around the known world. So the bracelet could come from anywhere. Sorry." She shrugged and left the kitchen.

By her watch it was almost time for Abel to pick her up, so she went up to her room and collected her things for diving that afternoon. So she hadn't lied, she picked up her tablet and typed in Abel Khan, cryptozoologist. Nothing came up. Odd, but then he might not have published anything that got him coverage. On the other hand, there were a lot of sites relating to cryptozoology. Maybe he just hadn't put his name to the site. He *had* mentioned that the field was frowned upon and that his background was in more traditional science. He could be trying to protect his professional reputation. She tried another search for Abel Khan, biologist. Still nothing, but it was quite reasonable that any papers he'd written back before his military service wouldn't be online. She tried his name again, with military as the search refinement and came up with a Facebook page—not his—and a variety of articles about anti-terrorism. She sighed.

So just what did this prove? He wasn't an axe murderer with a public profile. A lot of people didn't have an internet presence. Her parents didn't. Sure, Lila would, because she'd once been famous. Reggie would because of her jewelry. Did Chloe? She typed in her name, but aside from her recent work to put up a Facebook page about her healing practice, there was nothing. So Abel not having a lot of web presence wasn't so unusual.

Okay. She'd done due diligence. She checked her watch. Abel would be here any time. She wasn't going to back out at the last minute just because the guy had been a dick the last time she'd seen him. Everyone was entitled to a bad day.

Through the open window came the strains of guitar music. She ignored it and packed up her bathing suit, towel, and other toiletries as well as well as a fleece jacket and long trousers in case they were out late on the boat. She stuffed the lot into her daypack and grabbed her camera bag.

The music hadn't stopped. Instead it lifted in strains that brought her flashbacks of hiking with Séamus over the rugged hills of the Dingle and other times looking out at the Mizen Head, the cliff-sided, southwestern-most point of Irish land in the Atlantic. In the dawn light, the ocean and sky had been misty, with the stars still burning bright as the sky turned from black to azure and then orange. She edged to the window to peer out at the street.

Séamus still faced the water, but a small group of people had settled their beach chairs around him to listen. One of them produced a small pipe and the sweet, high notes played around Séamus' guitar strumming. There was no question that music was what Séamus should be doing—not causing trouble for her charity by undoing years of work.

He *had* seemed ashamed of what he'd done. Truly ashamed, because Séamus had always been honest about his emotions. Their lovemaking last night had shown it, because it *was* lovemaking. Tender even in the more athletic moments. Nothing like with Abel, where it was all about show and trying something new to amp the pleasure. Séamus was about the tried-and-true and bringing the pleasure through intimacy of mind and body. Too bad he hadn't thought of that before he ruined everything.

A rumble from the street announced the arrival of Abel's black Humvee. The vehicle cruised into the curb in front of the house and Ally pulled the window closed. Across the street the music died away. Séamus stood.

Oh God! Not that! He wasn't going to get into it with Abel!

She grabbed her daypack and camera bag and dashed down the stairs only to find herself following Chloe and Lila out the front door.

"What are you doing?" she hissed at them as Abel stepped down from the car, his black hair like an unexposed image, his ruggedly handsome features only made more so in the sunshine. He waved at her across the Humvee's hood and started around to her, but Séamus caught up to him and caught his arm. Not that! Not a fight! Not about her!

Ally started down the stairs toward them. *Séamus, don't do anything stupid, because you might be strong, but Abel is stronger.*

Séamus backed off and Abel came around the truck to greet her with an arm around her neck, pulling her into a passionate kiss as if he was marking his territory. Then he released her.

She couldn't help wiping her lips. Maybe this was a bad idea, even if he looked like a male model in a form-fitting black t-shirt and ass-hugging knee-length, denim cut-offs, but with bare feet stuck in athletic sandals. "Ready to go?"

"Sure. For the dive." She nodded up at him, hoping he got that she specified just what it was that she was ready for.

"Good."

"Abel, is it?" Lila stopped him with an outstretched hand before he could swing Ally around to the Humvee hulking at the curb. "I don't believe we've formally met. I'm Lila Weber, co-owner of *This and That,* and this is Chloe Main, one of my partners."

Abel released Ally and shook both women's hands. "Nice to meet you. Abel Khan, at your service." He bowed his head at each of them, a movement that would surely send both of them swooning, but instead Chloe's eyes narrowed.

"Just bring our Ally back to us. We have plans for this evening," Lila said.

Ally frowned a question at her. She knew nothing of any plans. But maybe it was a good idea to have Lila plant that idea. Lila simply smiled at her and stepped back as Abel handed her and her equipment into his vehicle and climbed in the other side.

Ally raised her hand in a wave at her friends, too aware of Séamus standing watching her from the other side of the road. Well, too bad for him. Then the Humvee pulled away in a low rumble and the others were left behind.

"Sorry about that—the gauntlet of people checking you out."

Abel only shrugged.

"What did Séamus want? The guy? He stopped you?"

He diverted his attention from the road to her. "He told me to keep you safe. He said you're in danger. That true?" His scrutiny felt hot on her skin.

"Nah." She shook her head. "They're all full of these stories about this bracelet bringing danger. She held it up to show it to him. "You might have noticed me wearing it all the time. The darned thing won't come off."

"Ah. You have taken it into a jeweler?"

"We have a jeweler on staff—at least the store does. Reggie Lewis. You might not have heard of her, but you will someday. The woman is going to be famous. But she couldn't get it off, either, at least not without cutting it off, and that doesn't really appeal to me."

So suddenly she almost fought him, he caught her wrist and studied the bracelet as he drove. Then he released her. "It really is most interesting. Not beautiful, but a unique thing."

And just as suddenly as she'd been mad at Séamus, she wished she was back with him. That he was the one driving the Humvee, not Abel. But that was so not going to happen. She'd made herself vulnerable to Séamus once too many times. She rubbed the bracelet and her favorite little door. But what did she know about Abel aside from his work and apparent wealth?

"So. You've never told me much about yourself, other than you have a home in Germany."

He didn't take his eyes off the road as he drove up Drought Hill and on into West Kelowna. "I was born in Minnesota, but work took me elsewhere. I spent time in Great Britain, but now I have my home in Berlin."

"Really? That sounds like an interesting life. What took you to Europe? Your studies? Or were you just traveling?"

He gave a perfunctory nod. "Initially it was school. But now it is business, really." A glance in her direction that was like coals smoldering and she swallowed and looked away. Abel was a sexy beast, there was no question about it.

"So what's on the agenda for today?" she asked, seeking a subject that wouldn't make her feel like she was expected to crawl into his lap right here and now.

"I picked up the camera housing and some additional lighting that should help in that murky water. I think we head out to the island and dive today and try to get some good photographs of that cave. I was hoping to stay out for the night and get in some additional dives tomorrow, but given you've got plans, I guess we can go back out tomorrow. If that works for you?"

"Works just fine."But at that moment she could have kissed Lila for her mention of an engagement this evening. For some reason, she didn't relish the thought of spending a night on the water with Abel. She sat back in her seat as he turned into his condo development and drove around to the marina.

He pulled in next to the security gate to the boats—locked closed. "I'll let you out here to lug your gear down to the boat. I'll just park the car and join you."

She hopped out, grabbed her daypack and her shoulder bag of camera gear, and watched him drive away. It really was a thoughtful action on his part. She punched in the code and lugged her stuff to the boat, but Abel caught up to her before she could board. A pat to her behind and then he pulled her into him so there was no mistaking his arousal.

"What do you say to a little play on board?" he said when he'd raised his head from what should be a toe-tingling kiss. His dark eyes peered down at her, smoldering. "I've been thinking about you soaking wet in that tiny bikini for two days now."

She swallowed. A part of her—the part she had lived with for almost fifteen years—was ready to peel her clothes off right on the dock. A less familiar part of herself took a cautious step back. "I am so sorry. I brought a different suit today—more suitable for diving. I'd really prefer to just focus on that, if you don't mind."

His hands slid up her sides to caress the sensitive undersides of her breasts, but then fell down to his sides. "Babe, I prefer you in no suit at all, but if that's the way you're feeling, then diving it is today."

See? She'd been right about him. It was like a giant load off her mind as he helped her aboard, and she went below to dump her camera and gear while he readied the boat. Lila had been so wrong.Tarps came off windows. Cushions were brought out for the seating. He took the engine keys up above and it burbled to life with a belch of blue smoke. Then he was back on the dock, tossing ropes up to her for careful winding as he boarded and began to back the craft out of the marina.

In short order they were outside the wood pilings into open water and he increased the speed, aiming the boat like an arrow across the water to Rattlesnake Island.

Ally climbed the ladder to the pilot deck and stood beside him as the bow of the boat sighted on the low hump of the Island. She was free of Séamus here. There was no way he could find her and that was a good thing. The wind tore her hair back from her face, but cleared her head.

Ogopogo was waiting.

§

Séamus watched the black beast of a vehicle rumble down Beach Avenue, spreading its blue diesel smoke into the clear morning air. His chest felt tight with—not anger, but fear—and that wasn't right. Not right at all. So Ally had another man in her life. He expected she'd likely had more than a few in all the years between Ireland and now. Hell, he'd had a woman or three himself.

Sighing, he turned back to the blue water of the lake, though it looked a little grayer now. The park bench was a tad harder, too. He picked up his old friend the guitar, and nodded at the bloke with the flute. The guy had a talent for improvising around Séamus' tunes on the strings. He plucked a few notes, but just couldn't feel them in his fingertips. Usually the notes flooded up through his hands and arms and into his soul, so he was singing from the heart.

At the moment it wasn't happening, though.

Shaking his head, he left the guitar in his lap and stared out at the water. The fella with the flute played a few ditties and then put the instrument away so there was only the sound of the water and of voices of the sunbathers. Out on the water came the drone of boat engines. He sat there until a larger boat appeared from the north, cruising across the lake toward the spot the barista at the café had said was Rattlesnake Island. Not a good place to be, by the sound of it.

Ally—and she was out there alone with some scoundrel. He had to do something.

"Séamus?"

He sighed and turned. "Lila. Hi. What can I do for ya?"

She came around the bench and settled herself beside him. "Can you see why we're a little worried?"

"Seems t'me that Ally's made her choice. Who're we to be unmaking them if that's what she wants? He's a good-looking bloke. A good match for Ally."

Lila scrubbed at her face. "I don't know what it is. That—that guy—he's a good-looking man. Any woman would fall for him. But I can't help asking myself, why him? Why now, when she's most at risk? Of course, when I try to explain it to her, she just resists. It's like there's no talking to her."

"I think it's because of the bracelet," said another voice. "It's like she's got a different resonance right now—at least that's what I felt like when I was wearing it. All the common sense you know I have just went right out the window. Weirdest sensation I've ever had," Chloe said coming up beside them.

The guy with the flute gave them the strangest look, then got up and moved farther down the beach with his friends.

Chloe had a strange look to her, that girl. Sort of like an earth-mother type, with her extra-long, plaited hair and her shapeless shirt—dress—tunic—whatever it was. She stood beside them looking out over the lake. "I just wish we knew more about him. I mean, Ally isn't about to go off and do something totally crazy, but there's a lot that can happen alone on a lake the size of the Okanagan..."

This was far too akin to his own fears to lend any satisfaction. Séamus blew out a breath and stood. "So maybe we need to learn a little bit more about Mr. Abel Khan, cryptozoologist and despoiler of women. What sort of computers do you have in that store of yours?"

§

It turned out that there were a few, and all had been well-maintained with current software, internet, and social media accounts.

After a while, Séamus looked up from the nook in the sunny kitchen in which he was ensconced. It didn't look at all like the dismal portal that Ally had so unceremoniously kicked him out of last night. Clear white walls and sunny yellow cupboards reminded him of his mother's kitchen, except his mother's had been white-washed old brick and stucco, with ancient fridge and iron stove instead of a modern affair with stainless steel appliances.

He opened his Linked-in account and started digging around for Abel Khan. He found a lot of Khans and a sizeable number of

Abels. But none in combination. Hmm. It didn't necessarily mean anything, but a man like him, in the service of cryptozoology, could be expected to have an internet presence, couldn't he?

He opened the Google search engine and typed in Abel's name. A listing of similar names came up but none of them included Abel. Stranger still. He tried cryptozoology, figuring he'd probably find him somewhere here even if the search of his name hadn't worked, but all he found were multiple websites full of hazy photos of lake monsters and questionable videos of Sasquatch sightings in Yellowstone Park.

That made no sense. From what he'd seen with Nessie in Scotland and the wee beasties said to inhabit the lakes and steep-sided bays of Ireland, the kind of person who researched strange beasts was the same kind of man to scream his suspect findings to the heavens. Abel Khan didn't seem to have done that. In fact, to Séamus' way of thinking, there was entirely too little of one Abel Khan on the net.

He looked up and found Lila pacing the center of the kitchen while she waited for him. She stopped when she saw him staring at her. "Anything?"

"Nothing at all."

"Don't internet searches usually yield at least a listing in the white pages?" she asked.

"Not Abel Khan, apparently." He tapped in a question for his address and phone number but came up with listings for a variety of other names, just not the one he was looking for.

Lila pulled out her phone, took off an earring, and dialed a number. "Danny. Hi. Are you and Jas busy at the moment? Any chance you could find an excuse to come visit the store?" She shook her head. "No, it's not an emergency." Then she caught sight of Séamus. "Well, maybe it is. It's about Ally. She's gone off with this guy she met named Abel Khan and when we've run his name on the internet, we come up with nothing. There don't seem to be any telephone listings on the net either. He's taken Ally out to Rattlesnake Island for diving and, frankly, I'm worried about her. He doesn't seem to be a local. Can you check around? I believe he's staying at the Waterford Condominiums." She nodded. "Thanks. I owe you one." She hung up and looked at Séamus. "It pays to have police as your friends. Danny said he'd get back to us this afternoon."

Séamus scanned the computer terminal again. There wasn't much he knew about Ally's fellow. Tall, good-looking as hell—the kinda bloke who stole another man's girlfriend—and with money to burn if his vehicle was any indication. "If he doesn't have a phone number, maybe he isn't from here. Is there a rental car company here that rents posh cars like the one that bloke was driving? And what about boats? If he's got some kind of yacht to ferry them over to the island, there has t' be a record?"

Lila sank down at the table to face him. "You're right. And Ally said something about him renting equipment for her photography—lights and so on. There can't be many places in town that do that!" She leapt up. "Do a search for *Through the Lens*. It's the biggest camera shop in Kelowna. I know because the photographer I used for some advertising shots had to rent some equipment there."

She grabbed the phone and slid in beside him. Séamus looked her in the eye but he still hadn't searched the number. "We need t'think about this a moment. Ya know that if we do this and Ally finds out, she'll never forgive us. She'll say we were spying and didn't trust her t' have common sense."

He met Lila's steady gaze and read her worry, but he'd already burned Ally once—make that twice—so she wasn't about to forgive him easily. If he did this, it would just alienate her further. Did he want Séamus O'Hearn t' have more black strokes in the negative side of her tally column?

'Course, if she was dead, that wouldn't really matter, would it?

It left him between the proverbial rock and a hard place, and either way he came out crushed; but if Ally was safe at the end of it all, it was worth it. He nodded and typed in the name of the photo shop.

Lila dialed as soon as they had the number.

"Hello, I'm hoping you can help me. A friend of mine is going out with this fellow who's here researching Ogopogo. I wanted to send him an invitation to a birthday party I'm throwing for my friend. Stupidly, I wrote down his address, but I can't recall the guy's name. Do I feel dumb. I'm pretty sure he rented some equipment from you, though. I'm hoping you might be able to help me out and give me his name. It started with an A—Axel or Abe or Abel or something? Could you possibly check your records?"

She smiled briefly in his direction and tapped one manicured finger on the tabletop, then, "Abel Khan! Yes, that was it. Thank you so much. Can I ask you one more thing? Mr. Khan rented a large yacht to conduct his research. Any idea where he might have rented it from?" She listened a moment and thanked the store clerk again before hanging up.

"Okay. Abel Khan did rent some equipment so he must have identification in that name. They also told me that the only place in this part of the valley that rent boats of that size and type is the Kelowna marina. They rent yachts to people who want to cruise the lake for a few days as their summer vacation."

"They could probably help with outfitting the boat for diving, too," Séamus said. "But all this doesn't show anything nefarious. Doesn't it prove he's on the up-and-up?" And that he was honestly losing Ally to another man. "Lila, I know yer trying to help, but haven't I screwed with Ally's life enough? If she's decided this is the fella she wants..."

Ye Gods, it hurt to say it and even more to think it. He couldn't quite bring himself t' believe it, though. Not his Ally-girl. He'd found her again. He wasn't going to let his own idiocy wreck things once more. He'd find a way to win her around—if he could keep her safe so he could do the winning.

He scooped the phone from Lila and dialed the marina, got the manager, and gave a story that was a variation of the one Lila had given to the photo store. The manager said he'd call them back. Séamus gave Lila's number and then sat back and sighed.

They'd done all they could. Now came the waiting.

Chapter 17

It had taken an hour and a half to get out to the island, but the wind tugged at Ally's loose hair as the boat slowed as they neared the low hump of the island. The sun beat down as she went forward to ready the anchor for Abel's command. She wore cut-off shorts that showed a lot of leg and a slim-fitting t-shirt in indigo blue so that she felt like she was part of an editorial shoot of blue on blue: clothing, lake, and sky, with the white fiberglass of the boat and her blonde hair as counterpoint. A little shapely thigh and the image would sell a million on one of those online stock image sites.

The breeze carried the scent of the once-burned-off mountainside. Pine and sage and perhaps an old scent of ashes. She looked in the direction of the breeze—straight down the boat's axis from the pilot's deck.

"Drop anchor," Abel called and she frowned.

"We're farther from the island than the other day!" she called.

"I don't want to take a chance of hitting the cave," he called back.

Reasonable. She hit the lever to let the anchor fall and heard it splash into the dark blue water beneath the boat. The chain went rattling after, and for a moment she wondered what it would sound like under the water. A rattling death knell.

Crap, she was in a weird headspace today. One moment she'd been feeling all the sexual tension of Abel's presence and the next feeling almost creeped out by it and something else she couldn't quite put her finger on. She made her way around the cabin by way of the narrow walkway and stepped down on the deck.

"So should we grab a light snack before the dive?" she asked, looking up at the pilot's deck. Abel wasn't there.

"Abel?" She stuck her head in the cabin. More silence. Just the creak of water against the hull.

A shiver ran through her as she stepped into the lounge area with all its mysterious equipment. "Abel? You here?" Still nothing and she crossed through the equipment to the head and the bedroom beyond.

"Abel?" she rapped on the head door. No answer so she swung the door open. Empty.

That left the bedroom. The door hung half-open, and she caught a whiff of something burning but there was no sound. All the little hairs on the back of her neck stood on end. She shoved the door fully open with her foot. There was nothing. The twin beds filled most of the space in the bow, with only a small space for standing right by the door. Her heart was going kathump-kathump-kathump.

Just what the heck had happened to Abel?

A shift in the air, a slight movement of the deck, and she spun around and almost fell. No Abel, but the whiff of smoke was in the air and—crap—what if the boat had caught fire? In a rush she spooked out of the cabin and onto the rear deck, stubbed her toe, and almost fell. She plunked down on one of the bench seats and nursed her toe.

"So what's going on?"

Abel's voice startled her so she squeaked and turned. He was standing right there behind her as if he'd just come from the cabin, but *he hadn't been there!*

For a moment she didn't know what to say. The ka-thunk of her heart had gone wild and she swallowed and drew in a deep breath. "Abel. Where were you? I was looking all over."

He shrugged. "Right here."

As if she was blind, and a splinter of something like fear ran through her. There was no way he'd been inside—not even if he'd purposely been hiding from her. But that made no sense. There was no reason for him to hide from her.

"So I was asking if you wanted a snack before we dive?" she said.

"Go ahead," he said, stripping off his shirt. "I just want to get down to the cave to see if we can find anything like the body the previous divers found." He stripped down, abs rippling in the sun as he tossed the shirt aside and tugged down his cutoffs. He wore Speedo trunks and a tan that left nothing to the imagination.

Her mouth went dry and she went into the cabin to raid the fridge. The cool air was a balm across her skin. Just what was it about Abel? She was almost beginning to think it wasn't natural. She'd been with other attractive men before, but it had never been so hard to think when in the presence of a man. It was like his scent lit part of her aflame regardless of what her brain might know was best for her. Well, she knew what she was here for, so she'd just focus on the dive and getting her shots.

Abel, she'd come to realize, meant nothing to her. He could leave Kelowna tomorrow and it wouldn't break her heart.

Would it? She clamped her eyes closed and held on tight to the counter. Just what was she feeling? What was real? What did she want?

Brown eyes, tousled hair, a crooked smile, perhaps?

No darn way. Not that lying bastard.

She took a deep breath and sliced an apple and cheese and carried both on deck. Abel was already in his wetsuit, the zipper undone to expose his chest. He checked their air tanks, hoses, and gauges. "All good."

Nibbling her apple, she took her time settling her Nikon into the underwater housing, making sure that she had the settings correct for the new environment and that the dials on the housing worked. Once the camera was water-tight, she arranged the flash units on the housing so it looked like she held a metal-armed robot of some type.

"All done?" Abel asked. He was fussing with the lines attached to the small zodiac slung at the rear of the boat. He'd said it was so that they could leave the boat at anchor and still travel to other locations to dive. He really seemed to have thought of everything.

She nodded. "It all looks operational."

She stripped off her shorts and t-shirt down to the green maillot she wore, then finished the apple and cheese while she pulled the wet suit on.

The suit rolled up over her legs with no problem, but when it came to pulling it onto her torso, the bracelet proved troublesome. Again. Somehow it kept hooking onto the sleeve until finally she grabbed some electrician's tape and taped the bracelet to her wrist. Then the suit slid right on. The apple finished, she accepted the tank onto her back and checked the gauge herself.

"A diving watch?" she asked.

"Damn. I knew there was something I forgot." Abel shook his head and caught her shoulders. He bussed her cheek with his lips. "But I've got my watch, Ally. We'll be together so there's no need to worry about it. Just follow me and I'll make sure we head back to the surface in plenty of time."

The tank gauge was working fine and read the tank was full. When she tapped it, the gauge indicator held steady.

"Then I guess everything's ready. Ogopogo, here we come!"

Abel helped her shift the camera down to the diving platform at the rear of the boat, then climbed down himself. The day was hot on the heavy neoprene wetsuit as Ally slipped on her flippers and mask and let her legs dangle in the water. She slid into the cool water, the surface marginally warmer than where her feet dangled below. Abel, with his mask and flippers on, stood above her to hand the camera down.

She looked up at him, and for a moment thought his face had gone strange, his blue eyes almost red, the way the reflecting sun caught them. With the camera in his hands, she could almost imagine him bringing it down on her head. Then he grinned as if he read her hesitation and gently placed the camera and light constellation in her waiting hands. By the time she had the camera settled in her grasp and a tether attaching it to her waist, he had gone over the side, given her a thumbs-up, and disappeared underwater.

Pushing the camera before her, she followed.

The camera took getting used to. Although she'd used one before, she'd forgotten how the awkward bulk slowed her down in the water. Through the blue-green murk, Abel was a disappearing form below her and she had to kick like a madwoman to catch up. When she did, she touched his leg and motioned that she needed to take a moment to check the camera. He hung there in the water while she swam around him, taking photos, adjusting the flash and the natural ambient light until she was satisfied with the images in the SLR camera screen.

She signed to him that she needed him to go slower and rocked the camera to indicate that it was the problem. He nodded and started out again, this time at a pace she could follow. Good. At least this time he was listening to her.

Fish flickered around them again, and at the slower pace, some even ventured close enough that she tried a few photos. The general rule when photographing underwater was that unless the photographic subject was large like a whale or a dolphin, you needed to be within three feet. That was the only way the wide-angle lens on her camera could capture the image through the sediments and algae in the water. The silver image of a lake trout looked out from her camera screen. Yes, she had the camera set up properly. If there was anything to be seen, she could probably get the image.

At first they followed the long angled columns of sunlight down into the green world, but then the columns melted away into darkness and they turned on the lights mounted on their foreheads and the camera. The water glowed eerily around them, thick with the algae. The hiss of her air flow and the hollow sound of her breathing filled her head.

Abel led them at an angle from the boat toward the island until finally their light found its weed-covered rock side.

Abel didn't wait. He simply glanced back and turned deeper into the water. One hard kick that churned the sediment in the water and he almost disappeared below her except for his light. Well, at least the light gave her something to follow. She kicked after him, ignoring the darkness and the way the water resisted her muscles.

The granite stone of the island's side caught in her light. The weeds disappeared and were replaced by stunted marine grass and a thick algae growth. Fish darted around the algae, feeding. When she looked back below her, Abel's light was fading. She had fallen behind.

She kicked hard after him, but the camera housing and flashes were like pushing a shield through the water. She was just going to have to depend on Abel to realize that he'd lost her behind him. She kept a steady pace downward, following Abel's now-dim light. Surely it couldn't be much farther to the cave.

Then Abel's light steadied and seemed to grow. Finally she could see him caught in his light's glow as he explored around the entrance to the cave. He nodded when she came up to him and pointed inside.

It was like a black hole in the water, the darkness there. Their lights caught on pale, waving grasses growing on the floor and sides of the entrance, but the light couldn't beat through the cloud of particles in the water. A little tremor of primal fear ran through her and she could have laughed. She was playing with all of humanity's worst fears here. Drowning. The dark. Being unable to run because her legs were trapped in viscous water. She nodded her answer and followed him inside.

The water here seemed still, but their entry stirred it and brought sediments up from the floor and down from the ceiling. The cave itself was about thirty feet across at the mouth, but started to narrow almost immediately. The floor was a mix of stone fallen from the ceiling, clouds of algae, and what looked like thin, pale grass that flowed in the current her movement created. A few fish darted past for the cave opening.

Otherwise all was darkness and the cave narrowed around them so she felt like she was being swallowed. Her breath came in short, sharp gasps until she realized what she was doing and steadied herself. This was no place for a panic attack. Hell, this was no place to be at all. She didn't like it here. It felt dangerous as hell—foolhardy dangerous. Why take this risk? But then that was Abel, wasn't it? All about the risks, even in their sex.

Abel would say that the risks were worth the rewards. Orgasm. Possibly finding sign of Ogopogo. But she found herself wondering. Was life all about taking risks? Once she'd thought so. After leaving Ireland, she'd picked up where she'd left off in school—taking risks with men and her career. She'd parlayed it into her charity. That had given her satisfaction, but it wasn't the same as what she'd had in Ireland—or during a certain one night stand in Peachland.

Séamus, damn him. The damned Irishman had gotten under her skin again.

She almost banged into Abel, his light, trained ahead, almost invisible in the murk. The cave had diminished in width to about six feet wide. Wide enough for her and the equipment, but still not the best situation. If it narrowed much more, there'd be challenges getting turned around. Just how much farther did Abel intend to go?

As if in answer, his hand caught in her light and motioned her forward. Something obviously had his interest and he wanted her to document it. He slipped over against the wall and she kicked herself forward, camera up and ready.

Ahead the cave seemed to expand again, and as she swam forward, it was like a greater darkness reached out to swallow her. Her light caught on stone walls, on rock floor. Algae pillowed in deep banks along the cavern walls and grew in a thick, glistening slime up the walls. Small white creatures that looked like salamanders skittered through the cloud of stuff away from the brightest light they'd probably ever seen. She shot a few frames of them close up and then turned back to the cavern bottom. There was something about it and she couldn't figure out what it was until she realized: there was no algae on the floor. Instead, the smooth granite of the island was there, a layer of slime over it, but there was none of the billowing algae like along the walls. Almost as if something large bedded down here.

Ogopogo? The ancient legends said he lived under this very island... She shot a few more images and checked her air gauge. Nearing forty percent. For safety's sake, they needed to get going back to the surface.

She turned toward the entrance and Abel, but there was only darkness. Abel and his light were gone.

§

The little blonde, Kylee, had arrived for her shift in the store and so had Chloe while Séamus and Lila waited for someone—anyone—to call them back. It had been thirty minutes so far.

The kitchen nook had been too tight a fit, so he'd joined Lila in pacing the hardwood kitchen floor. The sunlight tracked his shadow a mite too harshly as he strode back and forth like a horse fretting at the fence. The minutes ticked past on the turquoise-faced wall clock and this was taking too much time.

He wanted to be gone. He wanted Ally safe beside him. *Anything* could be happening out there on the water. He never shoulda let her go with Abel this morning. His gut had told him something was wrong as soon as he set eyes on the bloke. There'd been something about him.

Or maybe his imagination was getting a hold of him. An Irishman was always good with imagining both the best and the worst.

No. It wasn't imagination that Ally was in danger. He was as sure of that as he was of the face that would look back at him from a mirror. He didn't fancy seeing that face if anything happened to her.

"I'm going out there. I don't know who this Abel Khan is, but I don't trust him."

The phone rang as he turned toward the shop. Lila picked up. "Hello." She listened. "Yes. Yes, we did call about the boat."

Séamus stopped and turned back to her. Finally some information.

Lila pulled a paper and pen to her. "Can you spell that, please." She wrote something down and Séamus crossed the room to read over her shoulder.

Schwarzenacht Corporation.

He knew that name. He just couldn't place where from. Something in the past day or so.

Lila hung up and he turned back to her. "I know that name. I do. But damned if I recall where I've heard it before."

"What's the matter?" Kylee said as she came into the kitchen. "You're getting a little loud in here."

Séamus shook his head. "Sorry to be disturbing the customers, but we're just trying to decide how much danger Ally's in and whether I should be high-tailing out to that damned boat of Abel's."

Kylee turned to Lila, her face gone stubborn, like a small warrior. "I thought you were waiting for information from Jas and Danny. What have you found out?"

"We called the marina where the boat's from in hopes of getting information on Abel, but it turned out that he didn't rent the boat though he's on record as the user. The rental was billed to a company called *Schwarzenacht*." Lila shook her head, obviously just as frustrated as Séamus was.

His hands curled into fists. Think, man, think. Where didja hear the name, ya sorry sod?

"I know that name," Kylee said and frowned. She looked thoughtful a moment, then beckoned them to follow her into the jewelry store. It was a sweet space made sweeter by the heady incense, but the place was empty except for Chloe.

"Hey, Chloe, remember that day you had that weird visitor in the store? The guy who totally freaked you out?"

Chloe went still behind the cash counter, her expression guarded. "Yeah. It was probably one of the scariest moments I've had in my life. It was like the guy just about read my thoughts." Her hands trailed up to the jet beads she wore in the mess of silver chains around her neck. More of the jet was around both wrists. "Jas was asking me about it. What of it?"

"Johan Fehr, right? That was his name. He was the guy from the limousine that Danny and Jas were looking into. Didn't they say it was rented by a company called *Schwarzenacht?*"

Chloe staggered a moment, but caught herself. Her face went ashen, her eyes almost black. "That was the name—the man's name that Jas asked me about, but I couldn't remember. Kylee—how? How did you know?"

"You told me, remember? I came back from lunch and the limo he was in was just leaving and you told me about the guy who came in and terrified you."

"But I didn't remember when Jas questioned me. The name was just gone. I don't even remember telling you. But now that you tell me, it's like veils falling away from my brain. I remember it clearly." She rubbed her temples. "Johan Fehr is the man who terrified me. He was the man in the limo that Jas has been trying to identify!"

She grabbed the store phone and dialed a number.

"Would somebody kindly illuminate a poor bloke from Ireland? What's this all have to do with Ally?" Because what they were saying was all Greek to him and had nothing to do with where he'd heard the company name before.

Lila and Kylee swung around to him as if just remembering he was there.

"If that boat was rented by Johan Fehr, then Ally's in real danger. Johan Fehr was quite likely the one behind Kylee's abduction—at least it seems likely. He was riding in a limo rented by *Schwarzenacht* and it was a limo that was planning on picking up Kylee for points unknown until Brent stopped it."

It was all he needed to know. He was slamming out the door and down the porch stairs as fast a man could go.

A boat. He fekking needed a boat. The marina was around the bay from here, but who knew if anyone was loading up to go out on the water? In the other direction it looked like there were a few powerboats planning on waterskiing. A boat with a powerful motor was what he was looking for.

He turned away from the marina and dashed across the street toward the boats drawn up at wharfs beyond the swimming area. A run like a madman up the street and then he was puffing beside a powerful looking red fiberglass boat's owner, a youngish bloke with shaved head in a sleeveless undershirt that showed off tanned shoulder muscles—probably to impress the brunette he was with.

"I need yer boat, sir. There's a woman whose life is in danger out by Rattlesnake Island. I need yer help t' get there."

The man frowned like Séamus was a crazy man, and Séamus knew he likely looked it. The man shook his head. "I'm not giving you my boat. Now buzz off."

Séamus grabbed him by the shoulder. "Aren't ya listening? There's a woman as like t' be killed out there. Will ya ferry me out there to make sure she's okay?"

The guy looked about to punch him and this might not be the time, but for Ally he'd get into a brawl.

"Aren't you the musician from the pub last night?" interrupted the brunette, a cute little number in extra-short cut-offs who was probably the bloke's girlfriend. Séamus swung toward her. "Yes, it is you. Remember, Simon. He sang those two Irish songs."

The guy looked him up and down, not looking friendlier, exactly, but at least like he was listening. "For real, there's a woman out there? She's in danger?"

Séamus nodded.

"Come on. I'll get you across the lake. I'm Simon Bell."

"Séamus O'Hearn." They shook hands as they climbed aboard the boat and pushed off from the beach. "Could you go to the jewelry shop—*This and That*—and tell them what I've done?" Séamus called back to shore.

The woman nodded so he had to believe she'd do it as the engine roared to life and the boat did a tight turn to head out onto the water. Séamus scrambled to a white leather seat beside Simon.

"Is she fast?" he asked.

"Fast? Just you wait and see." Simon pressed the throttle forward and the boat about leapt to the tops of the waves. She was a sweet craft with very little draft and a long, slim form that cut like a needle across the lake. Judging by her owner, she was built for speed and maximum testosterone. She fit Simon perfectly.

Simon aimed the speedboat toward the island that, from this angle, looked like a jut of the mountains into the lake. Even from here he could make out a large cabin cruiser apparently anchored to one side of the island.

"See there? That boat? That's where we're headed."

Simon nodded. Over the roar of the boat's huge inboard engine, conversation was almost impossible.

"So how'd the woman get out here?" Simon yelled above the roar.

"Ally—her name's Ally. She went with the guy before we knew about the danger. There've been two attempts on Ally's friends' lives in the last month or so, and now Ally's the target."

Simon was frowning and eased the throttle back a little. "How do you know this guy is targeting her? I mean, come on, guy. What are you, a jealous boyfriend or something?"

Just how did he know? Could he be overreacting? But there was something in his gut that made him certain. He shook his head. "We just identified who rented the boat. He was directly involved in the first attempt on one of their lives. This guy she's with—he's got to be working for him."

Simon, damn him, still looked doubtful.

"Listen, just get me there, will ya? There's a tank of gas and a hundred bucks in it for ya."

Simon shook his head, but he banged the throttle forward again and the boat positively flew.

If only he was in time. Ally had been out on the water a long time already.

Chapter 18

Ally's breath sounded too loud in her ears. The air lines burbled and the bubbles glistened silver for a moment in the light of her headlamp and then disappeared into the darkness of the cave's murky water. Cold. It was so cold—or she was, suddenly. Her heart was doing its ka-boom thing in her chest—she could hear it, too—at least the pulse of blood in her ears.

Where the heck was Abel? Was he all right? Had his light gone out? She didn't remember him checking it. A needle of fear exposed itself. *If hers went out, she'd be trapped here in the dark.*

But she was a professional and she could deal with her fear. She slowed her breathing and felt her heart slow, too. Good. Abel had been right there and so excited. She could understand why, because the darn cave, when she flashed her light around it one more time, looked a lot like a lair, a hidey-hole. Of course, at the moment it also looked seriously like some place she didn't want to be.

A few more photos of the walls and the floor and the large white stone in the back corner that she could imagine as an egg, and then she shoved the camera housing and flash before her and started out of the cavern.

Coming in she hadn't noticed the current, so that meant there was another exit from the cavern behind her. Now the current pushed against her and made it just that much tougher to make progress toward the exit. She kept going, the cave gradually widening around her as if she was traveling down a birthing canal. She was breathing heavily and had left the side of the island behind by the time she realized she was out of the cave. She turned back in the darkened water and the mass of the granite island was just a darker murk through the water.

But at least she was out of the cave. From here she could find her way up to the surface. She checked her air gauge—fifty percent. Odd. It had read forty percent in the cave. She shook it and the gauge dial shifted a little, but was still in the safe range. She turned the light around her, but there was still no sign of Abel. There was no way she could have missed him in the cave unless he'd found some side tunnel to hide in, but what would be the reason for that? If he had gone exploring on his own, the fact he hadn't turned up by now could mean that he was in trouble.

Leave him and return to the surface? It was against everything she knew was right when diving. But he'd already broken the rule to never leave your diving buddy, and this wasn't the first time.

She swam back to the cave entrance and shone her light inside. The murk ate it within a few feet. It was go to the surface or go back inside searching. Abel had other tanks on the boat. She could go up, and if he wasn't there, she would change tanks and come back for him without the camera. She'd be faster then, more maneuverable.

With a mental apology to him if he was inside the cavern, she struck out for the surface. The darkness was all around her as she shoved the camera housing ahead of her. Her arms were exhausted. Her legs felt leaden after the effort of getting out of that cavern. When she got to the boat, if Abel wasn't there, she was going to call for help. As exhausted as she felt, going back to find Abel might just lead to her getting herself in trouble.

She didn't try to angle out into the lake toward the boat. She'd get to the surface first. She drew in a deep breath, but the air didn't seem to be there. She tried again and felt starved in response. What the hell? She grabbed the gauge—still comfortably at fifty percent. But she wasn't getting any air and the surface was still just a distant glimmer.

She kicked up toward it while she tapped the gauge and fought with the tank, the camera momentarily forgotten to hang from its tether to her waist, a dead weight.

A small hiss of air into her mouth and nose and she struck out for the surface, kicking for all she was worth, dragging the camera up with her. The surface was a crystalline promise above her. Light leaked in long columns through the murk. She was strangling for air. Needed air and there was no way she could keep going like this, because the tank was giving up nothing and she was inhaling her own carbon monoxide in her mask.

The water was ink black around her.

She had to keep going.

So slow. Her arms, her legs were too slow. It was like something held her legs and pulled her back down away from the light and life and freedom. Away from all her problems. Away from Séamus and his betrayal.

So he'd betrayed her. It happened to people all the time. She was not going to give up because of that.

A few more struggling strokes for the surface. She was going to do it. Another thirty feet and she would reach the air. Thirty feet. She could hold her breath that long. She had done it free-diving off Pemba to see the reefs.

Of course, she hadn't been starved for air to start with.

She could do it if she didn't have things weighing her down.

She kept kicking toward the surface as her fingers fumbled for the tank. Undid the belt and chest closures and slipped it off. She shot upward a few feet. Keep going. Twenty feet.

Something plowed into her and caught her around the hips. Dragged her down.

She kicked, grabbed for the surface that was falling upward away from her. She had nothing to breathe. Wanted to scream. Pounded her fists on the back of the man who dragged her down.

Man. Abel. Abel was trying to kill her. Had killed her, if she didn't get up to the surface and fast.

But the light was disappearing above her and he wasn't letting go. Her fists were futile love taps in the water, all their force stolen. She had no other weapon.

The camera was still tethered to her waist. The housing was heavy. It might serve as a bludgeon.

She stopped fighting him and the surface sank away from her. She hauled the camera up to her and slammed it as hard as she could against him. It broke one of the flashes off, leaving a sharp-edged metal arm sticking sideways out of the housing.

His hold loosened for a moment and she yanked away, but the surface was so distant there was no way she'd make it back up. All Abel had to do was follow her and she'd run out of air and he'd win.

He hung beside her, shaking his head against the blow, precious air escaping him in a long string of bubbles. She needed that air.

She swam into him and brought the camera housing against him again. Again.

Hands caught her throat and she knew it was over. She had no air left to survive with. There was nothing she could do. Her hands clawed at his face, at his mask, as he floated above her. But the light still on her helmet only showed the blaze of blue eyes gone red. His hands were fire on her throat and the bracelet burned in answer. A last surge of desperate energy found her. Somehow her hands found the camera housing, the sharp edge where the flash had broken. She grabbed the housing and two-handed, with final strength, drove the sharp-edged stanchion into his belly. Felt neoprene resist and part under its edge. Ground it into him and flesh parted.

Hands loosed from her neck as thick blood pulsed into the water. The light on her helmet lit up the red water around his face. Shock. Fury. Hatred. Then the eyes went dark.

She needed air. Had to have air.

Numb-handed, she fumbled Abel's mouthpiece out of his mouth. Bubbles flooded up into the water as the weight of him pulled them both down into the depth of the lake. She took the mouthpiece and blessed air filled her desperate lungs. The mouthpiece tasted horribly of Abel. She spat it out, washing it in the lake before she took it back in. Fumbled with the tank closures as she fell farther and farther. She had to get the tank off of him if she wanted to live, and damn it, she wanted to live. Wanted to do the things that Séamus had said, and stop running; instead, finish off what she started.

Abel's body was limp and she was linked so closely to him because of the tank—if she wanted air. She couldn't get his body to cooperate and release the tank, and with every moment, the surface of the lake disappeared above them.

Above *her*.

She sank, alone in the lake with a dead body and dwindling air.

§

Even in Simon's high-powered boat, it had taken too long. Too long on what shoulda been the ride of a lifetime, skimming over the waves in the sunshine, the wind in his hair. Every schoolboy's dream of rich boy's fun, but Séamus could only think of Ally. Had that man killed her outright on the boat, or done something much more deadly and done her in while diving? The latter seemed more likely.

Rattlesnake Island raised its head above the water just ahead, its surface not much beyond bare granite and sun-yellowed scrub grass that grew in the cracks in the stone. A tumbledown structure stood there, long ago abandoned. Just out from the island floated a large white cabin cruiser, with a small Canadian flag fluttering its red and white maple leaf gaily over the stern.

Simon brought the throttle back and the high-powered boat settled into the water.

"What now?" Simon asked, his shaved head shining in the sun.

"Bring her alongside the cruiser."

Simon obeyed, the red boat easing in beside the cruiser's gunnels.

"Ahoy!" Séamus called. "Anyone here?"

No answer. Séamus stood. "I'm going aboard to check it out. Take me around to the diving deck there at the back."

"Hey man! That's another man's private space." But Simon shifted the boat around.

"Just hang tough a moment." Séamus leapt onto the diving deck and the boat swayed. He steadied himself on the stern of the boat and then scrambled up onto the deck. "Hello?" He stuck his head into the cabin. Still nothing. But he recognized the pack that sat abandoned on the counter.

Ally's. He looked inside it and noted the camera bag beside it. The camera compartment was empty when he opened the top. He returned to the deck. There were two diver's tanks in a rack and space for two more. A neoprene suit hung in a rack. Two spaces were empty.

Diving. They'd gone diving where anything could happen. An accident. Hell, a fekking run-in with fekking Ogopogo. Anything could happen under the water.

"Anything?" Simon called.

Séamus went to the stern, where Simon had the red boat.

"This is the boat. Ally's things are here. But they've gone diving." He looked back at the tanks. He knew as much about diving as he did rocket flying, which wasn't a damn thing. "You know anything about diving?"

Simon met his gaze. With his muscle and his muscle boat, he looked the kind who might. He shrugged. "Some. I've been down a few times on holidays. I took a course in Thailand."

"Good, then. Get yerself aboard and teach me what you know. I'm going after them."

"No way. That's a good way to get yourself killed, friend. Especially if you've never dived before." Simon shook his head and held his boat just away from the white cruiser—probably not wanting to streak his fiberglass paint job.

"Show me. Please. If ya don't, I'll figure it out m'self and go looking for her."

Simon blew out a breath in frustration. His palm slapped his steering wheel and he looked ready to turn tail for the shore. Finally he shook his head. "Your money better be good, buster."

He cut the red boat's motor and dug in a cargo compartment to pull out two white bumpers that he placed between the two boats. Then he tied the speedboat to the cruiser and climbed aboard, pushing past Séamus to examine the equipment.

It took him five minutes before he turned to Séamus and handed him the neoprene suit. "Put this on."

The thing hung on Séamus' hand like a fekking Selkie skin, but cold and clammy, even in the sunlight. But Ally was somewhere under the water and he needed to get down there and help her. At least he was a decent swimmer.

By the time he was tucked in tight to the suit, Simon had hefted the tank up and held it like it was a suit jacket. Séamus eyed the thing. "What's all this, then?"

"Put it on and I'll show you."

Obeying, Séamus accepted the weight of the tank on his shoulders and pulled the hip and chest clips closed.

"Put this mask on and this in your mouth." Simon held out a mask and a mouthpiece, then turned a nozzle on the tank. "How's it doing? You getting a comfortable amount of oxygen?"

Séamus shrugged. He was breathing as normally as he likely would be, given the circumstances and his need to get over the side and into the water. Simon caught his hand and showed him a gauge snapped to his belt. Air gauge of the amount of air he had left in his tank. "This is an eighty-pound tank. That means that you have about eighty minutes of air if you stay close to the surface, but if you go down thirty-three feet, your utilization will double, which means that your time under is down to forty minutes, and so on. The deeper you go, the less time you have. Keep an eye on the gauge. You should definitely be thinking about turning back when you hit the fifty percent. I've also hooked you up with a power pack to drive this." He hooked a light over Séamus' head. "In this water, you're not going to see much without light, plus it might help

Ally find you. Now climb in the water and practice around the boat before you try anything more."

Carrying a pair of ridiculous duck-footed flippers, Séamus climbed down onto the rear deck and sat down at the edge of the water. It looked clear green at the surface, turning oily dark just below. *Jesus God, Ally, what have ya got yerself into?* But he was coming. He was going to make sure she made it back to the surface.

He slipped his feet into the rubber flippers and then his legs into the water. Warm. He could do this. He gave a thumbs-up to Simon. "You'll be here when I get back?" he asked around the mouthpiece.

Simon gave him a tap-tap on his shoulder and Séamus took that as a sign. He slipped into the water.

The warmth of the water was an all-out lie. Within a foot of the surface, the water turned cold enough to make him think twice about his choice, but he kicked and gradually got used to the weight of the tank. It seemed to hold him up on the surface and he had to work to get deep enough to swim under the boat. When he came up he felt like he was puffing, but he swam for the deck and hooked an elbow over the edge.

"This is a bugger. I can't sink worth a damn."

"Hang on." Simon leapt up onto the deck and came back with small black squares. "Put these in the pouches in your belt."

Séamus did and felt his torso sink a little deeper. Good enough. Another thumbs-up and he sank back into the water.

Cold closed over his head as he sank beneath the surface. He looked up to the hulls of the two boats surrounded by glittering water. If the bastard was going t' fool Ally into going diving, and the island was the supposed home of the Ogopogo, then it was likely they'd be diving close to the island's side. He set off southeast from the boats, angling downward and trying to remember all of the things Simon had told him.

The light faded above him and became long columns like the dusty motes he might find in one of Cork's great cathedrals. Gradually they faded away and he was blinded by the light on his head reflecting in the debris in the water. How the hell any normal man could see, he didn't know. Why any sane man would do this for fun totally escaped him. This breathing through the mouth just wasn't working for him, either. He kept getting it mixed up and almost taking in water. What the hell had Ally been thinking, going down here with a stranger? When he found her, he didn't care how much she protested, he was going to make sure it didn't happen again.

He kept going, with the uneasy feeling that he should have found the side of the island by now. In all this murk, he could be going in circles for all he knew. He could be swimming like some great bleedin' fish out into the lake, never to be seen again. A spike of fear ran through him, because he didn't know how deep he was. How fast was his air going to run out? The watch he had said he still had time, but under the water like this, he didn't know whether to believe it.

The only light was his own and his breathing was ragged and too loud in his ears, as if he'd been running a race and his heart was pounding. That couldn't be good. Not good at all. *Hold on Ally-girl, I'm coming for you.*

Ahead, the murk changed and his light caught on something. He kicked himself smoothly through the water. Stone. Weeds growing out of it. God above, he'd done it—he'd found the fekking island. That was good. If that bastard, Abel, had said he was looking for the beast, then he had to be around here, didn't he. Left or right?

Beneath him the water was a wall of darkness. He swallowed. Left or right wasn't going to cut it. If he was a bloke intent on killing someone, he'd lure her deeper. Hadn't Lila said something about a cave at the island? That would be a perfect place to do the deed.

Ally-girl, if we get outta this alive, I hope you understand just what I've put m'self through fer you.

He started down, knowing that he was working against time. He pushed the thought aside. Yes, finding a woman in this blackness was like trying t' find the proverbial needle in a haystack with one hand tied behind yer back and blindfolded, but he had to try. He didn't look up at the surface. He had to be farther than thirty feet down, which meant that his time was further depleted. He was going to have to start for the surface soon.

The side of the island was his guide. He started traversing it back and forth as he spiraled downward.

A flicker of something caught his eye. Large. Silver. He turned toward it. Nothing there. What the hell?

He swam toward it. Another flash. It was like a shadow filled the murk, except something caught the edge of his light. A fish? It was a bloody big fish, if it was.

He spiraled after it again. Down. The side of the mountain barely visible to one side of him.

Another flash and he felt the water shift around him as if something huge slid past, pushing the water before it. Holy shite. What was out there? Abel? But the shift of water against him had been far bigger than he could imagine a man making, and if Abel had a weapon, why hadn't he attacked?

His hand fell to the knife at his belt. At least Simon had made sure he wasn't helpless.

He hung in the water and checked his watch. It was time for him to return to the surface. He knew he'd pushed Simon's brief guidelines to the limit.

But through the darkness another glimmer caught his eye. This one distant, diffuse. Not a flash, more like a star, glimmering through a pall of cloud. A light. There was only one reason for a light at these depths.

He kicked down toward it, praying to all the holies that he was right. That it was his Ally-girl and that she was all right.

The murk parted around him. Two figures caught in struggle as the mountainside swallowed them down. Leastwise, that was what it looked like. Cave. Cavern, and they were in the mouth, algae billowing around them as one figure fought with the other. Then he realized what was happening. The larger figure was a limp weight, floating as the smaller figure fought to get the diving tank off the larger one. Ally had no tank.

He kicked through the water, coming up across the body from her. Surprise registered on her face. Then her eyes closed and for a moment he thought she'd passed out, but her blue eyes flashed open, more brilliant than he'd ever seen, and they smiled at him as she pointed at the chest closure of Abel's tanks.

The man was obviously dead, and however that had happened, he really didn't give a damn. He nudged her hands aside and tried the closure, but it refused to budge no matter what he did. He checked the gauge on the dead man's suit. He wasn't sure what it meant except she didn't have much time at all. There was only one answer. He hauled the knife Simon had given him out of its place at his belt and sawed at the tough nylon webbing of Abel's chest closure. Finally it parted and together they slipped the tank off the dead man's shoulders. Ally pulled it on and did up the belt, adjusted it closed. Nodded.

He reached for her hand. There was no hesitation as she took it and they pushed off for the surface.

Séamus ran scared. He was almost dragging Ally as he followed the side of the mountain. How long had she been down there fighting with that dead body? What had Abel done to her beforehand? The darkness was all around him, the only light the small glow of his and Ally's lights, and he had no idea how much air they had—whether it was enough to get them to the surface. He had to do it. It all depended on him.

Let him see those columns of light. Let him see the glow of the surface. The mountain slope was just that—a slope. He needed to head directly for the surface.

He left the island's side and struck off upward. Kick. Kick some more, and kick again, ya wanker. There was only the feel of Ally's slim fingers and kicking upward, dragging the woman he loved with him. It didn't matter if it was over between them. What mattered was knowing she was alive. Ally in the world was a far cry better than a world without her.

He didn't notice the soft glimmer of columns of light until he entered one. Ally was almost a dead weight on his arm. He turned back to her and realized the stream of bubbles from her tank were almost non-existent. Damn it, she was out of air, and he had no idea how much he had left.

He grabbed her around the waist and shook her and her blue eyes flashed open. He pointed to his air hose and at hers, then helped her spit her mouthpiece out. He took a deep breath and slipped his mouthpiece out, placed it into her mouth. Her chest worked against his and a string of silver bubbles floated upward.

She handed the mouthpiece back to him and together they kicked upward, toward light. Toward air. If they could only make it. But his own tank wasn't giving him the air he demanded. He was gasping. And Ally's chest had to be bursting as he stopped again to share what air he had with her.

It was too damned far. Above, the surface was a crystal barrier there was no way they would reach in time.

He drove toward the surface with every bit of his strength, but the air was almost gone and every time he stopped to share with Ally, they sank down again.

She was going to have to hold her breath and he just prayed she could hold on.

The crystal barrier above him suddenly shattered and a dark shape plummeted deep into the water. Then it slowed and turned downward, seeking. Man. Diver. Simon.

Séamus understood what he saw, but it was so hard to keep kicking, when the most important thing was just holding onto Ally. He pulled her into him. Pressed the last of his air into her mouth. An embrace. He knew it was his imagination, but he swore he could smell her clove scent through the water.

And then hands were on him, on Ally. He almost punched the diver until the man shoved a streaming air hose in his face. He pulled it into his mouth and inhaled deeply, the life-giving air clearing away the darkness that had eaten his vision. He pulled the air hose out and shoved it in Ally's mouth. Prayed she was still breathing, as he added his kicks to those of the man helping them.

More suddenly than he'd expected, his head broke the surface. A roaring filled the air. He inhaled and a wave caught him the face. He gasped, coughed, and sputtered, but he was alive. Alive!

Ally? Where was Ally?

She sagged in the water next to him, supported by the diver. Séamus yanked her mask off and, with the help of the diver, he started mouth-to-mouth, praying it would work. A rumble sounded and suddenly something red was beside him. Two arms reached down and lifted Ally away from him, her damned camera thunking up the side of the boat. Then they helped him into the boat.

Simon slapped him on the shoulder. Not Simon in the water... Who? He had no time to check. He was on his knees beside Ally. He turned her on her side and slapped her back, praying she hadn't breathed in too much water. Then he started mouth-to-mouth again.

Come on, Ally-girl. Come on.

Was that a movement of her lips? Did her hand just twitch? The boat shifted under him again and the diver came up behind him as Ally's eyes suddenly flew open. She coughed and he rolled her onto her side, let her choke out water while he held her shoulders.

Damn it, he was crying like a schoolgirl, but she was alive. His Ally-girl had made it.

"You all right, man?" Simon asked.

"Just fine. Better than fine, in fact." He rubbed Ally's shoulder and helped her sit up, then turned to the diver. Neoprene-clad Jas Stone sat there, palming dripping wet black hair off his face. "I guess I've got a lot of thanking to do."

Jas raised his dark brows. "Seems to me you did most of the work, finding her and getting her that close to the surface. You made my job easy."

"I didn't know you dove," Ally whispered and Séamus pulled her into his side. She was shivering, not with cold, but with shock.

Jas shrugged. "I used to be on the RCMP's underwater recovery team. I'm still on callout. Good thing too, apparently. I got the chopper to bring me out here." He nodded to the island. A small spotter helicopter had come to rest on the top near the old structure. The rotors still turned. "So where's this Abel guy?"

"Dead," Ally whispered. "In the cave."

Séamus shushed her because her voice sounded raw. He told Jas where he'd found them and how they'd got to the surface.

"We'd better get Ally to a doctor," Jas said. "You ever ridden in a helicopter?" he asked her.

She shook her head.

Between Simon, Jas, and Séamus, they got her out of the boat, onto the island, and up the rough slope to the helicopter. Séamus helped her into the passenger seat and then looked up at her. She was pale, his Ally-girl, still dressed in her neoprene suit, but her gaze was the same—brilliant, intelligent, and quick to anger and quicker to laugh. She met his gaze and caught his hand. "Thank you," she mouthed as Jas gave a report to the pilot and asked for a dive team to come out to recover the body. The pilot made the call and then Séamus was forced to do the one thing he never wanted to do. He let his Ally-girl go again and she lifted off into the blue, leaving him behind again. Just like always.

As if it was just meant to be.

Jas opted to remain on the cruiser to await the dive team and give them directions to the body. He told Séamus that he was to come in to give a statement that afternoon. Then Simon took Séamus back across the lake to Peachland.

Chapter 19

The town was pretty from the water, all leafy trees and comfortable houses kept up nice. The long sweep of beachfront and the playing families were a nice touch to remind him of all the possibilities he'd lost with Ally. Sure, he might find another woman, but there just wasn't anyone he could picture himself settling down with other than Ally. The images that filled his head of blond-haired children—a boy and a girl—and a wee cottage amid green fields, they were holdovers from when he was practically no more than a kid himself, when he and Ally had first been together. All water long under the bridge.

He shivered and was thankful for the bright sun overhead as Simon drove the boat toward the shore and his girlfriend's waving form.

"You've got to be feeling pretty good," Simon said above the engine's roar as he throttled back and the boat settled lower in the water. "You rescued your girl. You're a hero, man."

"I just wish I felt like one. Ya see, saving her was the least I could do. I ruined her life, I did. I took away the thing she loved most in this world—ruined it for everyone else, too. It's a mite hard for a woman like Ally to forgive and forget something like that—even if I did almost drown m'self trying to help her."

"Does she realize that you've never dived before? The risk you took?"

Séamus just shook his head. "She doesn't need to know, does she? I did what I could as a bit of paying back a debt. It's all I could do."

On shore he paid Simon two hundred dollars—one for the boat and the gas, and one because Simon had had the good sense to call for help using the cruiser's radio. That had been the final assistance in getting the chopper to bring Jas out to the island. Still fair to sodden and dressed in neoprene, Séamus left them to their barbecue and struck off down the shoreline, carrying his clothes done up in a bundle. The white and red shop was closed up tight and he wondered what time it was. His watch, waterproof, but never meant for diving, had stopped at three o'clock, so the women had closed the store early. Knock on the door and let them know that Ally was all right?

It was more likely that the Kelowna hospital had called them already, given Ally would have arrived there long before he reached the shore. The others were likely on their way there as moral support. He looked up at the second floor windows. One of them gave onto the room where he'd thought his world had begun again, and then it had ended. He remembered her drowsy in his arms, the clove scent of her hair, the smooth silk of her skin.

All not to be. He kept walking, following the curving lakeshore past the people enjoying their summer. Past the log-built restaurant where Lila had thrown them together again. Past the pub where he'd sung for her and only her, no matter what the others might think. The dark green door gave onto the stairs that led to his room at the Beach Hotel. He unlocked his room door and went inside, his footsteps still squishy from the water that ran from the neoprene into his shoes.

Inside he slipped everything off, wrung his shoes out in the tub, and then set them on the windowsill to dry in the breeze from the window. The neoprene suit he hung from the curtain rod. He climbed into the shower and let the water run down his face and body. Give him water like this or a fekking good rain shower any day over water deep and dark and dangerous in a lake.

He was just toweling off when the phone in the room rang. Wrapping the towel around himself, he padded wet footprints out onto the carpet and picked up. "Hello."

"Séamus. Thank goodness," Lila's voice, rich with relief. "I didn't know where to reach you. Ally told me what you did and asked me to call you. She's going to be fine, Séamus. Thanks to you, she is."

"That's a good piece of news. She could barely talk when they left the island."

"It wasn't just the water that she breathed in. Abel tried to choke her before she somehow managed to free herself. They're letting her out this afternoon."

More good news. He just didn't know what to say... "Thank you for letting me know."

"Séamus, I was wondering if you'd like to come over for dinner tonight? Jas and Danny will be there, and the ladies, of course. And Ally. We want to celebrate being alive."

It was so damned tempting. Another evening with Ally. One last time. "Does Ally know what you're planning?"

Lila seemed to hesitate a moment. "Well, no. We thought we'd surprise her."

"Let me guess: the bracelet is still on and you're still thinking I'm the answer."

Dead silence this time. He sank down on the edge of the bed. "Listen, Lila. I appreciate ya trying. I really do, but this thing with Ally—it just isn't workin'. At least not fer her. I'm thinking it's better for everyone if I just cut my losses and head on out of here."

Before she could protest, he hung up on her and took the phone off the hook. He was tired. So damn tired, and he had a long flight ahead of him. Because he'd finally remembered where he'd heard the name *Schwarzenacht*. It had come to him as he was swimming through the pitch darkness of the lake. *Schwarzenacht* or *schwarzenacht*. Black night. It was Ally herself who had said it—the name of the corporation that had hired the boat that had tried to carry her to her death was also the name of the corporation that had ruined her Pemba Project. He'd already ruined one of the company's nefarious ventures. He'd travel home via Berlin and try to ruin another.

But not right now. His shoulders felt bowed with fatigue—the aftermath of adrenaline, probably. He couldn't imagine Ally feeling much better, so Lila had messed up this time with planning her parties. Odd. That didn't seem like the woman he'd met.

Finished drying off, he sprawled on the bed, used the remote to turn on the TV, and some sort of mindless drivel came on.

He must have slept because the sky through the window was dark when he opened his eyes. The light from the town street lights placed weird wetsuit shadows on his walls. A few hungry mosquitoes buzzed around his nakedness. The air smelled of lake water overlaid by cigarette smoke and beer. He could use a pint or two. Down the beach, undoubtedly some lovely women were celebratin' victory over an unknown foe.

Damn right, a pint or two were in order. He pulled on old faded jeans and grabbed a t-shirt from among those that needed washing, then slid his feet into sandals and padded down the stairs to the bar. There was a good crowd for a weeknight when no band was playing, but canned rock and roll came from speakers in the ceiling. The tables were filled with couples and groups of men who looked like they'd come directly from work. The stage was empty and dark, the microphone locked away. The bar itself wasn't made for seating, but Séamus wandered up to its shiny dark wood veneer and its brass railing and ordered a beer. His reflection stared back at him from the mirrored wall behind the lined-up bottles and an old photo of the lake, and something that looked like one of those wave formations that Lila had said were thought to be Ogopogo.

He paid for the foaming glass the bartender plunked in front of him and turned back to the dimly lit room with its three waitresses wending their way through the tables. The beer was elixir. He could feel his blood start t' move again.

"Hey, fella!" A man, older, in jeans and a t-shirt that had a moving company logo on the front, waved at him from a nearby table. The bloke was balding on top but still had hair like a bristle brush around his ears and a moustache to match that framed his mouth. "You can join us if you like. We've got room at the table." He motioned to an empty chair.

Though he didn't really fancy joining a group of friends, Séamus carried his beer over. "Thanks," he said and settled into the chair. "Name's Séamus."

"Shamus? Like a detective?"

"No, Séamus. I'm a—" Just what was he? A washed up businessman? A has-been musician tryin' for a comeback? "I'm between jobs at the moment."

"I'm Jim Harcort, Harcort Moving and Storage. These are my boys, Rory, Kent, and Dave." He waved at the others around the table. Younger, broad shoulders. The muscle a moving company would need. One wore baldness like a badge to show off a tattoo of an eagle up the side of his skull. While the two others looked like they were just out of high school with the patchy beards of new adulthood.

"You're the Irishman who played the other night, aren't you? Here? At the pub?" asked Jim.

"Ya heard that, didja?" Séamus sipped his beer.

"Yeah. I did. So did the rest of us."

There were nods around the three other men at the table. They all wore t-shirts like Jim.

"You're good," said the bald bloke, named Rory. "Better than a lot of the crap high school kids they get in here. No offense." He nodded at the two youngsters.

"Best music I've heard in a while," Jim agreed. "You should be playing tonight. Liven up the place."

"Sorry." Séamus shrugged. "I don't feel much like playin' tonight. It's been a long day." He glanced toward the door and the lake he knew waited beyond the dark-tinted glass.

"Say, you're not the fella who saved that woman today, are ya? He was an Irishman, too, if the news story's true."

The last thing he needed. People asking him to think or talk about Ally. He knocked back his beer and stood. "Listen, no offense, but I think I made a mistake coming down here. I'm knackered and m'bed's calling. Thank you for the company."

He excused himself and trudged up the stairs to his room and inside. He kicked off his sandals and collapsed on the bed.

The beer had been good enough, but not good enough to be peppered with twenty questions. He just needed quiet and time to be with his own head to sort out his feelings. Get them neatly compartmentalized and put away so that he could get on with life. He'd learned the art long ago after Ally left him the first time he betrayed her.

"What an all-out wanker ya are. Hurting a woman like that and then ruining her life's work." It wasn't the kind of man he'd wanted t'be growin' up. It wasn't the kind of man his ma raised him t'be. Wanker didn't half describe what he was. He might have saved Ally's life, but he'd left her with problems that she wouldn't have had except for what he'd done.

A knock came on the door and he turned a bleary eye on the offending panel. If he didn't answer, maybe they'd just go away. Leave him to nurse his black mood in peace.

Another knock and "Séamus?" said softly.

He sat bolt upright and swung his legs off the bed. It couldn't be.

"Séamus, please. I need to talk to you." The voice had a hoarse edge to it.

Holy God, it was!

He was at the door, throwing it open so fast his brain barely had a chance to catch up t' his body. "Ally."

She looked—good, in denim shorts and a blue denim shirt she wore loose over a white singlet. Blue eyes bright, blonde mane of hair around her shoulders, but her eyes had dark circles and there were bruises on her neck that just plain made him angry. He wanted to cry. He wanted to take her in his arms and hold her, confirm she was real and it wasn't some trick of a tired mind and the single watery beer. Instead he held onto the door edge like it was the only thing holding him back from doing something stupid that might send her away forever. She still wore that damned silver bracelet on her wrist.

"Can—can I come in?" she asked. "I need to talk to you."

Feeling numb, he stepped to one side, careful to allow her enough room to pass without touching him, but he could still feel the heat of her body. Her light clove scent was heady. He closed his eyes for a moment, then closed the door behind her.

She took the chair by the desk and he sank back on the bed again. God, she was beautiful—the golden goddess of a woman that he'd always been so surprised had picked him out of all the men in that pub way back when. He'd been sure it was just a joke, a fling, but then their time together had gone on and he just knew it had to end sometime. She was too beyond him. So he'd taken the choice from her and left instead. The trouble was, once you taste the fruit of the gods, nothing ever compares, does it.

She glanced around the room and her gaze settled on his guitar case leaned against the wall. "I thought you might be playing tonight. In the pub."

He shook his head. "Not their amateur night, I'm afraid."

"You're not an amateur."

It was too hard, looking into those intelligent eyes. He studied his hands, callused fingers. "It's been a long time since I made my living with music."

"But you want to, don't you? I made a few calls oversees. Seems the man who was responsible for the Lux International Pemba Project quit because he couldn't stand what his work was doing. Apparently his boss called him a fool because the guy said he was going back to music."

"Sounds like an idiot from where I'm sitting."

"Or an honest man with a conscience."

He looked up at her then, wondering where this was going. Ally stood and came to him and caught his hands in hers, the silver links of the bracelet jingling softly. "Thank you, Séamus. I'd be long dead if it wasn't for you."

He wanted to pull away. It would be easier that way, but his muscles refused to move. He looked up at her. "I did what anyone else would do."

"You risked your life. I spoke to the man with the boat— Simon. He said you had absolutely no experience diving. Do you know how big a risk you took coming for me? You could have gotten lost yourself. You could have died, Séamus!"

He shrugged. "I didn't, did I?"

"How the hell did you even find me?"

He looked up at her then, drinking her face in, feeling the heat of her hands. God, he loved this woman and would never stop loving her, but he'd made his peace with her decision.

"It was strange, really. I was down there where I never want t' go again, I'll have ya know. It was dark and I couldn't see a thing and it crossed my mind I could be swimming in circles fer all I knew. And then I caught a glimpse of something. It was big, but my light just caught the edge of it. I swam toward it. It happened again and again, until I suddenly saw your light below me. And found ya. Almost as if whatever was in that water wanted me to find ya." He shook his head. "Stupid, I know."

She squeezed his hands. "Not stupid. I dreamed there was something out there. Abel and I—we found a cave and went inside. We found a chamber that looked like it could be a lair. I got photos." She shrugged. "Ogopogo doesn't matter. He can stay hidden down there forever. But I can't. I had to come see you tonight, Séamus. I had to make things right between us."

§

It was like a light came on in Séamus' brown eyes. Like sunlight on good earth or peat after a rain, and she inhaled his fresh-cut-grass scent and the yeasty scent of beer. He sat before her, still as a portrait model, watchful and waiting even though his gaze said she might have rekindled hope. Hope in such a dingy room. Plain brown Berber carpet, brown bedspread, mussed from occupancy, half dry neoprene suit hanging in the window, and an abstract painting of a long-necked lake monster on the wall. Dismal, dingy, and by the look of Séamus, it was how he was feeling.

She went to her knees in front of him, caught his face in her hands. Had she ever done this before? Had she ever not run, and taken the time to forgive? She'd certainly never forgiven her father for leaving, nor her mother for being the cold fish that had chased him away. Sure, she'd come home to visit her estranged parents a time or two over the years, but she'd never forgiven how they made her life a living hell because of their drive for her to succeed and be more than they ever were. She'd slept with boys, and then men, just because she knew it would drive her parents mad and because she didn't want to be her mother. And then she'd run away to follow her dream and, she realized now, somewhere along the way she'd become a lot like her parents—just as rigid in her opinion of the people around her and how they should behave.

She'd done it to Séamus more than most. It took almost losing her life to make her face it.

"I was an idiot the other night—my God, was it only last night? You were doing your job. You weren't trying to betray me. And then you quit your job and came all this way to try to make it right?"

"I did." His hands left his knees for her waist. They were warm, lightly resting there as if to hold them both steady.

"Did you know I was a stubborn woman who wouldn't likely forgive?"

A slight curve found his lips. "How could I not know that? Ally McVay is about the most cussed stubborn woman I've ever known."

She bowed her head. "Sorry about that. It's a skill I learned at the feet of the very best. I'm trying to unlearn it. I thought maybe you could help me."

"Could I, now."

"You—you could forgive me. Show me how it's done…" She met his gaze then. His brown gaze was waiting and, dammit, she needed to get this out. "I've been an idiot, all right. All holier than thou about what you did. But I was wrong, too. All those years ago in Ireland. Like you said: I didn't do what I should have done and fought for you. Nope. I was too stubborn and proud and so I just walked away from the best thing I've ever had in my life." Darn it, her idiot eyes were filling when she'd been determined not to cry. "Help me, Séamus. I don't want to make the same mistake twice."

She closed her eyes against the mortification, but the stupid tears still snuck their way past her lashes. She released Séamus to swipe them off, but his hands came up to her cheeks, his thumbs scrubbed her lips. When she opened her eyes, he was looking at her so intently it was like looking into a too-bright sun and all her thoughts were bright refractions of the light.

Then he leaned in and kissed her. Softly. So softly she thought he was going to set her away again and say it was goodbye. Then his arms came around her and he pulled her into his chest so tightly she lost her breath.

"Ah, Ally-girl. What a pair of fools we've been that we have to half kill ourselves to realize what we mean to each other."

She snuffled against his chest until he hauled her up and onto his lap. A long time ago, they'd sat like that so many times in the small apartment they'd shared. They'd had an old couch, and many a night they'd sat like that, reading a book to each other, Ally trapped on his lap and loving the closeness of it.

"So let's see this famous bracelet of yours," he said, his arms warm around her.

She held up her wrist and examined the small doors. "Well now, that is strange, isn't it?" He lifted her wrist closer to look at the small gargoyle door. "It does look like the door on the farm, right enough." He motioned to his chest and she realized that he was wearing the door-patterned t-shirt that he'd worn to the bar.

Snuffling, she nodded.

"So let's see this closure then?" He flipped her wrist and examined the small skeleton key that had always stymied her, Lila's, anybody's, ability to get back through the keyhole that held the bracelet closed. "Clever little piece, it is."

His talented fingers grasped the key and it slid, as if it always had, back through the keyhole. The bracelet collapsed into a train of silver links dangling from his fingers, almost as if the bracelet had wanted to be released. He held it out to her and she caught it in her hand. Closing her fingers over it, he kissed her hair.

"Maybe—maybe there is something to this bracelet thing, my Ally-girl," he whispered.

Nodding, she rested her head on his shoulders and hoped he wouldn't let go.

Chapter 20

She and Séamus stayed that way for a very long time. In the quiet of the dingy room, with the moon rising over the lake and the breeze flowing in bringing the scent of gardens and—well—beer. Séamus tilted her head up and kissed her softly, sweet as misty rain on a green Irish field. She kissed him back, inhaling his scent of clean green grass, and for a moment she felt like she was young again and all the years between were gone.

"Ya know you've come away to me when all your friends are back at the store. What're they going to be thinking at your disappearance?"

She pondered a moment. "Given I had the bracelet on when I left, they're probably worried." Sighing, she straightened in his arms. "I guess all good things must come to an end."

"And just what are you speaking of, Ally-girl? Because I don't fancy letting you out of my sight for a day or two." He waggled his eyebrows and she tilted one right back.

"Only two? That doesn't sound like much. And then you'll be where? What the heck am I going to remember you by?" She shook her head and stood above him, caught his hand and shook it. "It's been very nice seeing you again."

He grabbed her waist and tumbled her onto the bed. "If ya think you can get away from me that easy, think again, Ally-girl. Yer mine because we were meant to be, by more than some infernal bracelet." Then he kissed her hard and passionately so she was left breathless on the bed.

Séamus, ever contrary, of course, chose that moment to stand. "So are we going to yer friends, or not?"

It was sorely tempting to just stay where she was and enjoy the night with Séamus, but she had friends waiting and they were throwing the party for *her*. She caught Séamus' proffered hand and stood. "Party it is," and dragged him to the door.

Down the stairs and outside, the breeze felt brisker than inside. Overhead, scuttling clouds half-obscured the crescent moon. The wind sent the waves rolling into the shore and there were whitecaps out on the lake as Séamus caught her hand and walked beside her down the lakeshore. The summer people were all gone, the parking stalls and picnic tables all empty. A few dog owners followed their canines, and a few joggers got their late-night run in.

Down the lake, the red and white house that was *This and That* had enough lights on that it was a beacon in the night. Séamus opened the front gate for her and together they went around the side of the house to the sheltered back patio. Small white Christmas lights hung from the eaves of the house and Reggie's workshop. They were slung in the branches of a lilac bush in the corner, and myriad candles were set on the ground, the table, and along the kitchen windowsill.

The others were there. Lila, holding court in a chair brought out from the kitchen. Chloe, sharing a chaise with Jas, who had plunked himself down by her feet. Kylee and Brett and red-haired RCMP officer Danny Forester sat around the table, and Reggie had settled herself cross-legged on the ground by Lila. They were all talking and enjoying glasses of pale white wine, but all conversation stopped when Ally led Séamus around the corner of the house.

"Well, well, well. I was just getting ready to send out the search party," Lila said, standing to greet them.

She wore flowing white trousers and a bronze-colored top that brought out the red in her burnished curls. Her gaze trailed to Séamus and then down to their joined hands.

"I won't ask where you've been. That's obvious." She stepped forward and caught Séamus' free hand. "Welcome. Truly welcome to our home."

Ally almost felt like crying again, because although this wasn't ever her house, at the moment it felt like home; and Lila's welcome seemed to make it official: Séamus was back in her life. And if she had anything to say about it, he was here to stay. Perhaps it was that he had saved her life, but it was more the effect of her time alone in the deep dark of the lake. She'd gained a lot of perspective when she'd been sure she was going to die.

Jas, looking casual in jeans and a black t-shirt, and Brett in his khakis and a blue polo shirt, brought chairs out from the kitchen for them, and Chloe poured them glasses of wine, and then they were seated in the group; but it was like everyone was waiting for them to tell them something.

"Before I forget," Lila said. "Your office in Nairobi called for you, Ally. Apparently, someone from Pemba contacted them. They're looking for your help in starting the project again. Something about the islanders realizing they needed to keep the project going and they needed help in dealing with the resort development people."

What could Ally say? A lot could be lost in the translation across international phone calls.

"Can I see the message?"

Lila produced a neatly folded piece of white paper from a pocket and gave it to her and Ally unfolded it and read. For a moment she felt like dancing, then she turned and threw her arms around Séamus.

"It's happening. Something good. They want me—us—the project back. I'm in business again!"

She had her chance to stand and fight for Pemba, too!

But Séamus' gaze belied the way his arms came around her. "I'm happy fer ya, Ally-girl."

"You'll come with me, right? You know the corporation. You can help to negotiate."

He held her away from him and stroked her face. "Ally, when I left my job with them, it wasn't just because I'd discovered what we were doing and who we were doin' it to. I wasn't happy. I knew I had to get back to my music. That's what I want to do—even if I just play pubs in Ireland and help my dad on the farm."

The pain in his expression broke her heart and she would not do that to this man. "Séamus, I understand. I totally understand, and I'm not going to take you away from your music. I can do my work from pretty much anywhere in the world, and I will. Ireland is as good a place as any—better, in fact. But I have to fight this fight. I have to finish what I started and try to put things to right—just like you did, coming here. Can I ask for your help in this? Come with me to Pemba? Help me deal with Lux International?"

A slow smile bloomed across his face. "If that's where you're going, then I guess that's where I'll be, too. I can pick up the beat of East Africa while I'm helping ya with your problem." He drummed his fingers on her shoulder.

She hugged him—hard—and planted a kiss on his lips that spoke of other things to come. A chorus of cheers broke out behind them, but Ally ignored them.

When she and Séamus broke apart, she turned back to them. "You're just jealous."

Séamus sat down and pulled her down into his lap.

"Did you find Abel?" she asked Jas to change the subject.

The dark-haired cop looked at Danny and nodded. "We got the diving team out and found his body deep in the cave. The current was tugging him farther in all the time."

Ally looked at her hands as her throat tightened. She thought of their few nights together and the vibrant man he had been. And she had killed him. It could have been her. The worst part was that she didn't understand why he'd wanted to kill her—there was no explanation except for a magic bracelet, and that just didn't make sense. She swallowed and Séamus wrapped his arms around her a little tighter.His warmth flowed into her, giving her strength.

"You got the camera, too?" she asked.

Jas nodded. "The coroner will be checking the wound that killed him. We'll want you in to give a statement."

She nodded. "How did you even know that I was in trouble? I mean, I'd been out there before and come back with no problems."

"That's probably what he was counting on," Danny said, rubbing his hands back through his red shock of hair. He shook his head. "It was Lila and Séamus who figured out that Abel was after you."

"Uh-uh. Make that Kylee and Séamus," Lila corrected. "We were trying to find out more about Abel to see if our feeling of ill-ease was warranted. We contacted the camera rental place and asked them where Abel might have rented the boat, and when we talked to the Kelowna marina, they gave us the name of the actual renter—Johan Fehr of *Schwarzenacht Corporation*."

Chloe visibly shivered. "That was the guy who scared the heck out of me when he came into the store looking for the bracelet about a month ago. That's when this whole thing with the bracelet started. But it was Kylee who remembered me telling her his name at the time. I didn't remember it until she reminded me. It was weird—like a fog in my brain suddenly burned off in the sun."

"I ran the name past the driver of the limousine that was coming for Kylee, too." Danny added. "He also suddenly got his memory back. It was like a spell got broken or something, because he suddenly could fill in all the description that he couldn't remember when Jas talked to him. He confirmed it was Johan Fehr. We've put out the call to Interpol to get the goods on the guy. In the meantime, we figured that Abel Khan was working for him."

"When we figured that out, we knew you were in danger, Ally-girl," Séamus picked up the story. "Lila called your friends, here." He nodded at Jas, who stroked Chloe's bare leg below her black capris. "And I took off looking for a boat on the beach that could get me out to you. I found one and the rest is history and you're safe and sound beside me." He put his arms around her, disregarding all the little quips from Chloe and Brett.

What could she say? All these people had worked so hard to save her and she loved them all, each one. She reached in her pocket and pulled out its contents, dangling the silver bracelet from her fingers.

"Oh ho!" Reggie chortled from her spot on the ground. "Bet we can guess what you two were doing."

"Well, you can guess, but you'd be wrong. We were sitting in Séamus' room—with our clothes on, I might add—and Séamus tried the clasp. It came right off in his hands, almost as if it wanted to. Strangest thing I've ever seen after the way none of us could get the darn thing off."

She leaned over to lay the bracelet on the table. The twinkle and candle lights gleamed on its surface, but oddly, the doors didn't look the same. Three of them seemed to catch the light and hold it. The other four were dull by comparison.

"Do you guys see that?" Ally asked.

"What are you talking about?" Lila asked.

She explained about the bracelet and the others gathered around. "Maybe it's just that as a photographer, I pay attention to light conditions, but there's something different there. The little arched door, the one that looks bound in iron, and the one with the gargoyle—they're all brighter than the others."

"Hold that thought," Reggie said and dashed into her darkened workshop, her black Cleopatra hair sweeping over her shoulders, her typical baggy camo trousers and singlet like a second skin. Lights flipped on, destroying the ambiance in the yard and exposing her world of hammer-wounded wood, fire, and ranks of well-used jewelry-making equipment. Then the light flicked off and she returned to them, holding up a loupe.

She bent down to study the bracelet links, shifting her study between the doors. Then she set the loupe down and ran her fingers over the bracelet. "It's strange, but it's like something dark has come off of them—the patina maybe. From all your handling?"

Chloe shook her head, her eyes gone a deep, dreamy lavender. "Something darker, I think," she said softly.

Jas slung his arm around his lady and pulled her into his side. "Let me guess. That's some of your mumbo jumbo coming out."

Chloe arched a brow at him. "Maybe. Whatcha going to do about it?"

Jas shook his head. "Not a darn thing."

"So who wears the bracelet, now?" Reggie asked and turned to them, the bracelet glittering across her fingers.

Her dark brown eyes had gone almost black. "I mean, we know that it has to be on someone's arm. You three have worn it. That leaves Lila and me and there's still two doors left."

She swallowed. "I don't want to be in love and I don't want to be in danger. I don't have time for it. I'm supposed to leave for Milan in three days with the jewelry designs to meet with the clothing designers and figure out what else they need so everything's ready for the show in September."

She looked from Ally to Chloe to Kylee to Lila, her eyes those of a trapped animal.

"I'll wear it," Lila said, but Reggie shook her head, her fingers closing around the bracelet in denial.

"I think—I think not." She slung the bracelet around her wrist, the key through the lock, and braced herself. Then she sighed and smiled, regaining her tough-girl exterior.

"Well, that wasn't so bad. No rush of danger or anything." She straightened and pushed her shoulders back, the Celtic knot tattoos on her biceps gleaming blackly. "All right." She looked up into the darkness of the heavens. "I'm here, I guess. I'm ready to step out of my shop and have an adventure!"

The stars only twinkled at her challenge.

Epilog

The useless phone call came just as Johan Fehr regained himself. He stood, panting, in the center of his living room, the sodden Berlin dawn slowly filling the floor-to-ceiling windows of his apartment overlooking the city. Outside, the piddling mortals were consumed in their futile morning commute, their taillights like gratifying streaks of blood in the rain down the glass, and at the moment he would be happy to add real blood to the hue. Female blood, preferably. One of the women from that dismal Canadian lake town most certainly.

He kicked the upended couch again and felt a toe break in this body. Pain stabbed through him, but he cut it off from his consciousness. The body only mattered because it was connected to a name and the name was connected to the power that gave him the ability to do what needed to be done. He had bided his time all these years, at first searching for the bracelet, then when the bracelet had seemed to be gone from the world, accumulating power in the ways of men. And then one day a feminine hand had held the bracelet with such longing that he had felt it through the ages-old connection of his power.

The bracelet found.

And still kept from him!

He heaved an ancient Assyrian terra-cotta vase across the room, shattering it against the fireplace. Nothing mattered. Nothing mattered at all except getting the bracelet back from those women.

The phone buzzed and he dug through the debris of kindling wood that had once been a side table. The smart phone vibrated in his hand and he stabbed it on. "Fehr."

Listened as the castrato told a sorry tale about how his *handpicked assassin,* intended to seduce and kill the woman, had failed in his duties and died.

"Do you think I need your phone call to tell me this?" Fehr's voice rose to a roar. "Imbecile, I was there. I felt your worthless one die!" He slammed the phone to the floor and crushed it under his heel, turned, and left the room.

In his book-lined office, he settled at his heavy, wood desk and stabbed his computer on. Three women, three doors. The power locked in the bracelet was dwindling and with it, his own. He had to stop this *now.* He sent the message he should have sent before this, but he'd thought he could deal with this quickly and easily through intermediaries. After all, it was only mortal women he had to deal with and he had never failed in that department before.

His hands cramped into fists, but he opened his fingers and sent the email: a request to know all there was to know about the women associated with a strange little store called *This and That,* in the insignificant town with the imbecilic-sounding name of Peachland.

When he was done, he sat back in his chair and studied his bloodied knuckles. There would be pain there, too, just like the foot of the man he wore, but those were minor injuries he could heal in an instant once he had his full power back.

No, send him the dossiers on the women and he would turn their lives against them. Then, when they were alone, he would pick them off, one by one. After all, if none were alive, they could not keep the bracelet from him.

About the Author

Karen L. Abrahamson (McKee) is a well-traveled writer who has explored cultures and countries around the world, but south central British Columbia, Canada is one of her favorite places to come back to. She is the author of literary, romantic, mystery and fantasy fiction including the highly regarded Cartographer fantasy series. She lives on the west coast of Canada with two Bengal cats that aren't quite as well traveled as she is.

When she isn't writing she can be found with a camera and backpack in fabulous locations around the world.

If you would like to get an automatic e-mail when Karen's next book is released, sign up at her website, *www.karenlabrahamson.com*. Your email address will never be shared and you can unsubscribe at any time.

A Special Request from the Author: Word-of-mouth is crucial for any author to succeed. If you enjoyed this book, please consider leaving a review at Amazon, Barnes and Noble, or any other e-tailer, or on Goodreads; even if it's only a line or two, it would make all the difference and would be very much appreciated.

To find more of her writing, visit

www.twistedrootpublishing.com.

Sneak Preview- Unlocking Her Dreams

Prolog

The mid-afternoon traffic of Berlin's Grunerstrasse and Karl Leibknecht-Strasse streets moved in a rhythmic pulse between the leafy confines of the sidewalks. The Fernsehturm, the bulbous Berlin television tower, glittered and fractured the sunlight as it poked out of the grey expanse of buildings like a periscope searching for prey. The thing that dwelt in Johan Fehr felt the same way.

All his plans so far had come to naught. But he had charted a new course when his pure frontal assault had not worked on the three women. Now he just had to make his new plan work.

Down below, the summer streets of the city were crowded with shirt-sleeved Berliners rubbing shoulders with the constant stream of foreigners who came to the city. Tourists, students, artists, businessmen crowded into the Mitte area with the glittering, golden chariot above the Brandenburg Tor, the grey arch of the Brandenburg Gate, the parliament buildings, the gray concrete and glass towers and modernity of PotsdamerPlatz. Humanity, all of it, and all nothing more than fodder for him.

Swirling his chilled crystal glass of scotch, he turned back from the view of the puny lives, the puny efforts to prove that humans were a great boon to the world. His apartment, repaired since his latest temper had led to his destruction of much of its contents, had a new, white, lamb's leather couch that formed a corner in the center of the room like a body curled on the floor, the huge, chrome-legged, zigzag-shaped glass coffee table set into its angle like an ancient tool of torture. The white wool rug that the couch and table sat on was like a field of new snow awaiting the destruction of footsteps. The two-story white walls held bold new paintings, red as splashed blood.

He sipped the whiskey and considered the largest painting of white background with vivid orange and red streaks down the canvas as if something had been disemboweled and hung there. One of the damnable women would be his preference. Who would think that four women from a place with the imbecilic name of Peachland could stymie him? HIM. The place was a scattering of houses, barely deserving of the name town, and he was—he was as old, as inexorable, as time. Had always taken what he wished from the puny humans—always until that fatal last time that had left him no more than a shade of himself, wandering the world, searching for what had been stolen from him. Yes, stolen.

Johan Fehr's fist tightened around the crystal glass, the knuckles white.

The silver bracelet was his. Though he might not have made it, it contained too much of his essence, too much of his power. All these years it had been lost, his power confined in its links, but so long as it existed he was safe.

Now, though, the bracelet had come to light and the ancient curse he had placed on the thing was coming undone, link by link, his power dissipating. If he did not reclaim the thing soon, he would be left with no more power than was within this body, and he had spent so much of that strength to reclaim the bracelet that if he was not successful, he could be left with nothing.

The body inhaled to quell the anger his emotions bred in the flesh and bone. He and this body had been together so long that they were almost one. They controlled the Schwarzenacht Corporation empire, which was another kind of power and one that he would use now to get what he wanted. He had been a fool to try frontal assaults on the women. As long as they were together—bound together in friendships so strong—they would defend each other. And he could not succeed. Or at least not without expending more power than he could chance.

So another approach was necessary. One that would break them apart. One that would destroy their friendship and everything it had built. One that would leave the bracelet wearer alone and easy prey.

The phone rang and he stabbed the receiver on. Listened.

"Good," he said and hung up.

It was four thirty in the morning in the place called Peachland and his plan was in motion. Now to see it through to completion.

This time he would succeed.

Chapter 1

The early morning hung brooding grey over the Okanagan Valley of south-central British Columbia; a storm off the Pacific Ocean had sent thick clouds streaming eastward over the coastal mountains and over the long valley that contained the eighty-mile-long Okanagan Lake. As a result, the rising August sun barely glowed in the clouds that filled the eastern sky, though the air was still warm—the thermometer on the porch post said it was almost seventy-eight degrees.

Ponderosa pine covered the folded mountains of the western shore above the town of Peachland, while on the eastern shore, fire had scoured the trees from the mountains. But life returned. Life always returned—grasses, the wild poppy and black-eyed Susan, fireweed and lupine would have been the first. Even the pines had started to grow again, their long-fallen seeds kindled to life by the flames that had killed the forest. At least that was what Lila Weber told herself, when a tingle of ill-ease had awakened her with the dawn this morning.

And with the new growth had come the wild mountain goats that, to Lila standing on her porch far across the lake, looked like tiny white flecks on the distant mountainside.

She smiled at the sight. It had been years since the herd had been on those rugged mountains. She stood, nursing her first cup of coffee of the day and hugging herself against her nerves, on the broad porch that spanned the front of the beloved red and white, two-story heritage house that she had inherited from her grandparents. It sat like a stately old dowager across Beach Avenue from the beach and the usually blue lake where she had whiled away many a summer as a child. But the lake was uneasy today and reflected how she felt. A cool wind from the south stirred the usually pleasant lake into a mass of whitecaps that only the most madcap boater would chance on. On shore, even though it was August, the beach was empty of its usual flock of summer people, though the diehard, Lycra-clad joggers and the silver-haired, Birkenstock-sandaled walkers still made their way along the promenade that paralleled the beach beside the road.

The wind smelled of heat and dry places and tasted of iron on her tongue. Heat lightning, maybe, but it reminded her more of dark, like the smothering dark in caves, instead of the dry desert hillsides of the Okanagan. No, something was unnatural about this wind. It soured her smooth, hazelnut-flavored coffee until it tasted only of chemicals. She wondered what Chloe, her friend, business partner, and resident 'psychic' would make of this change in the weather from her condominium down around the point.

A shiver ran down Lila's spine and she pulled her pale blue pashmina shawl around her shoulders, her light, three-quarter-sleeved shift of blue Indian cotton suddenly severely inadequate for the weather. After the attacks on three of her friends over the past three months, it really was no wonder that she feared the worst when the air was like this. Each of her friends had worn the same silver bracelet that she had brought into this house from an estate sale, so in a way, it was all her fault. And now the bracelet of seven perfectly-fashioned silver doors was on Reggie's wrist— Reggie Lewis of Regulus Designs, who was now winging her way home from Europe and Milan from her first in-person meeting about jewelry planned for the fashion runways of Europe.

It didn't bode well that she was due back today. This wind, this scent,made Lila's stomach clench and her scalp prickle despite her long auburn hair. Something was coming, and given the experiences she and her friends had had over the past three months, nothing that came on a wind like this could be good.

Lila roused herself and went inside, through the shop called This and That, the fashion jewelry store that she ran with her friends. They specialized in silver and gold jewelry of semiprecious stones that she found all over the world, as well as the astoundingly beautiful pieces that Reggie fashioned in her workshop out back. At this hour of the day, with lights turned off and only the light through the front windows that gave onto the porch and the view of the lake, the shop had a misty feeling with its lavender walls and dark wainscoting filling the space with a lovely light.

It was a good shop, with its glass cabinets and flowing displays of pashminas. They were selling well and making their mark with the marketing genius of Kylee, the latest addition to their little enclave of women.

And yet here she stood, actually sweating with—well—fear. Yes, that was what it was. She held out her coffee cup one-handed and tremors disturbed the top of the liquid. Definitely shaking. Definitely fear.

Well, enough of that, because she had nothing to fear. Her life was simple. It was good just being here with her friends and her business.

And a bracelet that brought danger into all their lives. Even Ally's. Her friend Allison McVay had come to town for a visit and had been the third woman nearly killed while she wore the bracelet.

Lila closed her eyes. She was not going to think about what could have happened. She pushed through the beaded curtain to the rest of the house and left it clack-clack-clacking softly behind her as she returned to the kitchen to flush the ill-tasting coffee down the drain.

The kitchen was her favorite room of the house and always had been. From her grandmother's domain of strictly functional summer kitchen, she'd remodeled the room into a thing of beauty and light. The rear wall gave onto the backyard through a French door, and a string of windows stretched over a long counter and sink. Pale yellow walls were offset by white cupboards. Stainless steel appliances had pride of place, with the gas range set off in its own alcove under a copper range hood. Bright accents of turquoise and tangerine were present in a turquoise-faced wall clock, a utensil jar, and salt and pepper shakers shaped like small orange tropical fishes. In one corner of the room she'd kept her grandmother's cozy kitchen nook, but had changed the cushions to tangerine and turquoise to go with the décor.

She pulled her darkest roast coffee beans out of the cupboard and set to making herself an espresso. Get rid of the chemical taste and get her day started, because along with the fear came a kind of lethargy at the inevitability of whatever was coming.

Her little espresso pot had just started its gurgling when the bell above the front door jingled. Hadn't she locked it behind her? Darn it, why was she so nervous?

"Lila?" came the melodious voice of Chloe Main, but the voice cracked. "You're up. I know it."

"Kitchen," Lila called and pulled a second cup from the cupboard.She turned around as Chloe entered the room, dangling her key from her fingers.

Chloe Main was a long-time friend and one of the most serene people that Lila knew—except when she'd gone through a bout of wearing a certain bracelet. But today, straggling into the kitchen with one of the three sets of shop keys dangling from her fingers, she looked almost as shaken as she had after a man had attacked her during that horrible time. Yes, her hip-long, lustrous brown hair was done up in its usual thick braid and she wore her usual thigh-length caftan and leggings—these in deep purple— but her deep blue eyes had a glazed, shocked look. Most of the color had drained from her cheeks, as well.

"Chloe! Are you all right?" Lila left the stove and caught her friend's arm to lead her to the kitchen table.

"I'm fine. Really. I am." Chloe pulled loose as she sank down into the nook. "I just had a bad dream and then—well—I woke up and went out onto the patio to get some air and calm myself but..." She shook her head, the jet beads clicked and rattled amongst the silver cavalcade of necklaces she wore.

"Then you felt it, too, and I'm not imagining things. Something's coming." Lila went back to the stove where the little silver espresso pot bubbled and spluttered. "Latte all right?"

Chloe nodded. "Just make it strong." She bowed her head as if seeking strength.

Lila pulled milk out of the fridge and measured it into a pot to heat.

"Something's coming. Some new disaster. Or danger." Chloe said, clutching at the string of jet. According to Chloe, they were protection against evil spirits. "I dreamt about a black wind, laden with sand. It blew through Peachland, tearing everything down. The sand ate away the red and white paint and the wood of the store. It tore down the marina and my condo. It stripped flesh from bones, and the worst of it was, the whole time I heard horrible laughter as if whatever sent the wind reveled in what it had done."

She looked up at Lila as she whisked the heated milk to a froth. Chloe's lovely, deep blue eyes had gone violet with emotion.

Lila pressed her lips together and nodded, then turned back to the coffee. She'd known Chloe long enough to know that Chloe's dreams should be listened to. She poured the steaming milk into two off-kilter shaped mugs reminiscent of something out of Alice in Wonderland, then poured in the thick black coffee with a little flourish so small flower designs blossomed on the top. She brought them over to the table and slid in beside Chloe.

"So what's coming? Any idea?"

Chloe shook her head. "You know me. I get impressions—emotions. I don't get details. When I realized that it wasn't just a dream, I got dressed and came right over. I was scared something had happened to you. Or the others."

"I'm fine. I heard from Reggie that she'd gotten on the plane. Everything was fine—great, even. She should be home this afternoon."

Chloe nodded. "That's a good bit of fortune, but it brings the bracelet back here while something's happening. Have you heard from Kylee?"

Lila smiled thinking of her high school BFF, who was now fully ensconced in the life of Peachland and the store. "Undoubtedly she's with your baby bro. Brett'll keep her safe if anyone can."

From the store came another bright jangle from the bell above the door. "Please tell me you locked the door behind you." Lila said.

"I did." Chloe looked toward the hallway where the bead curtains clicked behind somebody.

"Lila?" Kylee Jensen's bright voice travelled down the hall. The third person to have shop keys.

"Right here in the kitchen. If your ears were ringing, Chloe and I were just talking about you." Lila stood to greet her diminutive friend with a hug. "You okay?"

Kylee's bright blonde cap of hair was disheveled as if she had just gotten out of bed. She wore a pair of capris and a bright red blouse with an overlarge men's black hoody clutched around her neck. She nodded.

"Just flipping freezing. I woke up scared to death so I got up. Brett's still sleeping. So what's happening?"

"We're having a coffee and trying to figure it out. Want one?"

"Sure." Kylee headed for the table, then stopped. "Have you checked the house?"

Lila paused in refilling the espresso pot's water reservoir. "Why?" She filled the filter with fresh, finely ground coffee.

"In case anything's wrong. The store looked fine, from what I saw."

Lila screwed the top on the pot and placed it on the stove. "A good idea. I'll check upstairs. Maybe you two can check down here. Any idea what we're looking for?"

"Anything that could spell trouble," Chloe mulled. "We'll know it when we see it."

Lila took the espresso pot off the burner and headed for the stairs. As usual, Kylee's idea was a good one, but Lila couldn't see where someone breaking into This and That could bring on this disastrous feeling. She hadn't felt this way even when the shop was broken into and all of Reggie's prototype pieces made for

Milan had been stolen. But those pieces had been recovered and were all safely with Reggie. From what Reggie had said, the pieces had been a triumph with the clothing designer.

Lila checked the guest room, recently vacated when her friend Ally had left for East Africa and now ready for its expected next guest, the assistant designer who'd be arriving home with Reggie. The bed with its patchwork lavender duvet was made, the chalk-painted dresser standing primly against the wall complete with a vase of white lilies and baby's breath. The window blinds were open onto today's grey view of the lake. Nothing here. She headed for her office and had just poked her head inside when a shout came from the rear of the house. She clattered down the stairs again and back to the kitchen.

The back door was open and Kylee and Chloe both stood outside on the patio deck paving stones. The yard wasn't large—just room for the flagstone deck, barbeque, patio chairs, and a small flower garden—because most of the area was taken up with Reggie's jewelry workshop. Initially she had worked at home in a smallish shed. That had changed when This and That had opened and she'd needed more space. So she'd moved all her equipment here and had bought more until she was able to produce the jewelry that met her inspiration and vision. At the moment the door to the workshop hung open.

Chloe stood frozen in the middle of the patio, her arms wrapped around herself. Kylee stood at the door to the shop as if afraid to enter and glanced back at Lila when she stepped outside.

"The door was open when I came out. You better see this," Kylee said and motioned Lila forward.

Lila crossed the flagstones and peered inside.

It was a long, narrow room, with a workbench surrounded by smoke-dimmed windows at one end and counters with kilns and grinders and other equipment that Lila would prefer not to know about stationed neatly along the walls. Regardless of the general grime that came from the heated work of jewelry making, Reggie always kept the place tidy, with jeweler's tools in neat racks up above, cupboards for supplies, and a cabinet where Reggie kept files on her pieces—molds and processes used, the provenance of stones, etc., for each of her designs. At least that was how the place was supposed to look.

At the moment it was more like a hurricane had passed through it. The room reeked of spilled chemicals and kiln charcoal. Lila wrinkled her nose and cautiously stepped inside. The large pieces of equipment still stood where Reggie'd left them, but the small anvil and tools that Reggie kept close to hand at her work bench had been scooped off the table top into a pile on the floor. The cupboards, too, had been emptied, spilling small plastic bags of semiprecious and precious stones through the mess. Here and there the dark gleam of ruby, garnet, topaz, and sapphire caught the gray light from the door. No one was here.

She picked up a pale moonstone at her feet. Everything was devastation. It would take Reggie to make sense out of this mess. But Reggie wasn't here.

Lila swung around, her gaze falling on the yawning filing cabinet drawers.

Empty.

The sense of disaster flooded in once more.

Chapter 2

The Boeing 727 jerked slightly as it rolled to a halt on the tarmac. Its engines powered off and from outside the plane came the welcome hum of the staircase being driven up to the aircraft's cabin door. Fresh air would be a godsend after the long haul of connecting flights from Milan to Paris to Vancouver and now to the blessed tarmac of Kelowna International Airport in the heart of the Okanagan. The circulated air seemed to carry a sour pall of sweat and bad coffee that just underlined Reggie Lewis' fatigue.

Out the windows the low mountains surrounding the Okanagan valley gleamed summer-brown—sunburned grasses and sage mixed with the dark green of ponderosa pine and the fluttering green-gray leaves of poplar that followed the seams of the land where there was running water. The afternoon sky was brilliant, cloudless blue and the afternoon sun would be like an old friend on Reggie's shoulders. She might be returning triumphant from Milan, but she sighed with relief and cast a glance at her travel companion as the passengers beat the clicking off of the seatbelt sign and stood to deplane.

"Let's just let the others push and shove and we'll gather our things after the crush," Reggie said. Around them the overhead bins were releasing carry-on luggage large enough to be lethal if one fell on their heads. Her single suitcase was similar in size because she'd only been away for five days and it was packed in the overhead bin, but Victoria Angelucci didn't travel quite so light so they'd be waiting for the luggage arrival anyway. No reason to hurry.

Victoria nodded and sat back down.

The woman was the epitome of a fashionable Italian, even though she wasn't what you immediately thought of as Italian. Victoria was a honey blonde, with hair in thick soft curls à la Brigitte Bardot, and with the voluptuous curves to match. She wore what had to be a custom-fitted Armani suit of navy, with red piping along the collar of the peplum jacket and a pair of flowing trousers over towering, stacked red heels that Reggie was in awe of. Even after the sixteen hours of travel, Victoria looked just as wonderfully put together as she had at the start of the trip, while Reggie's grey-blue knit pants and tunic felt like rags and her makeup had probably melted on her face. Oh, to return to her usual garb of camo pants and sleeveless top and the comfort of her workshop.

Five days in Milan had felt like forever. She missed her space, her friends at the shop, and most of all her daughter, Thalia.

The cabin door opened and the smell of jet fuel, heated tarmac, pine, and lake water filled the cabin. Reggie inhaled like a hungry woman. Home. She was home. How the heck had Kylee and Chloe managed to stay away so long? How did Lila stand those long buying trips? The Okanagan was home and, at the moment, she didn't want to leave it again. Ever. Well, maybe not ever, but at least not until Milan fashion week. Then she'd go back to see her jewelry grace its first European runway. If the response of Erminio, the designer, was any indication, she might be seeing a lot of fashion weeks in the future. A little frisson of excitement ran through her.

Maybe next time she could take Thalia with her. Thalia would love the adventure of it.

Finally the other passengers had mostly shuffled past and she stood to hand Victoria down her various and sundry belongings— three bags from duty free, a coat, a hat, a briefcase and small suitcase to go with the larger suitcase she had checked through as luggage. With Reggie helping juggle Victoria's belongings, they trailed between the empty passenger seats, said their goodbyes to the cabin crew—in Victoria's case it was "Ciao, bella"—and then descended the long set of stairs to the tarmac and the painted walkway to Kelowna's small, one-story terminal.

"This eeze charming," Victoria said as she scanned the hillsides. "It eeze very dry. My skin will feel this very quickly." She plunked on a wide brimmed hat that matched the peplum on her jacket, placing her classic features in shadow. "The mountain are—how do you say? Rugged? Is that the word? And not so green as Lombardy. There are no tall, snowy mountains, either." She pouted her disappointment.

"The tall, snowy mountains are along the coast or east of here. The entire province is ridges of mountains, but this is one of the folds of valley in between the worst of them." Reggie tried to parse whether Victoria was really serious. Reggie still hadn't been able to figure the other woman out, though Victoria had been with her throughout her time in Milan. She was a wonderful host and had made sure Reggie saw the best of Milan and nearby Lake Como during her brief stay, as well as chauffeuring her around from her hotel to Erminio's design studio so that she and the Great Heir to Italian Fashion—as the fashion pundits were calling him—could discuss his vision for additional pieces of jewelry for this season and the next. The meetings had left Reggie just a tad ecstatic and a heck of a lot terrified. There was so much work to be done.

"Come on! There'll be people waiting for us."

Trundling their bags, they followed the last of the passengers up the ramp into the low-slung glass and concrete terminal. The gaggle of passengers had stopped there like a flow of silver, congealing in the mass of welcoming family members. Reggie and Victoria stalled at the door, Reggie craning her neck for a familiar face. Then she spotted welcoming auburn curls. Lila Weber waved over the heads of the crowd.

"Follow me." Like inserting a jewel into a delicate setting, she started easing them through the chattering families until suddenly Lila was there, looking lovely and cool as ever in a sky-blue sleeveless three-quarter-sleeve shift and white ballet flats with a cascade of silver chain and seed pearl necklaces. But her large hazel eyes had a hint of worry in them.

"You're home safe and sound and thank goodness for that." Lila tugged Reggie into a hug and then clasped Reggie's right hand to inspect the bracelet around her wrist. "Still got it on, I see."

Reggie shrugged. "Was there any alternative?"

Lila grinned. "I thought maybe one of those Italian studs might have swept you off your feet." She held out her hand to Victoria. "Hi. I'm Lila Weber, Reggie's friend."

"And co-owner of This and That, a little jewelry store we have in Peachland," Reggie added.

"Welcome to the Okanagan," Lila finished.

Nodding graciously, Victoria shook. It was like the two women were inspecting each other; both seemed to like what they saw and both relaxed.

"Victoria came back with me to help me with the final designs for the fall show and to discuss concepts for next spring."

A hesitation and then Lila grinned. "Are you telling me that they want your designs for a second season?"

Reggie could barely contain the need to shout it to the moon; that had been bursting in her chest since her last meeting with Erminio. Now it bubbled up and she squeezed her eyes shut. "This is one of those squee moments, where I want to dance like a kid, but I'll leave that to Thalia."

A congratulatory hug from Lila, but then the baggage carousel buzzed and they went with the crowd to retrieve Victoria's other bag.

While Victoria went carousel-side, Lila turned serious. "I want to hear all about your trip, but first, about the bracelet— there were no problems?"

Reggie held up her wrist for inspection. It was, without a doubt, the most intricate piece of jewelry she had ever laid her eyes on—more so than anything she had ever attempted. Yes, the Italians might have their way with jewel-encrusted torques, rings, and bracelets, but this bracelet was solid silver and very old—at least she'd put her money on it being old given the patina and the signs of slight corrosion.

It was made up of the most intricately cast and created doors she had ever seen. Seven doors—each unique—formed the bracelet. One was a tiny arched door with a gargoyle, one an iron-strapped heavy wooden door, another of wood and edged with ivy. Still another had what looked like scrolled fairy hinges, while another had hinges shaped like leaves. The sixth door looked like a Dutch doorthat would split at the middle so the upper area could be open to the air.

The final door had heavy, square-carved lintels above the door as if it had been removed from a place of some pomp and importance. A tiny silver Fatima hand hung as a door knocker. Some of the doors had tiny padlocks on miniature chains holding them closed. Reggie didn't know the provenance of the bracelet, only that it had been amongst the jewelry of an estate sale. She and her friends had found an old diary belonging to a British colonel who had owned the bracelet. He'd written that he had found it in the North African desert during the Second World War. Said colonel had always considered it lucky, but Reggie wasn't so sure, given the danger that the bracelet's other wearers had gone through.

She ran her fingers over the linteled door—the one she found her fingers straying to over her time with the bracelet. She raised her eyes to Lila's. "Problems? Only the fact that the darn thing won't come off and I had to choose my jewelry around it. People like Victoria notice things like that."

She nodded at the Italian woman who was hefting her bag off the rotating carousel with surprising strength. Victoria might look like an exotic bird in this environment, but she clearly had no expectation of being waited on. But fashion—all aspects of it down to the tiniest of details—was clearly important.

"But no attempts on your safety?"

Reggie shook her head. "I felt safe as a baby. Victoria was the perfect hostess," she said as the other woman rolled luggage almost as big as a smart car toward them. Reggie grinned. "Now

I just hope I—we—can be as gracious. They set a pretty high standard, Lila. They set me up in the Hotel Principe Di Savoia and I felt like a princess." She turned to Victoria. "We could still set you up in a hotel in West Kelowna. There is a nice place down on the water."

"No, no, no." Victoria held up her hands. "I came because I want to see where the magic of your jewelry comes from. If your friend is kind enough to let me stay in her home—please, it will be enough. And Reggie tells me it is near the water—like the villas of Lake Como? How can I turn such a pleasure down?"

"Well..." Lila said. "You're very welcome. Just don't be expecting a villa. It's my home—was my grandparents' and the place I always came to in the summer. Now it's also our shop. But you are more than welcome."

Lila led them out to her little Ford Escape SUV and Reggie thought of the limo that they had used to whisk her away from the Milan airport. Welcome back to the land of working folk. They loaded the luggage—no minions to do it for them—and climbed in. Reggie took the back to allow Victoria to have the better view. Then they headed to Peachland.

The highway took them through the sprawl of Kelowna's strip malls and hotels and then up and over the floating bridge over the narrow waist of the lake before winding up through West Kelowna's light industrial and commercial areas, all the while catching glimpses of the lake and the mountains and hills that at this time of year were tinder dry.

"Still no rain, huh?" she asked Lila.

"A thunder shower the other day. We all held our breath, praying there'd be no lightning strikes."

"We've had a couple of bad forest fires near Peachland," Reggie explained to Victoria. "A few years back they had to evacuate half the town. Luckily we weren't affected."

"This must look very different from Milan," Lila said as she guided the SUV down the long, steep slope that was known as Drought Hill and turned toward the lake.

"Here it is very dry—compared to Lake Como. There it is all

trees and flowers and streams pouring down from the mountains. The mountains are taller, too."

"Well, the Okanagan is technically a desert, but just add water and you can grow anything. We have lots of flowers and orchards and more and more very good wineries."

The familiar lapis shimmer of the lake lay ahead and all the tension of the five days of meetings and trying to be fashionable enough to get by in a city like Milan—in other words, trying to be something she was not and would never be—faded from Reggie's shoulders. Thiswas her turf and Victoria was just going to have to accept it. She grinned a little, certain that Reggie Lewis in camo and singlet was going to be a bit of a shock for fashionable Victoria. Lila, now—she was the fashionable one.

Lila turned down the lane that ran behind This and That and the other houses and businesses that fronted the lake.

"We have many wineries in Lombardy, as well. My family owns one."

"Really? Well then, I know someone who'd love to chat with you. Our friend Chloe's brother is part owner of Elkhart winery here in Peachland. You'll meet him, I'm sure."

Lila turned into the carport of the large, two-story, red-trimmed white house and turned off the engine. Reggie opened her door and inhaled the moist heat of the lakeshore. Roses and honeysuckle from Lila's rear garden, heat off the patio paving stones, and the permanent, slight under-taste of kiln charcoal from her shop. She closed her eyes and realized she'd missed the sweat and the heat and the ecstatic god-struck feeling that she always got in the midst of creation. Milan had been good for discussing ideas with Victoria and Erminio, for Victoria was a designer in her own right, but this—the fire, heat, and hard metal tools of her shop—this was creation. As if she was one of the mythical silversmiths of the dwarves or an apprentice of Vulcan, the god of the volcanoes.

"Reggie? You all right?"

Lila had unloaded the luggage and was leading Victoria toward the house.

Reggie shook herself. "Yeah. Sure. Fine. Just tired from the trip, I guess. And itching to get back to work in my shop. My head and my notebook are full of designs that I need to get to work on."

"Well, let's get Victoria settled and then I'll give you a run back to your place so you can get a shower and some rest before your start everything. Thalia called here three times this morning asking if you were back yet. She must be driving your parents crazy."

They crossed the patio—scorchinghot in the afternoon sun, regardless of the shady maple tree at the rear of the yard—and went into the air-conditioned cool of Lila's sunny kitchen with its welcoming nook and its bank of windows onto the back of the house.

Reggie sighed, closed her eyes, and could have just planted herself at the table it felt so good to be here, but this was only her home away from home and she wanted to see her daughter. It had been like a constant ache since she left even though they'd talked every night. Lila and her friends might be a big part of her life, but Thalia was her everything. She needed to get home and hug that ten-year-old body. Hard.

"You're here!" Chloe's voice came from the shop at the front of the house and the rush of footfall came from the hallway. Two figures pushed into the kitchen: Chloe Main clad in her usual knee-length caftan and leggings, these ones deep purple, with her hip-long hair kept confined in its ubiquitous heavy braid. With her came the blonde sprite that was Kylee Jensen, wearing a pretty little floral sundress that no one in Milan would be caught dead in because it was much too simple and probably too inexpensive. Her cap of bright hair framed her gamine face and large blue eyes.

"Reggie!" Kylee threw her arms around her in a hug. "We missed you."

Chloe grinned and turned to Victoria, who stood in all her finery. Chloe's eyes widened slightly at the larger than life hair, makeup, and suit. She stuck out her hand. "I'm Chloe Main. Welcome to the madhouse." She leaned in to buss Victoria's cheeks. Trust Chloe to have an Italian welcome for an Italian. She stepped back with a tiny frown.

"I'm Kylee," Kylee said, separating herself from Reggie and shaking Victoria's hand. "You must be exhausted after the trip. Would you like some tea? Coffee? Something to eat?"

"Whoa! Would you whoa?" Reggie said, stepping between her friends and Victoria. "This is Victoria Angelucci. She's Erminio Biondi's partner and she's here to work with me on the designs. But she's been through a heck of a long flight, just like I have, so let's let her have some space, okay?"

She looked from one enthusiastic face to the other. Both nodded.

"Of course. I forgot," Kylee said. "Those international flights can take it right out of you."

"But it is very nice to meet you both. Perhaps a cup of tea would be nice after a chance to freshen up?" said Victoria with a smile.

"Then let me show you to your room and then I'm going to run Reggie back to her place. Chloe, Kylee, I'll ask you to play hostess while I'm gone. Maybe you can show Victoria the shop and help her get settled. I should be back in twenty minutes."

She left, hauling Victoria's largest suitcase up the stairs to the guest room on the second floor. Reggie hoped it would do. It was a lovely room—or at least she'd always thought so until they put her up in what amounted to a suite that had looked like it was something out of a castle when she was in Milan. Totally outside her expectations and she wondered if Victoria would be able to handle the down-home comforts of Peachland. Well, she'd check with her tomorrow and if it wasn't working, she'd get the woman moved into a hotel. But she'd deal with that tomorrow.

"Lonely. That's the word for Victoria. I get the sense she doesn't trust many people," Chloe said, looking thoughtful.

"So how was it?" Kylee asked. "As exciting as it must have been?"

"Sure. It was." But God, she was so tired. She really needed to sleep because she certainly hadn't on the plane.

"So spill, girlfriend. What about the men? Meet anyone?" Kylee tugged her toward the nook's turquoise and tangerine seating.

"No, there were no men. Why the heck would I be interested in an Italian man? They're all hands and leers and rude comments." "Now that sounds like sour grapes—like maybe someone who's carrying a little disappointment that she didn't get swept off her feet," Chloe crowed.

Reggie batted her arm. "It sounds like someone who had better things to do than moon over a man. I have Thalia. I don't need another person to take up my time—not with all the work I have to do. And don't you two have a shop to tend or something?" she ended as they started tittering. "Get outta here and leave me alone."

She waved them away, but not before they each gave her another hug.

"So glad you're home safe, hon," Chloe whispered in her ear and then they were gone.

Reggie was just pondering whether she'd be able to get up again if she let herself curl up in the nook when Lila came back into the room.

"Victoria's settled. She's talking about taking a shower and maybe going for a walk on the beach. She seems very nice."

"She is. She—everyone—treated me like royalty over there. I just hope our homey little Peachland is enough for her. I mean—well—you saw her."

Lila caught her arm. "Don't worry. A lot of Europeans pine for the simpler life Canada offers them. Now let's get you home. I've got to talk to you about something."

They piled into the SUV again and Lila backed out and onto the lane. Then she stopped and bowed her head into the steering wheel. "I wasn't going to tell you until tomorrow, and then I wasn't going to tell you until you were home, but I guess I'm having a crisis of conscience."

"Just what are you talking about?" Reggie tried to understand, but her jet-lagged brain wasn't quite putting the pieces together. Lila wasn't helping, either. In fact, her auburn curls tumbled around her cheeks effectively blocking her face from Reggie almost as if she'd planned it.

Lila sighed and turned to her. "It happened this morning, I think. I was outside and it was as if the wind blew in change that smelled like hot iron. All the little hairs on my arms stood on end and the next thing I knew Chloe was here, and then Kylee, too. We searched the house looking for something that would match the disaster we were all feeling." She shook her head, her hazel eyes settling on Reggie. "It wasn't in the house. It was your shop. The door was open and everything easily moveable had been thrown on the floor."

Frowning, Reggie shrugged. "That's not so bad. I can sort stuff out again."

But Lila was already shaking her head. "Let me finish. They did that, sure. And it was a mess, but they got into your files, Reggie. They took everything."

To read more of Unlocking Her Dreams, look for it at your favorite bookstore or on-line retailer.

Romance and Adventure
from Twisted Root Publishing

If you enjoyed this book, you might enjoy other titles available from Karen L. Abrahamson in your local bookstore or wherever e-books are sold.

www.karenlabrahamson.com